THE DRAGON'S SECRET

THE DRAGON'S SECRET

DONNA MACQUIGG

FIVE STAR
A part of Gale, Cengage Learning

GALE
CENGAGE Learning

Detroit • New York • San Francisco • New Haven, Conn • Waterville, Maine • London

GALE
CENGAGE Learning

LIBRARY OF CONGRESS CATALOGING-IN-PUBLICATION DATA

MacQuigg, Donna.
   The dragon's secret / Donna MacQuigg. — 1st ed.
     p. cm.
   ISBN-13: 978-1-59414-868-2 (alk. paper)
   ISBN-10: 1-59414-868-6 (alk. paper)
   I. Title.
   PS3613.A283D73 2010
   813'.6—dc22   2010003972

First Edition. First Printing: May 2010.
Published in 2010 in conjunction with Tekno Books.

To Kathryne Kennedy, author of the Relics
of Merlin series, my dear friend and critique partner.
Thanks for your encouragement to put
some magic into this story.

ACKNOWLEDGMENTS

For the most part, I am known for my Western historical romances, but my first published book was a medieval romance. I have always loved medieval stories, but I've been so enthralled with my friend and fellow author, Kathryne Kennedy's fantasy series, *The Relics of Merlin,* that I wondered if I could break into such a fascinating genre. *The Dragon's Secret* began as a medieval romance. That was how I presented it to Kathryne who quickly fired back the suggestion that I try something different— something magical. Although I was reluctant to do so, I tried it and was pleased with the end result. But writing a book and getting it published are two different things, especially when changing genres. I took the chance, and it paid off because of a bunch of people who have had faith in me and have supported my ideas.

Therefore, I want to extend my sincere gratitude and appreciation to Kathryne Kennedy, author, Brittiany Koren and Rosalind Greenberg of Tekno Books, and of course to my *amiga,* Tiffany Schofield, acquisition editor, Thorndike Press/Five Star Gale and Cengage Learning. And one last word of thanks to Alice Duncan, my line editor who has put the final polish on this and my last four books.

CHAPTER ONE

Wales, 975

Sayrid rose slowly and tossed aside the furs on her small pallet. She yawned, remembering the dream that had kept her from peaceful sleep. The warrior's features seemed vividly real as they crept into her mind once more. She saw him, as she had in her dream, camped in the forest. He relaxed against a log as he oiled his sword, surrounded by many other battle-hardened soldiers preparing for war.

She thought him a fierce-looking man; his features hardened from years of doing battle. Broad of shoulder and narrow of girth, he appeared, by his rich attire, to be a warrior-knight of high rank. When he raised his eyes from his task, they were the blue seen in the deepest part of the sea with thick black lashes— eyes that demanded obedience. His dark brows contrasted sharply with his shoulder-length, tawny-gold hair.

She shook her head, for even now, wide awake, it proved difficult to ignore the odd fluttering that started in the pit of her stomach as she thought of him. A frightening stranger, yet somehow familiar. She quickly cast the odd feeling aside, assuming the closeness resulted from the dream.

'Twas worrisome to think that this new threat would be able to vanquish Aswyn and his Viking cohorts who had plagued her people since before she could remember. At least she'd learned how to deal with them. However, this man she knew naught, yet she sensed he wanted more than to rid her homeland of Aswyn and his intruders. This man hungered for Aswyn's blood, but there was something even more worrisome that nagged at her. He wanted something that she always felt belonged to her and her people. He wanted Dragon's Head and the magical power hidden deeply within.

She lifted a long, tousled strand of curly ginger-colored hair and groaned, regretting that she'd not taken the time to braid it. The curly mass cascaded down her bare back to her buttocks, and now, because her unsettling dreams had caused her to thrash about, 'twould take longer to remove the tangles.

After starting a fire, she filled a small cauldron with water from a stout wooden barrel in the corner of her cottage before placing the pot over the flames. When steam wafted upward and the fire had warmed the room, she poured the water into a basin. Her breath caught when she stared into it.

Ebbing in and out on the crystalline surface appeared the same warrior, his eyes glittering with contempt, his face partially masked by the narrow nose-guard of a bronze helm. And though she knew naught whom he fought, the sight of his blood-splattered surcoat sent a jolt of fear slithering spider-like down her spine. A highly detailed dragon with red eyes dominated a noble crest—its wings out as if in flight—its mouth open, exposing frightening teeth and a thin red tongue. Clutched in the dragon's talons hung the dead body of a black raven.

She squeezed her eyes tight before she dipped her hands into the warm water and bathed her face. Reaching for a soft cloth, she dried herself, glancing at the basin once again. His handsome visage churned with the motion of the water, and, to her increasing distress, she saw him wounded whilst doing battle, reaching out to her when she backed away. Trembling, she waited until his image slowly faded.

Sayrid threw open the door of her cottage, carefully snatched up the basin and tossed the water out over at the hawthorn hedges surrounding her tiny home. The quick motion startled a flock of ravens. Startled herself, she watched for a few moments while the ravens circled above before perching high in the tops of two towering oaks. More afraid than she cared to admit, she hurried inside, closed the door and leaned back against it until she could calm the rapid pounding of her heart. Slowly she became aware that her shoulder ached.

Flexing her arm to ease her discomfort, she vaguely remembered teachings from her childhood that the raven was an omen, but of what she couldn't recall, though she sensed it boded ill. She had lived in the forest for five years—in the little sod-and-thatch cottage overgrown with vines and dense foliage, hidden so well in the forest that often Aswyn's warriors were only a stone's throw away and still couldn't find it. She had no memory of how it came to be her home—only that she'd always felt safe and protected, even when she had slipped into the village to visit friends and trade for a few supplies.

But now Sayrid felt afraid.

By the time she dressed and had all the tangles from her hair, the late summer sun had turned the day overly warm. She cautiously peered out the door, relieved to see that the birds had gone. Clad in a rust-colored gown, she carefully arranged her overgown. A verdant garment made of cord, loosely braided, with bits of moss-colored, leaf-shaped material sewn into it. Giving the appearance of a vine, it had saved her life on more than one occasion, allowing her to blend in with the foliage of the forest. Many times while wearing it, she had been able to observe King Aswyn's warriors without being seen.

Sayrid tossed her heavy hair over her shoulder, secured it with a simple, beaded-leather circlet then picked up her bow and quiver. Refusing to think about the bizarre happenings of the morning, she stepped outside and pulled the door tightly

11

closed, wishing she hadn't lost her dagger whilst hunting the day before.

'Twas not wise to travel the forests of Dragon's Head unarmed.

As the sun climbed higher, so did her optimism that today the goddess of the forest would provide a bountiful feast. Though each and every day she thanked the gods for her freedom from King Aswyn, the thought of another day of leeks and turnips made her most anxious to begin the hunt.

Sweat ran into Kyran's eyes. The battle was over. The master of Dragon's Head lay dead and bloating in the insufferable heat. Kyran glanced around, wiping the blood from his sword on a dead warrior's surcoat before shoving the blade into the scabbard. It had mattered naught to King Aswyn that Kyran had him surrounded, and his foolish quest deemed suicide. Even Aswyn's warriors had looked on in disbelief. Nay. The only thing the old king had on his mind was gutting his adversary.

Wincing, Kyran slowly removed his helmet and raked his fingers through his sweat-dampened hair, heedless of the broken and bloodied blisters on his palm. It had not been his choice to end the old king's life. He would have preferred to take Aswyn prisoner, and later have him drawn and quartered as an example of what happens to those who forsake their people. But the foolish old man had left the security of the castle walls to lead his warriors into the valley to fight. And quite a fight it was. For his years, the old warlord had swung powerful, arm-numbing blows.

Engrossed in keeping Aswyn's sword from chopping off his head, Kyran didn't see the solitary archer on the wall-walk—not until an arrow sank into his shoulder, piercing his shirt of mail. The sight of blood only intensified Aswyn's lust for more, as the old king bragged that the archer was his woman. With his sword arm impaired, Kyran barely deflected the savage chop of the master's blade. Nevertheless, in the end, Aswyn's arrogance had cost him his life.

As the remaining few of Aswyn's army surrendered, Kyran wondered if Aswyn, in his last moments, had recognized his executioner.

The thought brought a cynical smile to Kyran's features as he swung up and into the saddle of his enormous gray destrier. He turned the animal toward the forest in search of some shade and a drink of cool water, away from the stench of battle. On top of the rise he stopped and looked back over the valley, patchworked with crops and edged with a jumble of thatched sod houses. Old, bitter memories threatened to surface, but he pushed them aside, the pain in his shoulder enough to bear for now.

His gaze traveled upward from the village to the mound, dotted with grass and coarse-grained rocks, then to the stone gatehouse, covered with ivy, and then to the outer curtain that stood twenty feet tall and five feet thick. It followed the rise and fall of the rugged terrain emanating from the rocky crag from which a narrow waterfall fell in frothy folds to the lush green valley below. The huge wall continued for a hundred more feet to the right before disappearing over a sheer drop.

Two slender drum towers partially covered with moss and ivy were built into the wall and stood like fearsome sentinels, pockmarked with arrow slits, their merlon heads crowned with rusted iron spikes. Behind the wall rose four huge towers—two with turrets constructed in the same fashion. The castle appeared as if it had been carved from the craggy face of the mountainous cliff, and, when the sun set, the long shadows made it look like a huge dragon's head.

Kyran unconsciously touched the dragon on his surcoat, his fingers brushing against the bronze medallion he'd taken in a previous battle. In the far reaches of his mind he remembered the tellers-of-tales and their stories about how long, long ago, dragons lived to protect the people, and the people loved and cared for them. Their leader was a great and powerful dragon that for many years gathered gems and shiny stones to place before his mate. Because of this, the neighboring royals grew jealous and sent warriors to steal the dragon's jewels.

Powerless to help against so many warriors, the people watched as first the smaller dragons were hunted into extinction. When only the fierce old dragon and his mate survived, the pair took refuge in a giant cave in the sacred mountains overlooking the Mystical Forest near the sea. But they couldn't escape the greed and hatred of the warlords. The soldiers wounded the old dragon and killed his mate. Heartbroken, the aging beast shed two almandine tears before he hid deep inside the bowels of the cave. There, he tore his heart from his chest. Magically, it turned into a large almandine.

The moment the old dragon died, the mountain mysteriously closed over him. The skies darkened and the earth began to shake, splitting solid rock, forming a huge and frightening castle that terrified the warriors and sent them away. After the dust settled, and with only the castle to protect them, the villagers named it Dragon's Head.

The mere mention of Dragon's Head sent a spark of fear into even the most formidable warriors, as the castle still appeared to be more an enormous cave than a castle, making it almost impossible to seize. Yet feasting his eyes on it now, Kyran nearly forgot the price he'd paid to take it. Nay, he'd come to face the old traitor and settle a blood feud, and nothing short of his own death could have prevented him from accomplishing his task. In the end he avenged his father and reclaimed his ancestral home. Too bad it bordered the lands of Aswyn's sworn ally.

A savage grin slanted across Kyran's sweat-dampened face—

too bad for King Oddrum.

The wind changed and wafted through the trees, bringing with it the acrid smell of smoke. The cries of the dying and wounded rose up from the valley's floor and settle in Kyran's skull—the pain merging with that in his right shoulder. He glanced down at the broken shaft protruding from his upper chest, pinning his doublet to his flesh.

The bitch had to have used a magical bow to be so accurate at such a distance—and, he hoped, a bodkin. But he suspected differently by the feel of the wound and the knowledge that he had seen Aswyn's personal guards, being creatures of little or no honor, using broadheads after they learned Kyran's army had no armor.

Kyran carefully lifted his leather doublet to inspect the wound. Blood clotted around the shaft, acting as a bandage. It gave him some peace that he'd not bleed to death whilst he rested in the forest. There'd be time to tend the wound after the castle was breached and all those who still boasted fealty to Aswyn were either hanged or banished. 'Twould be their choice, but he'd have no prisoners stinking up the dungeon—no dissension among his ranks.

'Twas a fact well known that Aswyn and his warriors had cast their lot in with Oddrum's tribe in hopes of conquering all of Wales. As the Norse had done before him, so did Aswyn underestimate the power of the dragon. It mattered naught to Kyran whether or not all of Aswyn's warriors died, for he'd been raised to believe a traitor deserved no mercy, and to cast one's lot in with those who would suppress the true people was worse than being a traitor. But he had promised Cyric, his lifelong friend, that he would spare them if they pledged fealty to their new king.

Kyran urged the stallion deeper into the forest. Three days he had fought. Three days without decent food or proper rest.

Weary to the very core of his being, he turned the stallion down a small ravine to where he remembered a river that ran deep and fast. The sound of rushing water acted like a balm for his weary soul. More tired than he'd thought, he slowly dismounted, dropping the reins so the gray could feast on the lush grass. Kyran walked to the bank and eased down on his knees between the ferns to bathe his face and drink from the noisy river.

A flash of light—the sun glinting off a silver blade reflected on the water. Inherent caution caused him to turn with weapon in hand. A sword crashed down, barely missing his head. Escaping it sent him sprawling on the dew-drenched bank. He raised his sword just in time to ward off another strike. The battering blow sent pain reverberating through his shoulder as steel glanced off steel.

"Cursed Viking," the man yelled, chopping with his sword.

This time Kyran grabbed a fallen branch with his left hand and deflected his antagonist's strike. Hindered by the mud and his fatigue, Kyran tried to scramble to his feet, but only made it to his knees before being set upon again. He raised his sword once more to defend himself, the reciprocate motion reviving the pain of his wound.

The other warrior moved swiftly, and with both hands on the hilt he chopped and hacked, his relentless advance forcing them both into the river. Blood began to flow freely from Kyran's shoulder as he tried with failing strength to defend himself.

His vision blurry and his head pounding, Kyran caught sight of movement in the trees and grabbed the man to use as a shield. His attacker jerked up before he slumped forward—an arrow embedded between his shoulders. Too exhausted to hold the dead man's weight, Kyran dropped him into the water and tensed, expecting the impact of the archer's next shot, but it never came. For a morbid moment, he glanced at his assailant's body as it floated downstream. The arrow appeared to be carved with runes, painted, and tied with braided ribbon resembling those he remembered from his childhood.

Sayrid swallowed down the urge to be ill. Never in her life had she killed a human being. Stunned, she leaned against a slender birch wondering what had gone wrong. By the dead man's clothing, he'd been one of Aswyn's warriors—of that, she felt sure—and a painful lump formed in her throat as she remembered how many of her people had been pressed into his service. She glanced down at her bow—the runes painted on it—certain she'd had the Norseman in her sights with her last arrow. But he'd moved at the last moment with the strength of two men and saved himself.

She sank to her knees, watching as the warrior used his sword as a staff to help himself up the bank. She assumed he thought to seek protection in the trees, but he collapsed before reaching them, rolling onto his back with a low, painful groan—his body partially hidden by the tall grass and thick ferns. She glanced around for a weapon, but to her dismay, could find none. She looked at the river, wishing that the dead man had not floated away with her last arrow in his back.

At the base of a tree, Sayrid placed the hare she'd killed earlier, and she leaned her bow against the trunk. She searched until she found a sturdy branch, thinking a small weapon better than none. She watched the warrior, wondering about the blood on his surcoat, but could see nary a sign that he still lived. A quick glance over her shoulder told her the sun would soon disappear between the distant mountains, and, with the ebbing of daylight, so did her courage waiver.

Carefully she crept forward, watching—listening. An almandine twinkled in the filtering sunlight, catching her eye. The large blood-red stone crowned the elaborately carved hilt of his dragon-headed sword, pinned beneath his hip. A smaller stone glittered from a ring on his long, tanned finger; as on his sword, the jewel was held fast by the carved claws of a dragon.

The moment she saw the warrior's face she froze. Instinct told her to leave, but she knew as soon as the thought came that she couldn't leave him to die. She jabbed him lightly in the ribs with her stick and was rewarded with another low groan. When he made no effort to defend himself, she stepped closer.

His leather boots were laced over tan leggings, darker now that they were wet. A broad leather belt bound his oyster-colored surcoat to his waist, and his right shoulder appeared to be entirely covered with blood. None of these things frightened her as much as the dragon crest upon his chest.

"Norseman?" she called in a soft voice. "Can you hear me?"

A raven screeched from the treetop in answer, startling her. Did the bird watch over his master, she wondered? She swallowed her fear and knelt, cautiously lifting his dagger from his belt. Taking a moment to admire the jewel-encrusted hilt, she placed her hand upon his chest. His heart still beat, and, though his breathing seemed faint, 'twas steady. Her nimble fingers relieved him of his ring and of a heavy pouch. She paused to examine the contents, delighted to find it filled with gold and silver coins.

"You're a rich lord," she whispered softly, stuffing the pouch and the ring into the deep pockets of her gown. Her gaze fell upon a bronze medallion that rested face down upon the grass, its thick chain still around the warrior's neck. With a flick of her fingers she righted it, catching her breath. Even after she sensed the warrior had opened his eyes and stared at her, she could not draw her gaze away from the amulet. She started to rise and would have left, but he caught her wrist with surprising strength—his touch shooting pain into her own shoulder. Tiny beads of sweat trickled down his brow, and he blinked several times as if trying to focus on her face.

18

"Water," he said in a hoarse whisper. Her gaze narrowed. His accent sounded foreign to her—barely discernible. "I need water."

For a moment she felt his despair—a warrior unaccustomed to being weak and defenseless, now unable to rise or get the drink he'd nearly sacrificed his life for. She dragged her eyes from his and cast another glance at the medallion. When his fingers slackened, she scooted back before she stood, torn between leaving and staying.

"Wait," the warrior commanded, his voice barely audible over the rush of the river. "You . . . you were . . . in my dreams." His voice faded as he bit down and tried to rise. The effort proved too great, and he groaned again as he lay back down.

His confession frightened her. Had he dreamed of her as she had dreamed of him? For a second time she was overcome with indecision. He said something in a language she didn't understand, but knew it to be the native tongue of the fearsome warlord to the north—King Arcas.

She scanned the area to make sure they were still alone, then, tucking the dagger into her girdle, headed to the river. Her fingers trembled as she pulled a large leaf from one of the many plants that grew near the bank. Using her hands to support it, she shaped it into a small cup, filled it with water and carried it back.

Through a haze of pain, Kyran's eyes scanned the woman's vine-covered garments for a weapon, but no dagger lurked in her strange attire. Nor was his still in its scabbard. A warrior unarmed and at her mercy. A long-forgotten memory about a mystical sorceress flickered in the depths of his consciousness—a woman who'd been blessed by the Ancient Ones with extraordinary beauty. The storytellers said that she had the gift of melding with the forest, surviving by casting paralyzing spells on her prey to make them more easily hunted.

He battled with the thought, wondering if this sorceress, this phantom of a storyteller's imagination, could be the same that had haunted his dreams whilst he camped outside of Dragon's Head.

Or could she simply be a thief?

As he stared at her, her features twisted and change into those of the witch he'd pictured in his mind. Yet the longer he looked, the more the beauty of the girl before him denied his vision of ugliness. Her eyes were bright green and enchantingly wise. Hair the color of sun-kissed copper shrouded her back and shoulders, glistening in the muted light filtering down through the trees.

"Are you of this world?" he asked, his voice husky with fatigue. He swallowed against the dryness in his throat. "Or of another?"

She knelt beside him once more. The moment she touched him, he felt comforted. She slipped her hand under his head but he could no longer keep his eyes open. He felt himself supported and when something touched his lips, cool water trickled into his mouth. He drank, not caring that the one who gave it to him could have easily poisoned it or could have used his own knife to slit his throat. Using the last of his strength, he forced his eyes open as the water and the helping hand was removed.

The breeze tugged at her hair, enlivening several wild curls to caress an ivory cheek as she tossed the leaf away and gazed down at him with a wide-eyed, wondering expression. Soft, pouting lips parted as the tip of her tongue darted out to moisten them.

"The arrow is deep. Your lifeblood flows from your shoulder; if it is not stanched, you will die."

A fresh wave of pain stabbed into his shoulder as she pried away the surcoat and heavy mail. Using his dagger, she cut away a piece of the padded doublet. He raised his left hand in a vain effort to see if she were flesh or a figment of his imagination, but his fingers only grazed air as she stood and disappeared from his sight.

Low, curly wisps of fog began to crawl toward him, and for the first time in days he felt cold. He dragged his hand across his eyes wondering if he hallucinated. She returned and knelt once more by his side, and oddly her presence soothed his rising alarm.

"Wh-who are you?" he asked gruffly, then sucked in his breath as she pressed something cold against his shoulder that turned too quickly hot. Cursing himself for believing she was good, he shoved her away. The agony in his shoulder intensified to the point that he dug his fingers into the damp earth and bit down hard to keep from crying out.

"Do not resist," she soothed, her small hand cool on his forehead. " 'Tis for your own good. Though it feels like fire now, 'twill temper the wound and make the arrow easier to remove."

"What manner of witch are you?" he ground out through clenched teeth when finally the pain eased enough to allow him to speak. A fair brow tilted upward as if she found his statement amusing.

"I am only a woman," she answered calmly. He watched her clean his dagger in the grass before she examined it more closely. Grunting in pain, he feebly reached for it. She moved swiftly, holding it out of his reach. "Nay, my lord. 'Tis payment for the drink."

She laughed a warm, lilting sound that denied the thought she was evil. Too weary to stop her, he could only watch as she removed his medallion from around his neck and quickly slipped it into her pocket.

"Are . . . you a witch . . . or a thief?"

Her smile appeared coy. "I prefer to think of myself as an

advocate of the poor and oppressed."

Through half-closed eyes he watched her stand, but in his muddled state he could not tell if she stood on her feet or simply floated above him.

"Your possessions will bring many of my people a small measure of relief."

"Take my pouch, but leave . . . the amulet," he muttered. She laughed again, but her voice faded away to nothingness as his mind played more tricks. The birdcalls from above became the eerie screeches of a witch. In the distance, banshees softly wailed his name as fairies appeared in the darkening sky. Too weary to care, he closed his eyes and sank into painless unconsciousness.

The rustling of brush in the direction the warrior had come from caused Sayrid to crouch down, placing her hand on the Norseman's chest. Beneath her fingertips his heart beat strong and steady, and she knew he would survive. Male voices grew louder over the forest sounds as two men searched for their fallen comrade.

Afraid of what would happen if they found her, she slipped the warrior's dagger back into her belt, gathering her bow and the hare she'd killed. Using the dense foliage as cover, she disappeared into a copse of leafy bushes. She thought to run, but felt torn between her urgency to flee and her desire to know of the warrior's fate. She hesitated a moment longer, unwilling to give much thought to her reasons.

"There," came a voice from the rise. "Kyran?"

Kyran? 'Twas a name she would remember. She watched two men approach. One, dressed much in the same manner as the fallen warrior, sheathed his sword before he knelt by his side. The man took off his helm and placed his ear on the warlord's chest while the other massive man glanced about the area and poked the thick foliage with a deadly spear. She fought the urge to scrunch down. She knew if she remained motionless she would not be seen.

"He lives," she heard the first man say, drawing the big one's attention. She watched as the brute hoisted the fallen warrior up and over his broad shoulder. The other man caught the stallion, leading the animal as they passed by her hiding place—unaware as the beast locked his wild-eyed gaze on her.

In stealth, she kept to the shrubs and trees, following their departure. When darkness finally hindered her view, she vanished into the mist-shrouded forest.

Brynn pressed back against the rocky indentation, her black-leather gambeson helping to keep her concealed. Holding her breath, she dared not move until the strangers had passed—yet she longed to finish what she'd begun. Curse the stamina of Aswyn's killer. The man had to have the strength of two men to withstand her poisoned arrow. And curse Sayrid too—for her interference and her knowledge of the healing mud.

When the intruders had left, Brynn changed into her raven form, narrowed her gaze and searched her surroundings to see if Sayrid had stayed behind. It seemed the bitch's powers were growing stronger, and she could appear and disappear at will. Brynn smiled slyly. She had no desire to drain her strength by searching. She knew exactly where to find Sayrid. She'd deal with her in due time—after she came up with a new plan to get close to the butcher who had destroyed her only hope of being queen.

CHAPTER TWO

Sayrid hid her bow and quiver behind some rocks. The hare she'd killed had been carried off by a hungry animal. She touched her fingers to the rough stone of Dragon's Head and smiled as if greeting an old friend. Slipping between a heavy drape of vines, she pushed open a small section of stone blocks forming a door and ducked inside the secret entrance. After touching a taper to the wick of a fat saffron candle, she paused a moment to gather her thoughts. A warm draft blew down from the ancient spiral stairway, causing the flame to cavort wildly.

"Rest easy, great one, old Aswyn is dead," she whispered. As if her words had quieted a giant beast, the flame grew still. She began her slow and silent trek up the stone steps, unmindful of the spiders and crickets that scurried out of her path.

Well accustomed to finding her way through the maze of hidden doors and tunnels of Dragon's Head, she steadily climbed upward into the main tower. The sound of muffled voices could be heard as she placed the candle on a rusty sconce. Before her stood a smooth wooden wall, and, to any who did not know the castle's secrets, their journey would have ended at that point.

Though she could not remember who'd taught her, this old castle she knew well. She only had to brush her fingertips across a hidden latch and the wall before her would rotate, exposing a row of shelves that were laden with dust-covered plunder and battle relics. 'Twas easy to slip into the old lord's bedchamber unnoticed whilst he bedded a whore, take a few items to trade, then disappear through the hidden passageway.

From behind a small square of rusty iron mesh cut into the wooden planks, she could see into the chamber without being seen. To her amazement, she saw the warlord she'd attended sitting on a stool with his back to her, as the men she'd seen in the forest worked to remove his clothing. Another young man joined him. Handsome in his own way, he wore rich clothing and looked to be slighter of build. The wounded warlord acknowledged the man's arrival with a nod and softly spoken "Cyric."

"Is it very painful?" the young man asked, his reddish brows tightly drawn together.

" 'Tis bothersome," the warrior murmured, and Sayrid scoffed at his understatement.

Two boys, clad in their master's same oyster-colored tunic, worked with the men, the smaller of the two handing a jeweled cup to the warrior, whilst the other added a log to the already blazing fire.

The large man, who'd carried Kyran away, shook his shaggy head as he inspected the bloody doublet. He nodded to the other man with the dark curly hair. "Bynor, cut this off whilst I hold it from the wound."

By the giant's size and the way his long red hair fell in braids on the sides, he was clearly Norse. She watched intently as the other man placed the ruined garments on the floor.

"What manner of mud is this, Morven, to be stuck thus to the wound?" the dark-haired man asked, and now she remembered where she had heard the big man's name. She had learned about Morven the Red whilst listening to stories of past wars between the Welsh and the Vikings. A terrifying giant, said to be the spawn of Thor who, after he consumed tainted mushrooms, could rip a man's head off with his bare hands. A huge man indeed; she saw more gray hairs than red in his bushy beard. But then she remembered how easily he had carried Kyran out of the forest, and had no doubt the tellers-of-tales had spoken the truth.

The warrior's shirt was cut away and added to the pile of discarded clothing. She looked closer, gazing upon a very broad, muscular back, wondering if the arrow had gone through, almost hoping it had because it would be easier to remove. Except for a few old scars, his back looked unblemished—each bulging muscle defined by the fine sheen of sweat that covered his torso.

Her attention was drawn away when Cyric repeated Bynor's question. "What manner of mud is this, Morven?"

"I know not," the giant Norseman growled, making a disgusted face, "but remove it."

" 'Twas a witch . . . a beautiful witch." Kyran's deep voice sounded calm, and this time, she heard no accent. " 'Tis magical. It took away the pain. I've need of more." The last was spoken with what sounded like a tinge of desperation.

"We saw no one," Bynor added, "yet the grass and ferns were trampled where you fought off your attacker. Are you certain you saw a female?"

"She came to me . . . after," he confirmed, so quietly that she could barely make out the words. He drained what he'd been given to drink and gave the boy the empty goblet. "She robbed me, and then gave me water."

Kyran's henchmen exchanged glances, and by their expressions she knew they didn't believe their lord.

"The draught will make you sleep. Will you lie down now?" Morven asked, his impatience apparent by his gruff tone.

"Nay. I stink of blood and battle. I need a bath."

Again, the older man growled orders to the boys to fetch hot water and clean cloths. They hurried to do his bidding, reminding her of frightened mice.

"Help him to stand," Morven grumbled, his voice now clearly laced with anger. "Steady, do not let him fall lest he knocks some sense into his thick head when he strikes the stone floor."

While the muscles of Bynor's arms bulged to hold his master steady, one of the boys untied the laces of Kyran's boots and braies then pulled them off. The boy tending the fire fetched the kettle and poured hot water into a bucket, but 'twas Cyric who carried it over to the giant.

Kyran drew in his breath when water flowed over his shoulders and back. Sayrid could not draw her gaze away. He appeared fit, and everywhere she looked he was hard, male-muscle. A firmer buttock she had never seen. She felt no embarrassment for, as Aswyn's slave, she had often brought food to him and his many concubines, and Aswyn had seen no reason to be modest, often bathing with his women before they joined.

Her thoughts returned quickly to the present as once more she heard the injured man swear. His two henchmen had eased Kyran back down on the stool. Morven dipped a cloth into the bucket then swabbed his back first and then his chest. After they rinsed him, Bynor took a large coarse cloth and dried him.

"Now will you take to the bed?" Morven asked. A subtle nod told her what she waited to hear. She nearly sighed with relief, and then caught herself. This warrior was her enemy—more so than old Aswyn as this one appeared young and virile, and worse . . . he looked to be Norse. At least Aswyn had been Welsh. This one was more likely loyal to King Arcas who'd staked his brutal claim on all of Briton and reigned over the people using his dark powers and black magic. Regardless of the strange sensations this warlord's manly visage stirred, 'twould not do to forget that.

Together, the men helped their lord to the bed. She could not draw her eyes away from him. A glimpse of a tattoo caught her eye—a dragon. She tried to determine if its color were green or blue, but too soon he moved out of sight, leaving her to wonder how he could bear such a mark when most of the tattoos she'd seen were faded black from the charcoal men must have used.

"A pox on the cowardly dog who did this." Sayrid recognized Cyric's voice, thinking it strange that like his comrade, his accent sounded slight compared to what she thought it should be. " 'Tis a broadhead."

" 'Tis indeed," she heard Bynor confirm. " 'Twas to be expected that Aswyn would use broadheads on humans. I curse his soul . . . if he ever had one."

" 'Twas a woman who loosed the arrow," Kyran confirmed. "Dressed in black with a feather-covered helm. I saw her on the wall-walk."

Sayrid shivered and her mouth went dry. Broadheads were the most feared—barbed to tear the flesh if pulled out, best for hunting wild beasts, not men. She knew with sickening assurance that it would have to be cut out, and now, without the healing mud, she did not envy the chore ahead for the warlord or his henchmen. There was something else that sickened her. She knew the woman he spoke of—of the black magic she practiced to impress Aswyn.

One of the boys picked up a poker, and after jabbing at the coals to break them from the roasting log, placed the iron bar in the center of the glowing inferno. The other boy filled a bowl with more hot water while Morven came back into view. He drew a long narrow dagger from the sheath on his belt, and then washed the blade. "We should wait until the potion works."

"Your potion is useless," came Kyran's voice from the bed. "Do it now and be done with it."

When Morven went back, she felt her stomach clench with dread. A moment later she heard Morven's gravelly voice as he asked his gods for assistance then told Cyric and Bynor to hold the warlord down. She placed her hands over her ears, expecting to hear him vent his agony, but other than the angry mutterings of Morven as he worked, it remained alarmingly quiet.

Time seemed suspended. The other boy ran to the table, lifted a thick cloth, then retrieved the red-hot poker and quickly carried it back to the bed.

"Hold him," Morven rasped, the distaste of his duty manifested in his voice. The smell of burning flesh assaulted her nose at the same time she heard a low, agonized growl. The terrifying sound came from the wounded man but seemed to spread through the chamber, reverberating through the thick stone walls and rolling down the steep winding steps.

Then silence, and Morven's gruffly spoken oath of revenge.

"Fetch that salve," the giant ordered. "And those cloths. I would have the bandage in place before he awakes."

Sayrid relaxed back against the stone wall, only now aware that she had been holding her breath. A mixture of emotions washed over her as she scolded herself for feeling sorry for her enemy—a rich enemy at that. Reminded of his possessions, she slipped her hand into her pocket and pulled out the Norseman's medallion. The rolled edge felt smooth with age and cool to the touch. The small almandine in the dragon's claws glinted reddish-brown in the candle's feeble light. Carefully she traced the carved runes with her fingertip.

Instantly she envisioned a battle, felt the heat of the flames as they burned a village. Her skin began to tingle as in her mind's eye she experienced the pain and suffering of those she saw. Writhing in pain, the medallion slipped from her grasp and landed in her lap. As quickly as it had begun, the vision and the pain ended. Breathing hard, she dragged the back of her hand over her moist forehead, wondering why the Norseman wore a mate to her own amulet and sacred crest she'd had since childhood.

A ground-hugging fog made the forest appear more ominous than Sayrid knew it to be. An owl hooted in the distance, causing her to cast a cautious glance over her shoulder as she traveled deeper into the forest. She hurried along the path, eager to find refuge in her little cottage. The sound of wings overhead urged her into a run, and, with one last glance to make certain she wasn't being followed, she slipped through the vine-covered door.

Once inside, she had no need of a candle to light her way through the inky darkness. She went directly to the stone hearth, placed a handful of twigs and dried moss, and poked the charred crust of a log. Soon a foundling flame sparked to life and quickly flourished to a more cheerful fire.

She stood and warmed her hands for several moments, her thoughts on the Norse warlord lying grievously wounded at Dragon's Head. She withdrew his dagger and ring, placing them upon the mantel. They would bring a good price when next the merchant came to the village. In all her young life she had never seen a stone of such beauty. A large almandine, smooth and round, yet perfectly clear. She felt sure that if she held it up to a light, the fire that danced in the gem's depths would stir to life and become even more brilliant.

She removed the leather pouch and the medallion. She tossed the pouch carelessly on the table. There was no need to count the coins. She had no use of them. In a day or two, after she felt safe, she'd sneak into the village and give them to Gwendolyn, her dearest friend. She and Dafydd would know best how to distribute the wealth among the people.

A cautious mixture of emotions washed over her as she glanced at the warlord's medallion. Again she asked herself why a Norseman wore the mate to her own treasured amulet. She scoffed, remembering at the river he'd called her a thief. Was it a profession he could also attest to? Though deep inside she sensed she'd been drawn to the river at precisely the right time, she felt there was much more she didn't know as she laid the medallion aside and began to undress.

Tired and hungry, she went to the basket atop a table and, lifting the cloth, took out a small crust of bread. There were nuts and a little bowl of berries, and they would do for now, she thought, as she dribbled honey over her meager feast.

Still musing about the happenings of the day, her gaze wandered to the wall at the head of her bed where her own medallion hung. The warlord's bore the same design, yet the runes on his were different and foreign to her knowledge of their tribes' written word.

Her meal was too soon devoured, and her pallet too inviting to think of anything else but sleep. She stripped before slipping between the furs, and offered a silent prayer that her dreams would be peaceful and not full of warriors and sacred talismans.

There would be time to think more upon this, she reassured herself, when the sun climbed high and her spirit felt less fatigued.

Brynn perched on the battlements, concealed by the darkness. She watched, as many of her kinsmen who'd been captured were bound and forced to sit on the cold damp ground before a huge fire. Many of them grumbled muted protests. Others remained silent as they all awaited their fate.

Her eyes darted around the outer bailey as she scanned the area, her mind awhirl with indecision. Should she leave and seek assistance from her brother? Never, she silently vowed. He already thought her a failure. What of Maldwyn? He always offered her encouragement—had taught her how to survive and many, many dark secrets. He would leap at the chance to help her succeed, yet she dared not risk the old man's capture. Without anyone's help, she would find a way to get inside Dragon's Head and finish what she'd begun.

She inched back carefully so as not to draw any attention to herself. Something moved below her, and she froze. She watched a scullery maid empty a bucket of dirty water over some bushes. Opportunity had presented itself. Without a moment's hesitation, Brynn made her way gracefully to the ground, smoothing her black-leather tunic. A sly smile curled the corners of Brynn's full mouth at the same time her fingers closed around the hilt of her raven-headed dagger.

The chattering of birds outside Sayrid's window announced the rising of the sun. She stretched, then tossed aside the furs and stood. Unmindful of her nakedness, she filled a cup with strawberry wine and drank, washing down the hazelnuts and gooseberries she nibbled for her morning meal. There was much to do, yet she could not be sure of her safety if she ventured outside without the cover of darkness.

Aswyn and his henchmen rarely visited the forest except to hunt and then only after the sun shone high above the treetops. The villagers who had been enslaved to work in the castle had been successful with their stories: they told their masters that, while fog blanketed the forest floor, witches and banshees lurked about, searching for the solitary soul whom they could carry off to the Otherworld.

Because of the villagers' fanciful tales, most of Aswyn's men had traveled in packs—noisy packs with deerhounds that could easily be heard and avoided. Now, a new threat dwelled in Dragon's Head, and their habits she knew not. She prayed they were as superstitious as those they drove out, nevertheless, she'd have to be extremely cautious if she were to elude them.

After she washed, she dressed in a moss-green gown—slightly tattered, but with deep pockets sewn into it that were useful for gathering berries. Because she'd been given the amulet for protection, she put it on and tucked it under her gown before stepping out from the security of her little cottage. Last night's fog still lingered and swirled around her ankles with each step. With no arrows, and no time to cut reeds for more, she left her bow behind. In its stead, she brought the Norseman's dagger, secure in her leather girdle under her vine-like overgown.

When her snares were relieved of their catch and reset, she headed back to her cottage. Two fat quails were placed into a pot to boil off the feathers, and more nuts and berries were added to those in the bowls. Wiping her hands, she strolled back to the table where she lifted the Norseman's amulet, softly speaking his name. "Kyran."

She had no sooner touched the amulet when a terrible pain stabbed into her shoulder and snaked down her arm, causing her to drop it. She inspected her fingers, wondering why they tingled as if she'd fallen in a patch of nettles. Drawing in a long, bewildered breath, she rubbed her shoulder at the same time she made a fist then opened it, repeating this movement over and over until the prickly pain began to ease. Frowning, she wiped the dots of perspiration from her forehead with the back of her hand, and stooped to pick up the bronze disk, holding it in her palm.

The next instant, her shoulder began to throb anew, and, the moment she realized the connection, she dropped the amulet onto the table, where it could stay, she decided, until she figured out what had happened. She forced herself to the unpleasant task of plucking the birds, casting several cautious glances at the warrior's necklace while she worked.

Only after she had the birds stewing in a pot with leeks, turnips and carrots—gifts from Gwendolyn's garden—did Sayrid dare another look at the amulet. Drawn to it, she took a step closer. Unwilling to believe that it held any special power, she cautiously traced the carved runes with her fingertip, ignoring the burning sensation on her skin. Once more she saw visions of a battle. Women cried. Men ran and fought amid the smoke and the onset of battle-hardened Viking warriors. She heard the wails of children being dragged away from their mothers and taken as slaves.

The burn intensified. With a gasp, Sayrid snatched her hand back, clutching it to her breast. She grabbed a drying cloth and covered the amulet, then quickly carried it to the mantel, where she laid it near the Norseman's other possessions. The cloth slipped and her little finger brushed against the cool bronze. A fresh wave of pain stabbed into her shoulder.

Frightened and confused, she whispered, "This cannot be happening." Slowly she backed away, casting one last cautious glance at the amulet as she gathered up quail feathers to save for a new pillow.

The rest of the day went by uneventfully. She boiled berries, to make a thick, sweet jam to be slathered over bread. She spent the midday hours sewing a new gown from a length of midnight-blue material Gwendolyn had given her last week in exchange for two plump rabbits. With strangers in Dragon's Head, Sayrid needed something dark to allow her the freedom to hunt at night if sentries were posted in the forest to prevent poaching.

After she finished her work, she rested. She'd be fresh and alert for her evening trek to the lake to fetch reeds, for new arrows, and fresh water, to replenish the small barrel in the corner of her one-room cottage. Fluffing her pillow, her gaze wandered over to the mantel and the amulet. This time, the moment she thought about Kyran, her shoulder started to ache, a deep throbbing ache. Perplexed that she hadn't touched the amulet, yet still felt pain, she rolled on her side, closed her eyes and tried to think of other, more pleasant things till the throbbing ebbed. Soon she relaxed enough to fall asleep.

Wispy fingers of fog floated eerily in the trees, and a thicker blanket of fog lay upon the ground. By the light of the moon, Sayrid finished her chores and even ventured to the other side of the lake and collected two dozen reeds for new arrows. All the while she worked, thoughts of Kyran nagged her, causing her to worry that the pain she felt earlier that day could not compare to his—if so, how could he endure it?

She shivered as she stepped inside her little house, aware that a flock of ravens roosted up high in the tallest tree. Once a fire burned in the hearth, she cut the reeds to length and fetched her little pots of paint from the shelf. She had only painted five shafts before her gaze wandered from the arrows to the hearth and then up to the mantel where an eerie glow pulsed from Kyran's amulet. She quickly looked away, forcing her attention on painting the arrow. She continued with her design with difficulty as her fingers had become less steady.

"Cursed man," she mumbled as she took a small rag and wiped away a mistake. But she didn't look at her work very long. Her eyes drifted to the mantel and once more she became engrossed in a vicious battle.

A night bird called from above. When Sayrid glanced up, she stood before the hidden doorway that led into Kyran's bedchamber. She had no idea how she'd gotten there. When she glanced down, she saw that she wore her medallion, and her leather slippers were wet with dew. She held a folded leaf from the river's edge. When she peeked inside, she saw that it contained more of the healing mud. She shoved her other hand into her pocket. Kyran's amulet grew warm under her searching fingers, as if it were a living thing.

Suddenly she knew why she had come.

He suffered, silently as a true warrior, but his pain was on the verge of agony. If she were to have peace in her life again, she must help him heal. She quickly made sure the dagger was still attached to her belt, breathing a little easier when she closed her hand around the hilt. Though she knew how to roam about the castle without anyone's knowledge, there was always great danger lurking where warlords reigned. Even now, memories of the battle she envisioned made her doubt the wisdom of her actions.

A short time later, with the stubby saffron candle flickering in the rusty sconce, she knelt down on the cool stones and eased back the little wooden shutter that concealed the iron mesh. The strange ache began again in her shoulder, and she massaged it for a moment, more interested in the activities in Aswyn's bedchamber than easing her discomfort.

As she watched, the one called Cyric placed a pitcher on the stone floor and rose from a chair. By his concerned expression, he must have asked the giant Norseman a question, and now she wished she had listened, because the big man's voice sounded laced with contempt and fatigue.

" 'Tis grim," she heard Morven say as she got more comfortable, realizing that Cyric must have asked about his master's welfare. "He cannot rest without the potion and he is hot to the touch, though he does not sweat or complain."

The fearsome Norseman stood and, after stretching, placed his big hands on his back and walked toward the balcony. The soft deerskin drape had been pulled aside to let in the cool evening air. "I fear his wound has turned sour. There is naught I can do for him now. 'Tis up to the gods."

"Methinks 'twas that black mud smeared on his shoulder," Cyric offered, his voice also edged with contempt. "I suspect it had been mixed with bloodroot to poison him."

How like them, Sayrid thought angrily, to assume that what she'd done to help their friend was now the cause of his distress. Foolish men. Had they left the mud in place, they would not have had to brand him. She idly rubbed her shoulder, refusing to admit that there was a definite connection—preferring to think she had strained it hunting. Surely that has to be the cause, she thought with more conviction than she felt.

"I gave him a draught to help him rest," Morven added. "He should sleep. Come. I would fill my belly whilst he rests."

The moment Sayrid heard the door latch click, her mouth grew dry and her palms began to moisten. She found the well-hidden latch and silently slipped through the secret passage. Kyran shifted his weight and muttered something angrily under his breath, causing her to hurry to a darkened corner where she could hide, yet still observe.

He slowly opened his eyes and looked toward her hiding place. The hairs on the back of her neck began to tingle, yet she felt positive she could not be seen.

"A drink," he said in a hoarse whisper, "I need a drink."

Sayrid held her breath and watched, even though she had not made a sound. 'Twas bizarre how he knew her whereabouts. She briefly touched the amulet, hoping its feel would calm her nerves, but as soon as her fingers grazed the cold metal, the pain in her shoulder intensified. And as before, the moment she snatched back her hand, the pain diminished.

He asked for a drink once more, and she immediately glanced around the room in search of one, suddenly thirsty herself. Cautiously, she stepped closer. The warrior grew restless on the bed, his wounded arm bound tightly across his chest. A bold man even ill, seeing him again revived her fear. She cast a quick glance at the passageway. How easy it would be to slip away unnoticed and forget his existence.

He shifted fitfully, wincing as he tried in vain to free his wounded arm. Odd, she thought, to restrain him so. She fought the urge to release him to alleviate his feelings of being trapped. But she knew, the moment she thought it, 'twas more to alleviate her own sensation of repression. She stared down at him, aware that, as she witnessed his distress, she also felt his pain—his feeling of vulnerability. She carefully took one finger and moved the bandage enough to get a better look at the tattoo she'd caught a glimpse of before.

It was even more startling than she expected, and in the muted light the scales of the creature appeared to be iridescent, not quite green and not quite blue. The dragon, though not large, had been done in great detail, from the tip of his horned snout to the tiny claws at the end of his bat-like wings. The beast itself had rusty-colored, bone-like protrusions down the full length of its scaly spine to its spear-shaped tail. Long white teeth and red serpent's tongue visible from its snarling mouth gave her reason to frown, but she couldn't suppress a shudder seeing how the beast used its talons to hold open its own chest, exposing a blood-red heart. Odd, she thought again, wondering why this man would bear such a beautiful but gruesome tattoo.

Kyran slowly opened his eyes. The sorceress from the forest had returned. Did he simply have to dream about her to make her appear? A long-lost memory flickered in the depths of his consciousness as he swallowed to ease the dryness in his throat. He wasn't afraid of her. If she came to end his life, he believed that a better world awaited a fallen warrior.

Pictures of arrows carved with runes and tied with ribbons floated in the far reaches of his mind, and now he wasn't sure if he had fought her or someone more powerful. Had there been a battle, or had he simply been ambushed and robbed? He vaguely remembered a terrible pain that had eased soon after her cool fingers had touched the wound. But then the fire had returned tenfold—if she had come to finish the deed, death would be a welcome reprieve.

"I knew you'd come," he said thickly. Her brows rose in question and he realized she didn't understand. "My shoulder . . . ," he murmured. "In the forest, you touched me and the pain went away. I know not how it happened, I only ask you do so again."

" 'Twas not I, but the mud that eased your pain. 'Tis a gift from my ancestors' spirits who reside within the ancient trees." *And this ancient castle.* He frowned, wondering why she would say such a silly thing. "I—I brought more."

She took a step closer and placed a folded leaf on the table, then touched his bandage. He groaned as the pain seemed to grow stronger then ebb ever so slightly, as if she took some of it upon herself. At the same time, he saw her squeeze her eyes tightly closed and give a little sob just before she jerked away, clutching her hands to her breast.

"W-what magic is this that passes between us?" he demanded in a gruff whisper. He tried to rise, but couldn't.

"I know not. I thought the connection was through the amulet."

Breathing hard, he grasped her medallion in his fist, yanking her down upon his chest. Slowly he opened his hand, staring at the amulet for several moments before he relaxed back on the bed to watch her under heavy lids. She took several steps back, rubbing the back of her neck where the chain had dug into her tender flesh. Staring at him cautiously, she left to fill a cup. She returned and, after only a moment's hesitation, slipped her hand under his head. The cool rim of the cup was pressed to his lips and he drank.

"No more," he rasped. " 'Tis Morven's potion. I cannot stomach it."

"Hush," she whispered harshly. "I will not be able to help you if the others hear you." She placed the cup on the bedside table, then searched for a different pitcher, seeing one on the floor by the chair. This time, the wine tasted cool and quenched his thirst. He rested back against the furs, closing his eyes until the pain from moving passed. The woman stood above him, his dagger clutched in her fist. Using the last of his strength he caught her wrist at the same time voices sounded at the door. Too sick to hold her, she easily pulled free and disappeared into the shadows.

Sayrid hesitated for a moment before she slipped into the safety of the hidden passageway, pausing to see who'd entered. Her heart quickened its pace when the light from the torches in the corridor washed over the woman's smooth features. The guard who stood in the doorway urged the raven-haired young woman to quickly do her duties and leave.

Brynn, Aswyn's most recent whore, carried in a pitcher and a few clean bandages. She looked different dressed like a scullery maid, foregoing her usual finery. But Sayrid knew her well, shivering at the evil that radiated from her being.

Unaware that Sayrid watched, Brynn placed the pitcher on the table next to the bandages. Casting a cautious glance over her shoulder, she carefully lifted a small pouch from her apron pocket, loosened the strings with her teeth and sprinkled the contents into the pitcher. She paused, saw the folded leaf and gave a slight smile before she tucked it into her apron pocket. She filled a cup and would have offered it to the warrior, but the impatient guard ordered her from the chamber.

Sayrid's heart beat heavily against her breast as she waited a few moments before she hurried back to Kyran's side. His eyes were closed, and she thanked the gods that he'd fallen into a restless sleep. She lifted the cup and sniffed, wrinkling her nose at the faint smell of a very potent poison—the same that had coated the arrowhead. Instantly, Sayrid saw the archer. Brynn, dressed as a warrior, her features so clear in Sayrid's mind, little doubt remained. Brynn had been the woman on the battlement—her longbow poised and ready—just as the warlord had told his henchmen.

Wondering why she could suddenly see things that had transpired, Sayrid shook her head in disgust as she poured the contents of the cup into the pitcher and carried it to the balcony and emptied it over the side. Although a Welsh woman, Brynn had no sense of right or wrong, to wound a man from afar engaged in mortal combat with an equally fierce warrior.

Casting one last look at Kyran, Sayrid knew that they would both have a troubled night without the help of the healing mud. Afraid too much time had passed and Morven would soon return, she tossed the cup and the pitcher over the battlement before she reluctantly crossed the room to the hidden passageway.

"Tomorrow," she whispered, casting one more glance at the warlord. "Tomorrow I will bring more mud." There came no answer from the bed, only a very low, frightening growl that seemed to fill the dimly lit chamber.

Bynor moved aside some ferns, frowning even more deeply when he discovered a woman's body. Her small white hand had been barely noticeable, covered with the bits of leaves and dark soil. From her clothing, he guessed her to be one of the castle's scullery maids. Since there was no stench of rot, her death had been recent. He motioned to several nearby men and gave them orders to exhume the body from its shallow grave and take her into the castle.

On his way to report his findings to Cyric and Morven, Bynor hesitated, spotting several black feathers crushed into a small footprint. He knelt and traced the print. Too small for a man, he scowled and, at the same time, unconsciously placed his hand on the hilt of his dagger. He'd heard stories that the women of Dragon's Head were as capable of defending the castle as their men, but he hadn't thought them capable of murder.

Chapter Three

Kyran dared not move, for each time he shifted his weight he remembered that his right arm had been bound tightly to his chest. The mixture Morven had given him had caused frightening, fitful dreams—dreams where he battled warrior women without a sword or the protection of a shield, using only a tree branch. And more. Dreams of a once-sleeping dragon, awake now, and watching from the shadows. He'd heard its low, rumbling growl and felt its hot breath, yet could never make out the beast's features.

He dragged his left hand down over his dry, burning eyes, longing for just a moment's relief from the agony in his shoulder and the insufferable heat. Heat that caused his tongue to feel thick and his head to throb relentlessly. Had he died? Had he been denied the peace of the Otherworld and cast into hell? He forced his blurry eyes open, reassured by his mortal surroundings that he had not passed.

A single candle burned in the grand chamber that used to be Aswyn's, but its light blinded him. Its flame distorted and licked at his flesh, causing him to wonder if the old warlord's spirit still lingered and yearned for revenge. Or perhaps it was the dragon's fiery breath.

So be it. *Kill me now and be done with it,* Kyran thought, too weary to worry about doing battle with the old man's ghost or a long-forgotten legend. The balcony doors stood open, the thin leather drape flapping vainly like a bird with a broken wing. The breeze caused the flame on the candle to dance and cavort, casting shadows on the wall that seemed ominous and threatening.

The next moment, he knew someone was there. Had the woman dressed in black returned to avenge her master? He glanced at the bedside table, his gaze settling on Morven's forgotten dagger.

"Kyran?" Sayrid whispered.

She watched him struggle to reach a weapon on the table. She'd waited until Morven and Cyric left to eat before she slipped inside the chamber. She stepped closer, and he seemed not to notice her and strained harder, gritting his teeth in frustration as his fingers barely grazed the hilt before knocking the dagger to the floor.

"Foolish warlord. I will not harm you," she said with a perplexed frown. "In fact, I saved your life again last night."

Exhausted, he collapsed back against the pillows with a frown so deeply carved into his forehead she worried about her safety should she get too close. Memories of his fingers biting into her wrist by the river caused her to massage her arm while she approached the bedside. Cautiously, she pressed her hand to his forehead. Alarmed by the increased heat of his skin, she placed a little pouch on the table then hurried to the basin and filled it with cool water.

"Free me," he ground out, trying to push the thick pad of bandage from his shoulder. She caught his hand, amazed at his strength even though he was terribly ill.

He paused as if trying to collect his thoughts before he spoke again. "Free my arm."

She pulled the dagger from her belt and sliced though the cloth, silently cursing that she hadn't taken the time to do it before she'd left the night before. The moment the bandage fell away, he relaxed back against the pillows, breathing as if he had run a great distance. He swore softly then muttered something else, and she assumed he'd thanked her.

A late summer storm toiled outside, and convulsive lightning began to streak across the starless sky. As the candles fluttered wildly in the salt-tinged breeze, she pulled aside the furs, and began to bathe him. Once more she admired his physique—hard and muscular from wielding a heavy sword and with many a small scar to prove him unafraid of battle. Odd, she thought, for a king to risk his life in such a manner. Nay, she amended. Foolish. Should he fall, so would his army and many of her people who had sworn fealty.

"The wind and the water will chase your fever away," she whispered, as she continued to bathe his burning flesh. Aware he watched through half-closed eyes, she put aside the cloth and took the folded leaf from her pouch, placing it in her lap as she sat by his side to remove the last piece of the bandage. As Morven said, the wound appeared spoiled, red and festering in spite of being cauterized. One look confirmed her suspicion that the tip of the arrow had been dipped in poison.

"I have brought the healing mud, but you must not cry out when I place it upon the wound. 'Twill feel like a thousand wasp stings, but 'twill pass, I promise."

As gently as she could, she packed the wound with the mud. He tensed, but the only sign she saw that revealed his agony was the way his jaw clenched and his fingers curled into fists in the fur throw. After a few moments he relaxed, but when she reached for a clean bandage, he caught her hand in his firm grasp.

"Do not tie me down," he whispered hoarsely. When she nodded, his fingers went slack and his hand fell to his side. From a pitcher of water on the table, she wet a clean cloth and placed it over the mud, then covered it with a thicker pad and bound his shoulder. Her reward for the lighter bandage was a slight smile that made him appear a little less threatening.

She filled the cup with water and added a pinch of a yellow powder that the old sorceress, Derwyn, had given her ages ago. A loud crack of thunder caused Sayrid to jump slightly. A few moments later, rain pelted hard against the deerskin. Afraid the drop in temperature would aggravate his condition, she quickly pushed aside the leather drape and closed the wooden doors, pausing to wipe the raindrops from her face. When she returned to his bedside, she retrieved the cup.

"Who are you, and why have you returned?" he asked softly as she helped him sit up so he could drink. She wondered about his accent—why it wasn't as pronounced as those Viking warriors she had seen before.

"I am Sayrid," she replied, unwilling to divulge more. He seemed pleased that she had given her name.

"I am . . . I am Kyran."

"Aye, I heard your henchman say so in the forest." She let him have another drink. "Why are you here?" she asked.

He eased back down then closed his eyes. "I—I have come to free. . . ."

Much to her disappointment, his words stilled upon his lips, her potion taking effect more quickly because of his weakened condition. She watched him for several moments whilst he slept. This time, when he shifted to a more comfortable position, he showed no signs of pain. She moved a strand of damp, tawny hair off his forehead. Delightfully warm sparks tingled up her arm when she touched his skin, as if she sat too close to a fire on a cold winter day. Something sleeping deep inside her stirred to life. She stared at him, transfixed by his strong features. He would sleep soundly tonight . . . but would she?

She stood and pulled the furs up over his chest. It would not do to have him catch a chill now that his fever had broken. Footsteps outside the heavy planked door drew her attention, and she hurriedly slipped through the hidden passage. She barely had the wall in place when Cyric entered, Morven and Bynor close on his heels. Watching through the mesh, she thought Morven moved quickly for his size. The Viking hurried to the bedside, his bushy red brows drawn together in a fierce scowl.

"In the name of the gods, what has happened?" Morven muttered as he bent down and inspected the new bandage. His master stirred, then slowly opened his eyes.

"Where is she?" he asked, struggling to stay awake.

"Whom do you speak of, my friend? We saw no one," Bynor answered.

"Sayrid . . . the sorceress. The woman I saw in the forest."

Morven's scowl deepened with confusion as he put his hand on his master's forehead, and Sayrid knew 'twas because their warlord's skin no longer burned. "No one came in here tonight. I've guards posted at the door."

"She came, and I am better for it."

"Nay," Morven added. "You dreamed it. 'Tis the mixture I gave you for the fever. Your mind is playing tricks." Morven examined Kyran's new bandage again, while Cyric checked the balcony doors. Slowly Cyric turned, scanned the room, then looked directly at the bookcase. He approached, running his fingers along the wood, his scowl so intense her mouth grew dry.

"Say you her name again," Cyric asked, still frowning deeply.

"Sayrid," Kyran said quietly, unable to keep his eyes open any longer. "She came to me . . . from the balcony."

Much to her relief, Cyric turned his attention back to the warrior whilst Bynor hurried to the balcony, lifted the leather flap and checked the closed doors. "He's right. These were open. I'm sure of it."

" 'Twas a dream and nothing more." Morven glanced

suspiciously around the spacious chamber, exchanging cautious glances with Cyric. "He sleeps. Come, we will search the grounds beneath the balcony, and post another man there to be certain this witch does not return."

Cyric walked to the bedside and looked down at Kyran. "Either mine eyes are playing tricks, or he appears some better."

Once again the redheaded young man came to examine the shelf, so close to the latch and the mesh screen that if he'd bent down he would've seen her. Strangely, Sayrid's fear vanished when she looked at the man, but she'd take no chances regardless of his gentle appearance. Cautiously, she backed away, licked her fingers and pinched out the candle before she hurried down the familiar steps. Careful to let the old door close softly, she silently bade good-eve to the ancient castle and the dragon she imagined lived inside, and stayed to the shrubs and hawthorn bushes until she could run into the safety of the forest.

Dawn came too quickly, but Sayrid forced herself to rise and dress even though she longed to stay beneath the furs on her pallet. She'd spent most of the night thrashing about on her bed, her dreams haunted by the Norse warlord. There had to be some way to rid herself of this unwelcome host.

But how? She knew very little about spells and potions, only about the healing mud and herbs. Yet she felt as if she should know—special things that came to her in fleeting moments before sleep and wakefulness. She splashed some water on her face, thinking about her problem, when suddenly she stopped and stared into the basin. Startled at first, she soon felt relieved by what she saw.

Derwyn, the sorceress. Her wrinkly face smiled at her from the water. Sweet old Derwyn. Sayrid hadn't thought about Derwyn for many months, nor dared she visit lest Aswyn's spies learn of the old woman's whereabouts. Aswyn's hefty bounty for the capture of the old sorceress had served him poorly. Derwyn had done too much for the villagers, and they wouldn't betray her for mere golden and silver coins. Nor would Brynn betray her, for she knew more than most the power of Derwyn's spells and potions.

Sayrid's urgency to seek out the old woman encouraged her to dress swiftly, pausing only to grab a cloth-covered jar of gooseberry jam.

Fog as thick as dragon's breath swirled around Sayrid's feet as she walked down the overgrown path until she came to the side of a steep ravine. It took several moments to get her bearings, but she soon recognized, twenty feet ahead, the overgrown hawthorn hedge that protected the door of Derwyn's cottage. She cast a cautious glance over her shoulder to make sure no one watched, and then turned to knock, but the door opened before her knuckles touched the weathered wood.

"Sayrid, come in, come in, child. I've been expectin' ye," Derwyn exclaimed. "Thank ye for the gooseberry jam. I've a need of it." Derwyn lifted the jar from Sayrid's hand and carried it to the table.

Brynn paced before the black-clad soldier who stood at attention, white-faced and repentant in his human form.

"I told you never to let her out of your sight," Brynn hissed, thrusting her face so close to the soldier he flinched. "I need to know where she goes, whom she sees. Everything, do you understand?"

The man nodded. "Aye, my lady."

Brynn slapped him hard across his cheek. "Never speak to me again of your failures. To do so will mean you're no longer needed." She cast him an evil glance over her shoulder. "You know what happens then, I'm sure."

Sayrid stepped into the cave-like cottage, wishing she knew how the old woman knew of the jam. A fire flickered in the small, raised hearth. Above it, a blackened cauldron hung, and from that the aroma of mint and saffron filled the air. Various bunches of dried flowers adorned the walls, held there with thin strips of rabbit fur. On the far wall hung several small animal bones, also bound together with strips of hide.

"Do not be scar't of me and what I know," Derwyn reassured her. "Sit and rest yerself. Ye are tired from the lack of sleep, and I've got water boiling for some marigold tea."

Sayrid smiled. Several times in the past she'd sought out the old woman for healing herbs and advice, and each time old Derwyn had known Sayrid's reason before she could voice it. "Tell me, wise one, how you knew of my gift, and that I did not rest well?"

Sayrid hurried to help the old woman fill another pot with water. Derwyn seemed smaller, bent over more than Sayrid remembered from the last time she had visited. Her shoulders hunched forward, and she walked with the aid of a staff carved of blackthorn. The favorite wood of wizard and witches, Sayrid thought to herself. And how long had it been? Two years? Perhaps three?

"Three, lass. 'Tis been three. I'd begun tae believe ye'd forgotten auld Derwyn. And blackthorn is thought tae be magical by the Ancient Ones, as well."

"Forgive me. I had forgotten." Sayrid smiled again, feeling terrible that she'd not come to check on the old woman's well being in such a long time, settling instead for reports from Gwendolyn. She pushed her guilt aside, remembering Derwyn's ancestry. How foolish to fear this old woman clad in a worn blue gown and a cream-colored knitted shawl. Wisps of silver hair that had escaped from a discolored white cap floated around her wrinkled face.

A kind, sweet face. When Sayrid escaped from Aswyn's warriors and did battle with Brynn, had it not been for Derwyn she would've died from her wounds. But Derwyn found her in the forest and only the gods knew how such a small, feeble woman carried her to this little cave-like cottage.

Sayrid had little memory of those days, only that the old woman had tended her wounds and nursed her back to health, speaking in soft tones and singing strange songs about the Ancient Ones. She'd hung a medallion on the wall above Sayrid's bed with the promise that it would bestow good fortune and protect her from evil.

While Sayrid had convalesced, Derwyn had told her stories of myths and omens and magic to pass the time. Especially interesting were the stories of Dragon's Head Castle. When she began to heal, and could move about, the sorceress took her on short walks where Sayrid learned about herbs and roots; which would heal and which would harm when boiled or ground for magical potions. She learned how to tie snares and how to make arrows, and that was when Sayrid discovered Derwyn's secret.

Derwyn came from a long line of warrior-women. Her ancestors had learned to fight to protect Dragon's Head alongside their life-mates long, long ago. Derwyn had trained many of the village women to stand by their mates at times of war and defend their lands and families from enemy tribes. Although the old sorceress gave her few details, Sayrid had been eager to accept the intricately carved bow when Derwyn pulled it from under the bed and offered it as a gift.

Derwyn spent many hours teaching Sayrid how to use her new weapon, always with stories of how the bow was magical. Sayrid's blister had broken open during one of these training sessions and the old woman had showed her where to find the strange healing mud, explaining that she'd used it many times.

Much to Sayrid's surprise, after the initial burn, the pain had disappeared.

The skills and knowledge the old sorceress shared had proven very useful and made Sayrid feel even more guilty for not visiting. She touched the amulet, remembering the tears in Derwyn's eyes when she placed it around her neck, insisting she take it—that it belonged to her—had belonged to Derwyn's long-dead family.

Aye, Derwyn proved a kind soul, but Sayrid thought her a little mad as she believed in faeries and banshees, and the powers the dead wielded over the living. Good magic and bad. And there was something else Derwyn believed—that special souls could see the future—sometimes in their dreams whilst they slept, and sometimes in visions whilst awake. 'Twas a gift from their ancient ancestors who'd sworn to protect the dragons. Like the beloved dragons, most of the women with this power had been killed, but those who survived soon learned to hide their magic and use it only to help their people.

"Derwyn, forgive me. I did not realize it had been so long since my last visit."

"Ye've been busy stayin' alive," the old woman confirmed. "If naught from auld Aswyn then from those who have taken Dragon's Head."

"Aye, 'tis true, but I have come—"

"I know, child. I know why ye have come as I know the auld king is dead, replaced with a new, more potent one. Ye've seen him in yer dreams and then again in a vision and 'tis worrisome tae ye since ye dinna believe in the auld ones and their ways."

"Aye," Sayrid said, stunned by the old woman's ability to know exactly what had happened.

"Though my back is bent and mine eyesight grows dim, I still see many things the sighted cannot."

Once again, Sayrid's heart picked up its pace. "How?" Sayrid managed to ask, her voice barely over a whisper. "How do you know and see so much, yet you rarely leave this cave?"

" 'Tis as I said—a gift handed down from one to another." The old woman gave a toothless grin. "And Gwendolyn's little girl told me much when she delivered the eggs."

Sayrid smiled at the teasing twinkle in Derwyn's faded eyes.

"Now, come, sit and share a cup of marigold tea. 'Tis no' of'en I have a visitor." The old woman hobbled to the hearth, grabbed a thick cloth and lifted the kettle from the coals. She poured the boiling water into a chipped clay pot. A few moments later she added a sprinkle of precious spices from a small jar, a dab of honey, and then handed Sayrid a cup of her special brew. The old woman pulled up another stool and, sighing happily, sat and began to sip her tea.

Sayrid sank down upon a fleece-covered stool before she took a drink, trying to control her growing impatience. She had not traveled this long distance to sit quietly and sip tea. She had much more important matters to discuss, like those of the Norseman and the capture of Dragon's Head. She put down the cup and started to speak.

"Aye, child," Derwyn said, nodding toward Sayrid's cup with a knowledgeable grin. "In due time we will speak of the warrior and his army, and of the legend of Dragon's Head, but first we must take a moment tae enjoy our tea. 'Twill too quickly grow cold." She smiled and nodded at the same time. " 'Tis best served hot."

"Derwyn, you do not understand. This man . . . Kyran. He's wounded, and I'm in need of your advice."

"Ye've done all there is tae do. He's better as we speak."

"But there is much I need to know about—"

"In due time." Derwyn continued to sip her tea, closing her eyes and savoring the spicy aroma. "There is much to gain with patience and a good cup of tea."

53

Sayrid heaved a resigned sigh and picked up her cup. When she took another sip, she forced herself to breathe deeply of the pungent marigold and spices Derwyn had added. In truth, it tasted sweet and enjoyable, almost relaxing if she didn't have so much to tell the old sorceress. "Derwyn, please. I—"

"Very well, I can see ye will'na rest till ye know. But I can only give ye a little as he is still very much a mystery tae me too. I am auld and my powers are no' as strong."

Sayrid's brows came quickly together. "Then I shall tell you what I know. He is Norse. Of this I am certain."

Derwyn nodded and took the interruption as an opportunity to pour a little more tea. "So ye say, but even now ye harbor doubt, wondering what ye hear in his speech." Derwyn put down her tea and closed her faded blue eyes. "I see the mark of the dragon, and I see that many fear him, but judge him no' by his Viking speech."

"He has an accent—faint, but noticeable. It reeks of King Arcas' tribe."

"Aye. He's different from his cohorts, but how, I've yet tae discover. There's a large one, nearly a giant. . . ." Derwyn stared into the dregs of her cup. "A Viking, who's sworn a blood oath to protect the one you called Kyran. And a warrior friend, and. . . ." Derwyn's brows drew together. "Another young man, friend to Kyran, but no warrior." Derwyn looked up and grinned. "Though ye know yer way round Dragon's Head, beware of the big brute till he comes tae know yer purpose. Then he could well prove tae be a friend. Ye must also beware of an auld enemy . . . Brynn. Even though Aswyn is dead, she's evil and seeks to better herself with—"

"With Kyran?" Sayrid cried. "But she tried to kill—"

Derwyn held up her knobby hand. "Hush and ye shall hear. Now that auld Aswyn's gone, she seeks to restore her standin' with Oddrum and thinks she can accomplish this with the new king's death."

Sayrid nodded, wondering why it felt as if the whole time Derwyn spoke, she seemed to be trying to remember something. Sayrid looked up from her tea. "Oddrum's kingdom is leagues away. Why would she join with him?"

"She has good reason. They are kin. Oddrum cast her out and took her rightful place, declaring himself king. She's a crafty one, she is, and I sense that she's become more powerful—more of a threat. She was sent tae Aswyn to become his queen, but instead became his whore with no hope tae become his life-mate whilst you lived. If'n Aswyn could've found ye, he would've tried to make ye his queen. 'Twas why she tried to kill you so long ago. But now the old traitor's dead, leaving her with little chance tae become queen unless she—"

Derwyn wagged a finger. "If she kills the new king, she can go tae Oddrum with the news and make peace with her brother." Again Derwyn's expression grew vague. "I should know the reason she wants this . . . but it escapes me. . . ." She waved her knobby hand. "Never mind. 'Tis known by only a few that Oddrum's wife died in childbirth last spring. Brynn knows, and she hopes it softened Oddrum's heart. Yet her intentions are vague—I feel she seeks his death so she can become queen."

"She would kill her own brother?"

"She would. But she may no' have to. 'Tis no' uncommon for a man to die after losing his life-mate," Derwyn said with a nod. "He'll be seeking a new one and that's why ye must not venture too far from Dragon's Head." Derwyn took several sips of tea. " 'Tis no' Brynn and Oddrum ye came to speak of. Ye are curious about the new king. Ye nursed the warrior back to the livin'—rid him of the poison as I did ye so long ago. But then ye discovered something frightening, did ye no'?"

Sayrid nodded. She slipped her hand into her pocket and

withdrew a small pouch. She emptied it on the table, spilling out the amulet. "I took this from the warlord. When I touch it, I see a battle."

Derwyn's faded blue eyes widened a moment before they narrowed. She continued to stare at the bronze medallion, gingerly touching the smooth stone with a crooked finger. "Aye, ye see his past, but there's more yer no' tellin' me." Derwyn's faded eyes narrowed even more when she looked up. "Ye feel his pain."

Sayrid nearly choked on her tea, but could find no words to express her astonishment.

With the amulet still cradled in her palm, Derwyn fell silent for several moments before she looked up at Sayrid. "How did ye come by this?"

A thousand questions sprang to mind, but Sayrid didn't ask them. " 'Twas around his neck when I found him by the river."

Again the old woman touched it, lifting it and placing it in her palm where she gave it a closer, squinting look. " 'Tis special indeed. Looks tae be the mate tae yer own. Curious this is."

"The mate?" Sayrid asked, troubled by Derwyn's expression. The twinkle in the old woman's eyes had vanished, replaced by something Sayrid sensed to be much more serious. "But you gave me the amulet after I escaped. You told me it would keep me safe."

The old woman placed the warrior's medallion back in the pouch before she pushed it toward Sayrid. "Put it back in yer pocket. Hide it, and yers as well, lest someone sees them and does ye harm tae have them."

Derwyn stood slowly, tugging her shawl more closely around her shoulders before she placed another log on the fire, quiet for several moments as if she were trying again to remember something. She turned and her expression changed to one more cheerful as she retrieved a small sack and placed several things into it before she gave it to Sayrid. "Take these. I've plenty enough to share."

Sayrid took the sack and started to speak, but Derwyn turned back to tend the fire, adding a few small logs until the flames grew strong again.

"If ye bring me a lock of hair, I'll be able tae see him more clearly. There's no' much I can give ye with only the amulet. I fear 'tis not his, but stolen from the true owner."

Sayrid quickly pulled out his dagger. "I have this."

"Aye, a ring and his coin as well." Derwyn sat down and took the weapon, muttering about the difference between thieveries and restitutions for deeds done. She admired the hilt, turning it over in her heavily lined, calloused palm. "An almandine, and a fine one too. Like those in the amulets. There are legends of such stones—stones believed tae hold the secret to the creation of Dragon's Head—tears of the old dragon, hisself."

Sayrid's forehead crinkled, but before she could ask Derwyn to explain, the old woman spoke again.

"I see him, but no' clearly. A strappin' brute he is and a fearsome warlord . . . of mixed . . . nay, noble birth."

Sayrid felt certain she heard more than a touch of surprise in Derwyn's voice. "Noble? 'Twould explain much," she agreed. "His henchmen are never far away."

Derwyn's bushy gray brows nearly touched for several moments. But, this time, the old woman forced a smile before giving the dagger back. " 'Tis a weapon. All it tells me is that he's a skilled warrior gifted in dealin' out death." Derwyn shivered, and raised her hand when Sayrid went to speak. " 'Tis all I can tell ye till ye do as I've asked."

Sayrid sighed, certain there was more, but knew nothing she could say would make Derwyn admit it. "I wonder if our people will ever rule their own lands again."

"In time," Derwyn muttered as she added some honey to a

second cup of tea for Sayrid and herself. "I saw the ravens the morning Aswyn fell. They are of'en symbols of death and destruction."

"Then they have appeared because Aswyn is dead and his treasonous grip on Dragon's Head has been destroyed?"

"Perhaps . . . perhaps no'. The ravens hav'na left. I know ye saw one whilst tendin' the warrior by the river. 'Tis a special bird—one to be wary of."

Sayrid stared at the old woman. "Then you—"

"Know that ye killed a man?" Derwyn finished with a sympathetic smile. "Aye, lass, but fret ye no more about it. What happened 'twas meant tae happen, and there was nothin' ye could've done tae prevent it. Trust me when I say, the dead man was no' Welsh, but Norse, a mercenary loyal to Aswyn only for the gold he received for doin' his dirty work."

"How do you know this?" Sayrid asked with a worried frown, swallowing down the last sip of tea. The sooner she finished, the sooner the old sorceress would examine the dregs and perhaps disclose some more helpful information.

Derwyn shook her head. "Ye do no' remember all that I taught ye, lass?"

"Only bits and pieces," Sayrid replied, shaking her head. " 'Twas very long ago."

"I suppose 'twas tae be expected that ye'd forget as there was so much ye had tae learn and so lit'le time tae teach ye." Derwyn took a sip of tea. "Death and destruction are part of it, aye, but the warrior wears a dragon on his chest—a dragon clutching a dead raven. Dragons and ravens are both symbols of prophecy."

"What prophecy?"

"Too much knowledge too soon is arduous for even the most stalwart tae digest. Methinks I will remember more later." Derwyn's kind smile appeased Sayrid's impatience.

"You've been very kind to me over the years at great risk to yourself. Why, I wonder?"

Derwyn's expression grew serious again. "Ye remember nothin' of yer childhood, do ye?"

Sayrid sighed and shook her head, handing the old woman her cup when she reached for it. "Only that I am the daughter of Llewellyn and Nerys Emrys, but they died when I was four winters old and Aswyn took me into the castle after their deaths."

Derwyn muttered something under her breath that Sayrid didn't understand. Instead of repeating it, the old woman inspected the dregs. "Ye will have a long life and bear many children." She grinned again, only this time Sayrid sensed it to be forced. Without being asked, Derwyn retold one of her many stories about herbs and the good things provided by the goddess of the forest. Afterward, she sat back with a pleased smile and yawned. " 'Twas nice to see ye." Derwyn covered another long, loud yawn. "All this talkin' has worn me out. I've need of a nap. Come back another day and I'll tell ye about the legend of Dragon's Head."

"I'm in no hurry," Sayrid hurried to say.

"Another day," Derwyn repeated.

Perplexed by Derwyn's dismissal, Sayrid stood, watching as the old woman went to her cot and lay down. She yawned loudly, thwarting any more questions.

CHAPTER FOUR

Sayrid stood before Derwyn's small cottage, seeing it much differently than she had before. In Derwyn's story, she spoke of how the spiny hawthorn hedge surrounding the moss and ivy-covered sod had been placed there for a purpose. As old as Sayrid's cottage itself, each bush and vine had been planted by the Ancient Ones to protect anyone who took refuge in the little house. And so it was with the rowan trees, one in front and the other near the rear, both designed to chase away witches and evil sprites.

Sayrid looked at them with renewed respect after assuming their only purpose was to grow berries to feed the birds. And then there were the huge, towering oaks, there to draw any dangerous lightning, and to bind this world with the Otherworld so the Ancient Ones would never be forgotten.

She wrapped her arms tightly about herself, thinking about Derwyn and finding her unusual stories easier to believe. Even though she'd been sorely disappointed that Derwyn couldn't give her all the answers, she'd found this new knowledge very interesting, and promised to try to be content with her predicted future. She'd be the first to admit that the thought of children pleased her, but she hadn't made such a precarious journey to watch Derwyn read tea leaves and tell tales about trees.

She placed a sack of apples, spices and dried marigolds on the small table, thinking more about Derwyn's story. Her gaze landed upon her broom—a forgotten gift from Derwyn. She remembered when Derwyn gave it to her, how the old woman had crafted it from the birch tree, and told her it had magical powers to sweep away not only dirt, but harmful spirits.

Sayrid took two eggs from her pocket and placed them in the basket next to the bread. The eggs reminded her about Gwendolyn and Dafydd. She wondered what would happen to them and all of the villagers now that the new king had captured Dragon's Head. There was only one way to know of their fate. She would wait a day to let things settle down before she would visit her friends in the village.

Bynor spent most of the morning tending to the needs of his fellow soldiers in Kyran's place. Much had to be done. Bynor realized that Kyran wanted to see to it himself, but his best friend was much too ill to do so. Too ill to be told about the murdered servant woman.

Bynor strolled among the warriors, bellowing instructions, assisting some of the young ones in the use of their weapons. He motioned to the younger men to gather in a circle, calling one to meet him in the center with wooden sword and wicker wood shield. Bynor held a wooden staff and urged the man to attack. With an upward swing the young man's sword went flying, and with a downward sideways swing the man landed hard on his back. Bynor quickly straddled him, wrenching the shield from the startled man's grasp. Bynor came down with the edge of the shield, stopping within inches of the man's windpipe, hearing a unified gasp from the crowd. Bynor grinned. "A little harder, Erwyn, and you'd be missing your head."

"Aye, my lord," the young warrior said, accepting the captain's hand to rise.

Bynor nodded to him and gave him back his shield. "Now, fetch your sword and go practice what I've shown you." He raised his voice to be heard by the others. "Tomorrow I shall pick another opponent, so practice well."

The men were soon back at it, surprising Bynor with their renewed enthusiasm.

"Many are much younger than I," Cyric said as he came up behind Bynor.

"Aye, 'tis true, but they are all good men who would gladly lay down their lives for you." Bynor turned from watching the men and looked at Cyric. "We both know there cannot be peace without an army to ensure it."

"The irony of it troubles me. 'Tis like tying a white cloth to a bloody sword."

Bynor grinned again. "I need not remind you, I'm sure, but we both know life is much sweeter after a brush with death." He looked back at the men in the practice field. "They are ready to fight to the last man if we are attacked."

"Pray to the gods they won't have to," Cyric stated with a worried frown. "I fear if Kyran isn't better soon, we could lose all that we have worked for."

Bynor nodded, walking with his friend toward the inner bailey. "He will survive. He has always survived."

"True, but this wound is, by far, the most serious. Morven says it is because of the poison."

"Then perhaps we should send some men out to find the witch Kyran insists helped him." Cyric gave him a skeptical glance, and Bynor said, "I found a woman's body partially buried and covered with some ferns behind the scullery. Her throat had been cut—possibly by this witch. We needs find her before more are harmed."

"She appears and disappears at will, and you tell me with a straight face that you can capture her?" Cyric frowned. "Me-thinks she's had many years hiding in yonder forest, and has places to hide where even the gods couldn't find her."

" 'Tis simple. We will move Kyran into a different chamber;

when she appears tonight, she'll find me."

"Simple, you say. Our friend is in pain and you want to move him?" Cyric shook his head. "So far, when she visits, she hasn't harmed him."

"How can you be so sure?" Bynor's brows snapped together. "A scullery maid is dead, and, for all we know, this witch could have done it. Are you so sure she couldn't have been the one who shot him? If she's still lurking about and loyal to the old king, she could very easily poison him."

"I understand your concern, yet I sense the death of the scullery maid is unrelated. Methinks there is someone lurking about still loyal to the old king, but surely all those who followed Aswyn have fled or been punished." Cyric met Bynor's dark look. "When we first found Kyran, someone had packed the wound with mud. At first I thought it the cause of his continued illness, but then he got worse after the mud was removed. Now as I think upon it, I believe it had been done to draw the poison."

Bynor scoffed. "Magical mud? 'Tis nonsense." He shook his head. "Legends of dead dragons, hidden treasure and now magical mud. All nonsense."

"Perhaps . . . perhaps not. All I know is that he claims she helped him . . . and I believe him." Cyric caught Bynor's arm when the soldier went to leave. "When I was a child I remember that my grandmother believed in such things. She's gone now— killed when I was captured, but part of me still believes . . . in magic and legends."

"Aye, and I'll believe when I see him well enough to walk down those steps."

"Fair enough. But, in the meantime, methinks you should drop your scheme to capture her. I've a feeling she'll come to us when she's ready."

Kyran came awake with a start, half rising out of the bed before he realized there was no threat. He'd dreamed of the sorceress who had saved his life in a magical forest. She had come to him a woman, but, when he'd caught her arm, she'd changed into a child, yet her eyes still sparkled with adult defiance. He raked his left hand though his tousled hair, somewhat annoyed that she plagued his dreams—and, now, his waking thoughts.

Morven slept on the floor, on a mound of furs before the hearth, his snores loud enough to rouse the dead. Tossing the cover aside, Kyran swung his legs over the edge, waiting a moment until he felt sure he could stand. Though August seemed usually hot and humid, the damp chill of dawn still lingered in the chamber. He made his way to the wood bin and none too quietly tossed a log on the coals.

Morven bolted upright with a short sword in hand.

"Curse you, you young pup," the Norseman growled, tossing aside the fur and standing to his full height as he stretched.

Kyran glanced at his henchman and grinned, even though he felt a little dizzy. "You sleep like the dead. Methinks you've grown soft. I remember a time I could not have approached without waking you."

Morven dragged his thick fingers through his tangled mane of hair. "When your shoulder is healed, I will show you who has grown soft. I will beat you to a bloody pulp with my staff."

"I accept your challenge, but before you crush my skull—"

Morven caught him before he hit the stone floor. "You should stay abed," Morven grumbled. "You are pale and weak."

Feeling a little foolish, Kyran accepted Morven's help back to bed, and then wearily lay back against the pillows as a knock sounded on the door.

"Enter," Morven called.

Cyric came in carrying a pewter tray piled high with roasted meat, crusty bread and ripened fruit. He hesitated for several moments before he smiled. He dragged a chair closer to Kyran's bed, aware his friend looked fatigued and needed a few more days of rest. "Praise the gods, I did not think you would be able to open your eyes for several more days."

"Indeed," Morven added skeptically, moving the fur aside to inspect Kyran's shoulder. "I suppose now that the fog has cleared from your thick skull, you do not remember who or what changed your bandage?"

Cyric offered the tray, pleased when Kyran plucked several fat grapes from the plate before he spoke. "I told you last night. The enchantress from the forest came to me. When she finished, the pain vanished, and I slept like a babe without the nightmares your potion provokes."

Cyric buttered a chunk of warm bread before he placed a thin slice of meat on top. "Here, you need to build your strength."

"Who's cooking?"

"A woman named Gwendolyn today, but the village women share it. Most of the villagers chose to stay," Cyric added, cutting a piece of bread for himself before Morven took the tray from his lap. Cyric took a large bite, watching while Morven tore a large chunk from the loaf. " 'Tis a good thing, too, I say. I'm sure Morven will agree when I say this bread tastes as if the gods made it themselves."

Kyran shook his head. "Nay, 'tis made by a Welsh woman and tastes all the better because of it."

A boy entered carrying a pitcher. He cast a cautious glance at Kyran then openly stared at Morven, who purposely scowled back. The child placed the pitcher on the table and ran from the room.

Cyric chuckled as he filled a jeweled goblet with sweet, spiced wine. " 'Tis cruel to scare the young ones that way. How are we to win them over if you keep acting like some kind of terrifying giant?"

"He is a terrifying giant," Kyran confirmed, accepting the offered cup.

"I care little if they like me," Morven grumbled over a mouthful of food. "I prefer they fear me. Then, and only then, will they leave me be." He unsheathed his dagger. "I swear to you, if the wound is not better, I will seek out this witch, and, instead of burning you with a hot poker, I will pitch her into the fire."

Morven ate the last bite before he pulled the bandage away from Kyran's shoulder. He swore at the sight of the wad of nearly dry mud, complaining that now the wound would have to be cleansed, possibly even cauterized again.

Kyran put his hand protectively over his shoulder. "It pains me not, so forego your torture. Leave it alone."

" 'Tis dry at least." Morven moved as if to remove it, but the clump fell before he could touch it. The wound appeared clean and closed. The Norseman's expression turned comical as he stared at it.

Cyric stooped to pick up the dried clod. "Perhaps only a witch with magical spells could have done this." He looked at Kyran, wondering if he remembered anything of their childhood—before the battle—before they were sold as slaves. "Or a Welsh woman gifted in the ways of the Ancient Ones." Cyric laughed. "As I think upon it, my mother always knew when I told a fib."

"The mud and its healing power are not the doings of a witch. Only evil comes from women who profess such an alliance." Kyran leaned his head back on the pillows whilst Morven applied a clean bandage. "Nay, methinks the woman who came to me is a healer—or a very gifted sorceress—and, because of Aswyn, is afraid to show herself."

Morven shook his head as he tied the ends of the bandage in place with a long length of cloth. "If she is not a witch, then explain to me how she can appear and disappear at will?"

"I wish I knew," Kyran confessed. "But, now—as you put it— the fog is cleared from my head: I am certain she saved my life at the river, then again last night." He heaved a tired sigh, refusing to voice that he'd also felt as if some beast watched him from the shadows. "You're free now, Morven. I've a beautiful woman who has taken your place as my guardian."

Morven gave a doubtful snort, pulling the ends of the bandage tight, ignoring Kyran's disapproving scowl. "Now who has grown soft? Women are for cooking and bedding . . . and slitting a man's throat whilst he sleeps."

Cyric nearly choked. "Is that a confession?" He exchanged comical glances with Kyran. "Methinks he's speaking of that scar on his neck . . . and his poor dead wife."

"Laugh again and you shall join her," Morven warned.

"Easy, my large friend. I was but jesting. It matters little to me what Kyran's woman professes to be or how she behaves— only that he recovers." Cyric tossed the wad of dried mud into the fire, amazed as it curled and hissed upon the coals before it melted away.

"I've a hunger for roasted boar," Morven muttered gruffly as he left Cyric standing in the middle of the chamber. He grumbled something under his breath about doing some hunting, and then hoisted his ax over his shoulder.

"Of all the men to have pledged their lives to you . . . ," Cyric stated. He shook his head. "You had to save the life of Morven the Red, the most fearsome Viking ever spawned. He most likely helped kill many of our people. Probably with his bare hands."

Kyran gave a soft, humorless laugh. "Aye, 'tis strange to have one such as he so faithful, but I have grown accustomed to having him around and prefer him this way to facing him in battle. Think you, how many times since I saved his life has he saved ours?"

"Too many to count, but had he and his barbarous kind not

invaded our lands, destroyed our families, and taken us as slaves and sold us to Arcas, there would have been no need for his protection." Cyric went to the shelves on the wall and lifted an elegant pewter goblet, blowing off the dust to admire the stones. "Bynor found a woman's body partially buried behind the scullery. Her throat was cut, but no one saw or knows anything. He thinks it could be the doings of the woman that you've seen. Last night, you said the woman told you her name was Sayrid."

"Aye, she did."

"My little sister's name was Jenalyn." Cyric replaced the goblet and picked up a simple gold bracelet. He paused, trying to put a face to the name, but his memories were too few and too long ago. He hadn't thought about his family in many years. 'Twas better to leave the dead buried in the past. "Would you recognize this woman if you saw her again?" Cyric cast a quick glance over his shoulder.

"Aye. 'Tis likely. She had blue . . . nay, green eyes the color of new grass in spring."

Cyric grinned. "Are you now a poet?"

"I was merely trying to tell you the color," Kyran grumbled.

"I think my sister's eyes were green . . . as were my mother's," Cyric blurted out. He quickly turned back to the bounty on the shelf, feeling foolish. Hadn't he just decided not to resurrect old memories? He picked up a nasty-looking double-edged dagger, wiping the dust from his fingers on his tunic. He stared at the wall behind the shelves, overcome with a peculiar feeling that he'd been in this room before. "Praise the gods we were sold to King Arcas and not butchered as many of our tribe were butchered."

Had Cyric not been paying attention to the plunder on the shelves, he would have noticed the darkening of Kyran's eyes— the tightening of his firm jaw.

"I would think more of our future and less of what has

transpired," Kyran replied, reminding Cyric of the hardships Kyran experienced under Arcas' whip. Many times Cyric had wanted to tell his friend that he knew about the abuse, but he also knew that Kyran would deny it ever happened. Having been chosen as a house servant and taught to do the accounts, Cyric had been spared the fate of his friend, trained to be a soldier good for only one thing: to fight and kill King Arcas' enemies.

And Kyran had learned his lessons painfully well—lessons that were instrumental in the king's overthrow and the taking of Dragon's Head.

Cyric knew, whilst a slave, Kyran had performed so well, King Arcas put him in charge of training many of the new slaves. With the help of men much like himself, pressed into serving an evil king, Cyric felt certain it had been an easy task for Kyran to convince them to join the rebellion. He had heard Kyran say many times, 'twas better to be dead than to live one's life under the whip, and he knew many shared the same belief.

"We cannot change the past, only our futures," Kyran said, voicing Cyric's thoughts. Kyran shrugged his shoulder as if he were trying to work out some stiffness. "If there has been an innocent murdered, we should double the guard around the castle. Have our men settled in?"

"Aye, Bynor has taken command. He is doing as you would do if you could. You trained him well. All are fed, and houses are being built for their families as we speak." Cyric grinned. "Our destiny is but a stone's throw away."

"And guards posted on every wall and in the village?"

Cyric nodded. "Aye, just as you would've done had you not been wounded."

"We can't be too careful. Oddrum's kingdom is but four days to the west. If his spies survived, by now he knows of Aswyn's overthrow and could well be gathering an army."

Cyric's gaze locked with his friend's. "I, too, am concerned about that. I've asked Bynor to post guards deep in the forest and on the highest cliffs. Dragon's Head is on high ground. We'll easily see any who dare to attack. Perhaps if Oddrum's spies tell him the size of our army, he'll consider our proposal and see the good in it."

"Do not fool yourself. He will come," Kyran said at the same time he yawned. "That is why I must get to him first. Mayhap he will listen once he learns that the prophecy must be fulfilled or all of the tribes are in peril."

"We will speak of this again when you are well. In the meantime, should he attack, we will be as ready as any army can be," Cyric stated with more conviction than he felt. "And, I will ask Bynor to look more closely into the death of the scullery maid."

"Sayrid," Gwendolyn cried, "you very nearly frightened me to death." A woman old enough to be Sayrid's mother put down a basket of clean clothes and held out her arms. " 'Tis been ages since we've seen each other, and you blend so nicely with the trees I did not even notice you. Derwyn taught you well."

Sayrid stepped forward and accepted a hug, placing a kiss on the older woman's cheek before she pressed a heavy leather purse into her palm. "You are well? The children and Dafydd?"

"I am—we are. Rhonwyn is nearly a grown woman. 'Tis been a long time since we last saw each other," Gwendolyn stated with a bright smile. "Look about the village. Our lot in life has changed for the better, praise the gods and our new master." Gwendolyn gauged the weight of the purse. "I would ask how you came by this, but I think I already know. 'Tis his, is it not?"

"Speak thee of Kyran, the new king?" Sayrid asked, frowning. She shrugged her shoulders. "I found it in the forest."

"Aye. Most likely attached to his belt." Gwendolyn laughed.

She went to the shelf over the hearth and took down a brown jar, placing the pouch inside. "I will share this with the others in the morning, but as you can see, our lives really have changed."

"Aye, for the worse," Sayrid countered. She made a sweeping motion with her arms. "Look about you, dear friend. We are surrounded by warriors. I have never seen so many."

"Aye, but not all are as tough as they look. Many are barely past boyhood, while some are just like us—taken against their will and trained to fight or die. I will agree that many of our people are still frightened, but no one has been molested or even spoken to harshly. The new king forbids it. One young man, with hair much like the color of yours, spoke to Dafydd and several of the village elders on the new king's behalf and told us we have nothing to fear if we pledge fealty to the new lord of Dragon's Head. Then, when I least expected it, the same man asked me to come to the castle to prepare some food— bread and meat for his men and broth for the new king. And gave me three chickens for doing so."

"This man came to you and asked?" Sayrid repeated skeptically. "Chickens?"

"Aye. He asked, and, of course, I agreed. Though I must say, when I brought up the soup, the young king did not appear well at all. He could barely swallow the broth."

"He took an arrow in the right shoulder the day of the battle," Sayrid confirmed.

"Aye, so Dafydd told me—an arrow in his sword-arm whilst he fought Aswyn. Dafydd saw it happen. Though the archer hid on the battlement, we suspect Brynn. Not a soul has seen her since, clever girl she is, and growing stronger every day. However," Gwendolyn said, grinning, "there are rumors that a beautiful witch found the wounded king in the forest, cast a spell on him, and saved his life."

Gwendolyn gave Sayrid a sideways glance. " 'Twas you, was

it not?" A quick inspection caused her to shake her head. "No wonder he thinks you a forest-witch, dressed as you are."

"Aye, he called me such. I assume, since you know of it, he still believes it to be true?" Sayrid glanced around to make sure they were not being watched, then picked up the basket and motioned toward Gwendolyn's cottage. "Let us go into your home. Whilst I help you fold these, I will tell you what happened."

Several small children looked up from their play with rag dolls, then ran over to receive welcomed hugs. "The children miss you," Gwendolyn chided. "Rhonwyn is helping her father fix the thatch. She will be angry with me if she misses your visit. You should come by more often, especially now that the danger has passed."

"Has it passed?" Sayrid challenged, reaching for a shirt. "King Aswyn is dead, but what know us of his replacement? Soon, Oddrum will catch the scent of blood and send his wolves." Sayrid shook her head. "I fear we have come out of the jaws of one dragon into another."

Gwendolyn gave a small smile. " 'Tis true, but better a fair and just king feast on our bones than a traitorous Welshman. Three days ago, I would have been afraid to leave my house. Now, there is work for everyone, building new houses for the soldiers and their families, and we are paid with land and animals, not the lash. Gwendolyn's eyes grew round. "Reyna told me the one called Cyric came and asked if she would serve the new lord, in the castle. In return, she and her husband were given a small parcel of land which they can farm. They'll be able to keep all but a small portion of what they produce."

Gwendolyn nodded. "And because of my bread and a promise to deliver more, I was given two ewes with lambs. When the lambs are old enough to be weaned, one stays with us, and the other goes back to the master."

Sayrid's mouth fell open. "You were given stock and land? How—I mean, why?"

"I cannot say, but we are not the only ones to whom the king has shown such generosity. There are others as well. Each of us must give a portion of what we raise to the new king. As we pledged our loyalty to him, so has he pledged to protect us from the other warlords." Gwendolyn shook her head. "Nay, my dear Sayrid, I am not afraid of this man. If he came to the village, I would get down on my knees and thank him. I cannot know for sure, but this . . . this security is what our ancestors must have felt when the dragons offered them protection."

"The dragons are long gone." Sayrid folded a well-worn gown. "Although I'm relieved that Aswyn is dead, there are times when I fear word of it will spread, and those warlords who have coveted Dragon's Head will test their skill against the new master. King Arcas and King Oddrum have long desired Dragon's Head. Already a new flock of ravens has come to the forest. I feel them watching my every move."

Gwendolyn's smile vanished, but Sayrid was too busy with the wash to notice. "Nay, Gwen, I fear this man's rule may be short lived, and much more innocent blood will be shed."

"Have you not heard the good news?" Gwendolyn asked.

"Heard what?"

"King Arcas is dead."

Sayrid clutched the dishcloth she was about to fold to her breast. "How is that possible? He and his tribe have long ruled the north. I thought he had nearly ten thousand warriors under his command."

"Slaves, most of them," Gwendolyn added. "Loyal only because they lived in fear for their lives and those of their families."

"You seem pleased with this news." Sayrid shook her head, folded the cloth and added it to the pile. "I'm puzzled why you view this as good news. If he is dead, his sons will seek revenge on the tribe that killed him. What if they come here in search of them? They will think we joined them and kill us all as well."

Sayrid went to the door and looked out. Most of the soldiers had shed their doublets and weapons; if she hadn't been told who they were, they would have looked much like any other villagers. Many were large, heavily muscled men, bearing black tattoos on their arms. She had no doubt that they could take off a man's head with one swing of their sword. She couldn't stop the shiver that crawled up her spine, looking at one particularly stout man who appeared to be of higher ranking. "By the gods," she murmured. "Now I believe. Only men like these . . . this legion of warriors could defeat Arcas."

"Aye, or so Dafydd told me after speaking with one of their captains. I believe his name was Bynor. 'Tis why I sleep better at night—knowing that we are well protected." Gwendolyn took the empty basket and put it in the corner. "Since you saved the king's life, I am almost certain he would want an audience with you." The older woman smiled when she cast Sayrid a glance over her shoulder. "Mayhap you will be rewarded." Gwendolyn slipped her hand into her purse and retrieved two coins, holding them for Sayrid to see. "As Dafydd and the other men are paid for building houses, I, and many of the other women, are paid for delivering bread."

"You jest," Sayrid scoffed, watching while Gwendolyn dropped the coins back into her pocket.

"Go to him. Wouldn't it be wonderful if you could move back into the castle and live among your people again?"

"Castle? I have no right to live there. If it was possible, and I doubt it, I would ask Dafydd to build my house close to yours."

"That would please me very much, indeed."

Her friend's cheerfulness didn't chase the uneasiness that had settled over Sayrid. " 'Tis too soon. 'Tis too soon for all of you to think our situation improved or to think him kind and just. It could be trickery—to make us compliant."

"Nonsense," Gwendolyn persisted. "Go to him. Tell him you saved his life and see if he doesn't reward you."

"I've no need of a reward, only the desire to free my people, and I can best do that if first I study mine enemy."

"You're so sure he's your enemy?"

"Aye, till he proves otherwise. That is why I have come, to ask for your help. I must find a way to get inside the castle." Sayrid frowned when Gwendolyn laughed.

"Why not enter as you usually do . . . right under their noses."

Again Sayrid glanced around, worried someone might hear. "Shush, 'tis a secret only you and Dafydd know, and I insist we keep it that way." She tossed her heavy hair over her shoulder. "I need a disguise so I may witness with mine own eyes this king's treatment of our people . . . especially behind closed doors."

"Very well. Remove your gown. I've an idea that will make you look much like one of my daughters."

'Twas only a little while later when Sayrid picked up a basket of fresh, crusty bread and stepped out of Dafydd and Gwendolyn's cottage. She smoothed the white apron over the pale blue gown. Though not a fancy garment, Sayrid wished she owned such finery. With her breasts bound and her long hair braided and covered by a short white wimple, both Gwendolyn and her eldest daughter, Rhonwyn, agreed that she could pass for an adolescent. Rhonwyn told Sayrid that she should give the basket only to the young, redheaded man—that he was the nicest.

The weight of the king's dagger in her pocket eased some of her trepidation as she followed the winding path toward Dragon's Head. The sun appeared high above the mountaintop, but 'twas not the thin fingers of dark clouds that caused her to shiver. 'Twas the solitary raven that perched upon a low branch of an oak tree. She expected it to move as she got closer, but it did not. Instead it hopped to another branch and looked at her inquisitively.

"What omen are you?" she whispered, aware that the bird might be there to warn her of some impending danger. The bird tilted its shiny black head, matching her stare. When she reached out to touch it, it hopped to a nearby branch on the next tree. And so it followed her until she pulled off a small portion of bread and threw it at the bird. Much to her surprise, the raven caught the offering, and then flew away toward the parapets of Dragon's Head.

Maldwyn, King Oddrum's old sorcerer, dragged his bony hand over his long white beard, appearing more troubled than Oddrum could remember as they listened to one of Oddrum's spies describe the battle at Dragon's Head.

"King Aswyn is dead," Oddrum repeated, unaware that his own expression appeared dark and foreboding—so foreboding that the messenger took a step back before reconfirming the king's death with a barely audible aye. Oddrum motioned to a nearby servant. "Take this man, feed him and prepare a chamber where he can rest."

"My lord," Maldwyn began. "I saw a man's face in my dreams, but thought little of it till now. Now, I suspect it to be the face of Aswyn's killer."

"Tell me what he looks like," Oddrum commanded. "Tell me and I will send an army to Dragon's Head to retrieve him." He listened to Maldwyn's description, drumming his fingers impatiently on the polished wooden arms of his throne, all the while thinking of how he would torture the man.

"I warn you to be cautious," Maldwyn replied, making Oddrum wonder if the old man heard his thoughts. " 'Tis no ordinary warrior who has taken Dragon's Head. Nay, this warrior is different . . . gifted. He has within his grasp the means to destroy us all and the desire to do so. Yet he holds back, but not of his own will. Methinks we should send a messenger to warn your sister."

"Think you my sister's in danger?" Oddrum shook his head. "She's too clever to divulge her true identity. You must stop worrying. She's no longer your concern. Did you not send several of your pets to watch over her and teach her your secret as well?"

"Aye, but what if she's captured—tortured to tell—?"

"She would die first. I believe she's well aware that should she turn traitor, her life would be over." Oddrum cast the old man a dark glance, aware that Maldwyn thought of Brynn as his own daughter. "This man you speak of, he is Norse?"

Maldwyn's shoulders slumped in defeat. "He lets the people believe it so, but I sense there is something more that was not revealed to me in my dream. I remember a name. Kyran."

"Kyran? Is that not a Welsh name?"

"Aye, another confusing morsel." Maldwyn took a long drink of wine, dragging his hand across his mouth.

"What else have you seen?" Oddrum asked, knowing full well that if the old man dreamed of the new king, he could well be a fearsome adversary. Oddrum raked his fingers angrily through his thick black hair. "Can you tell me the numbers of his army?"

"Nay, my lord. I have not had a vision, only a dream . . . and I dreamed of a great and bloody war, the like of which has not been seen since the day dragons flew in our skies."

Oddrum half rose from his throne. "Silly old man. I care little about the days of the dragons. They are long gone—the dragons long dead. In the end the warriors won. Speak, man, who fought the battle in your dream? Who won this great battle?"

Maldwyn heaved a long sigh and shook his head while he

stared into his goblet, contemplating telling his king the truth, knowing he'd never believe him if he did. "I cannot say. I woke before it ended."

CHAPTER FIVE

The savory aroma of roasted meats made Sayrid's mouth water as she wandered into the inner bailey with a small stream of villagers bringing supplies. Her slight stature made it easy to blend in with the older children as she hurried up the stone steps and into the keep.

Two large, heavily armed warriors with dark mustaches and beards stood guard at the door, but paid her little attention as she stepped inside the main entrance. While the other children continued toward the scullery, she stood and stared in stunned silence. It seemed as if most of the women from the village were there, armed with rags and brooms, buckets of water and mops.

She briefly glanced at the multitude of candles twinkling from the iron chandeliers and from the wall-mounted, black-iron sconces, but something else caught her attention. 'Twas the king's coat of arms. Unlike any she'd ever seen before, this one was superb, with a polished and heavily bejeweled sword crisscrossing an ax on a huge argent shield.

The outside edge had been encrusted with gold, the inverted pattern made more prominent by the outline of a blood-red leafy vine. It did not surprise her to see an intricately painted dragon in the center of the noble crest—its wings out as if in flight, matching the one she had seen on the king's surcoat. The dragon's eyes were large, sparkling emeralds. Its fearsome mouth was open, exposing a thin, red tongue. And, just as she'd remembered, clutched in the dragon's talons was a dead raven.

"If what you bring is food. . . ."

Sayrid spun to gaze up at a slender, young man. By his rusty-red locks, she instantly recognized him as the one called Cyric—the kind one, according to Rhonwyn. Where she expected to see a frown of disapproval, he quickly smiled, nodding toward his master's coat of arms.

" 'Tis impressive, is it not?" He didn't give her time to answer, only to wonder why, like the king, he spoke with only a trace of an accent. "I saw you looking at it. There's no need to be frightened. I assure you, the new king is more worthy of your love than your fear. His intentions are to unite his people and unify the tribes . . . to fulfill the prophecy given to us by the Ancient Ones."

She wanted to laugh—to express her opinion of the impossible, but held her tongue. King Kyran could hang his coat of arms all around the old castle and never claim it. She stared at Cyric, sensing him to be a good man who believed the foolishness he spoke. When he turned back to her, she dropped her gaze to the floor, in hopes of appearing submissive. She thrust out the basket. "I have brought bread for you and your king from . . . Gwendolyn."

"Ah, yes. Gwendolyn. Her bread tastes as if made by the gods."

She expected him to rebuke her for loitering. Much to her astonishment, he put a copper coin into her hand after he took the basket. His smile faded ever so slightly as his brow crinkled with a frown. "Is Rhonwyn ill that she couldn't bring it herself?"

Sayrid shook her head. "Nay, just busy helping her father with thatching the roof."

"Then take this to her for me." The young man pulled out a small, intricate brooch and pressed it in Sayrid's hand. "Tell her it's a little gift from someone who thinks she's very beautiful."

Sayrid swallowed hard and looked at the twinkling bronze-and-topaz trinket. Would she be accused of stealing if she left with it? Gwendolyn had told her the people were paid, but Sayrid experienced doubt. Would their homes be searched, and all of them accused of crimes? It had been done before to press the able-bodied into service.

"Give the coin to your mother," he said, walking toward the scullery. "And you may look all you want, but touch nothing." He gave her another generous smile as he left. "For a time, the king wishes to welcome all the people into his home."

"For a time?" she asked, hoping she didn't sound too forward. For a time, the king wishes to welcome all the people into his home. She wondered at the young man's words, convinced more than ever that behind their show of hospitality lurked some evil intent.

"Aye. Many of our loyal warriors risked life and limb for this castle. 'Tis my lord's wish that the people come to accept Dragon's Head as their deliverance from their enemies, not the opposite." He glanced around as if admiring a beautiful woman. "Be sure to look at the stones before you leave. The rock appears to sparkle with a bluish-green hue when scrubbed."

He shook his head as if he didn't believe it himself, then strode away before she could question him further.

She glanced around, somewhat taken aback to see that what he'd said seemed true. With years of smoke and cobwebs cleansed away, the large, brick-shaped stones glistened much like she'd envisioned the scales of her imaginary dragon would glisten.

Frowning, she slipped the coin into her shoe to keep it safe for Gwendolyn and pinned the brooch to the inside of her gown near the hem. If she were searched, they would find nothing but lint in her pockets. She turned her attention back to the women as they worked on the stone stairway to the second floor, noticing as she stepped down two steps into the great hall that the old, pulverized rushes had been swept away and the stone floors scrubbed clean.

Hanging from wooden poles were lavish tapestries of ancient dragons, their wings spread as they flew above the village. And, upon inspection of the intricately carved heads of dragons on the ends of the poles, she recognized the artistry of Dafydd. For a moment she marveled that in only three days he could produce such splendor, but, then, she knew that under the threat of death many a task could be done in half the time.

The caked-on soot above the massive fireplace had also been scrubbed away, and, for the first time since she could remember, the huge oak timber forming the mantel had been scoured and oiled, exposing the elegantly carved runes and the wood's rich hue. Upon it sat several gold and silver plates. A quick glance at the wooden balustrade confirmed that it had also been polished and oiled, the carved wood gleaming in the dancing torchlight.

Sayrid glanced at the stairway leading to the warlord's chamber. *Bring me a lock of his hair and I'll tell ye more.* Derwyn's words loitered in the back of her mind. Anxious to know all that she could, she started up the stairway, pausing to grab the balustrade when she felt the stone beneath her feet shudder. Never before had the old dragon awakened in the presence of others. A low, deep, yawning growl reverberated from the walls, causing her to glance quickly about to see if she were the only one to notice the strangeness. Everyone appeared unaffected, staying busy with their chores. She quickly scooped up a broom so as not to draw unwanted attention and continued up the steps.

The higher she climbed, the more the old castle resembled what she remembered it as being a long time ago—memories she couldn't place in time or even rationalize, but memories that had to have started when Aswyn captured Dragon's Head.

Her memories mingled with the stories about the ancient dragon and its mate—stories she liked to believe were more truth than myth.

On the second level the walls and floors were dirty and dull, badly in need of a good scrubbing. When a man dressed in Viking fashion came near, she pretended to be busy sweeping. He paid her no attention as he descended the stairs.

She cast a cautious glance over her shoulder then started upward to the third floor, pleased that no one seemed to care that she had wandered away from the others. Once she stood on the landing, she paused again to assess her surroundings and make sure she hadn't drawn attention to herself or been followed.

A moment later she opened the door to Aswyn's old chamber and peeked inside. In the corner by the balcony, Kyran's recently oiled and polished sword rested against the wall. The king slept, so she cautiously entered. She leaned the broom silently against the bedside table before she stepped closer. Slipping the dagger out of her pocket, she very quietly lifted a small strand of his hair. Her fingers tingled, but she ignored the strange sensation and sliced off the bit of hair—unprepared as his arm shot up and his fingers closed tightly around her neck. An angry growl filled her ears, or mayhap it was just the blood rushing through her veins that sounded like a dragon's snarl.

Sayrid opened her mouth to scream, but she needed more air to accomplish it. Instead, she gave a pathetic croak. She grabbed his wrist, nearly dropping her prize. As spots formed before her eyes, her fingers closed more tightly around her dagger, but the warlord froze and his grip loosened. He stared at her for several fractured moments before he released her and sank back down on the bed in obvious discomfort. She fought the urge to rub her own shoulder.

"How did you get in here?" he asked gruffly, wincing as he shifted his weight. He looked better, but there was an annoying ache in her shoulder which reminded her of his wound. When she didn't answer, he dragged his left hand across his eyes. "Well?" he demanded.

"Well what?" she countered, cleverly tucking his hair and the dagger into her pocket.

He swore under his breath at the same time that he tossed the covers aside and began to rise. She felt his gaze upon her, and she wondered if he thought she was the type to be embarrassed by his nakedness. Ha, she thought with a smug smile. He had nothing she hadn't seen before, although his body was somewhat more eye-catching and virile than old Aswyn's.

Nevertheless, after her quick inspection, she kept her gaze carefully focused on his angry face, even though she longed to study the dragon tattooed above his left breast more closely. 'Twas only when he repeated his question did she remember she hadn't answered—cringing as she felt the telltale heat of a blush warm her cheeks.

"Through the door, my lord." Her voice sounded weak and breathless, but suited her pretense as a child. He shrugged on a loose-fitting shirt and a pair of leggings. She bent and picked up the broom, and would have moved away, but he grasped her arm, and once more she noticed that the quick movement caused them both a measure of pain. "Why have you come?" he asked. His gaze searched hers before it drifted over her body for several moments, and then returned to her eyes.

"To—to clean my lord's bedchamber." She looked about. " 'Tis badly in need of it."

"Speak the truth." His brows snapped together tightly. "This chamber was scrubbed only hours ago."

"Think you it was done properly? See for yourself," she quickly replied. "Th-that yonder shelf is thick with dust." She would have swallowed her growing apprehension, but he kept his eyes fused to hers—his frown causing her mouth to feel as dry as the dust on the shelf.

"I have seen you before—"

"Nay, you have not . . . I am sure of it," she said with a quick shake and then a nod.

"Though you appear differently, I'm certain of it. I've looked into your eyes before." He continued to frown as if trying to remember. "I dreamt of this . . . this transformation of woman to child." He released her, slowly circling her as a predator might circle his prey. He stopped in front of her, but she turned away. He grabbed her wrist with his left hand then caught her chin gently between the thumb and forefinger of his right hand, turning her to face him. "What magic do you possess that allows you to change from a woman to a child?"

She gaped at him, amazed that he saw through her disguise so easily. Her skin tingled where he touched her. His long fingers encompassed her wrist—gently yet firmly enough to keep her hostage. Her heart quickened its pace, yet not from fear, from something strange and foreign to her—something she sensed would be her ruin. She twisted her wrist, but could not free herself.

"Tell me," he repeated. "What magic do you—"

"The same power that can change you into a . . . a swine," she snapped. "Let me go before you force me to show you."

He smiled, but didn't relinquish his hold on her wrist. "Not until you tell me why you've returned."

"Release me," she warned through clenched teeth, reaching for her dagger. She threatened him with it, annoyed when he scoffed. Though she was loath to cause him any more pain, she could think of no other way to free herself. Before she thought about the consequences, she drew it swiftly across his forearm, successful in freeing herself, yet worried about the burning sensation on her own arm. He uttered something she didn't understand, but she cared little about anything except escape. She spun and ran for the door.

"What is your purpose?" boomed a deep, gravelly voice as she nearly ran into the monstrous Norseman. He grabbed her clothing near her neck, lifting her several inches off the floor. He easily wrenched the dagger from her grasp and tucked it into his wide leather belt. Her heart slammed against her ribs and her throat closed so tightly she could barely breathe. Up this close, his features were truly frightening. "Do you know what we do to thieves?"

"I—I—am not a thief," she ground out. She struggled against his hold, her arms and legs flailing until her toe landed hard against his shin. His grip tightened. Her eyes watered with the pain, and then the giant gave her a firm shake, making her dizzy. Afraid for her life, she intensified her struggles. "You're hurting me, you . . . you big brute."

"I will do more than that," the huge man warned, shaking his finger in her face.

She sank her teeth into Morven's index finger—a mistake realized too late. He cuffed her across the side of the head. The blow sent her reeling. She stumbled backward and lost her balance, landing hard on her bottom, but within reach of the broom. Shaking the stars from her vision, she grabbed the broom, scrambled to her feet, and waved it about as if it were a sword.

"Stay back," she warned, inwardly cringing at the Viking's disgusted expression as he approached. With Morven to her right and Kyran to her left, she had no choice except to take a step back, inching closer to the sword that she'd seen in the corner by the balcony.

The king must have guessed what she intended to do, for in two steps he grabbed her, and, no matter how many times she struck him with the broom, it had no effect until she hit his wounded arm. Freed, she groaned with him—feeling his pain. She tried to resist, but the puny weapon was easily ripped from her feeble grasp by Morven and, in one fluid motion, broken over his knee and tossed aside.

Rubbing her shoulder, she frantically sought an exit, but the only route open to her appeared to be across the huge bed. Again, the king must have sensed her plan, for the moment she dove toward it, he lunged for her. She dodged him, rolling and scrambling off on the other side of the bed, immensely pleased she'd been faster than he. The feeling promptly died.

Morven moved swiftly for his size and caught her braid in his fist before she could open the door. Yelping in pain, she tried to tug her hair free, but to no avail. His bear-like arm wrapped around her ribs. Tears blurred her vision as she dug her nails into his forearm. He held fast, giving her another shake for good measure. She stopped struggling, hanging like a sack of barley, her toes a foot from the floor.

"I would have you leave her whole and with her hair still attached to her head," the king said tightly, cradling his right arm.

She lifted her chin and glared at him, ignoring the aches and pains, and the pressure on her ribs from Morven's arm. The king stood, his legs slightly apart, several strands of tawny hair falling over his forehead. He appeared slightly winded, but that wasn't what made her feel wretched. The neck of his shirt fell open, exposing a splotch of blood on his bandage where she had struck him with the broom. There was also a smear of blood on his arm, just above his wrist. Frustrated and ashamed, she tried in vain to pull her braid from Morven's fist. The more she moved, the more it hurt.

"If you'll allow it," she replied rebelliously, "I'll explain."

Kyran nodded at Morven. "Release her, but stay by the door." He waited until the Viking did as he asked, then went to the table and sloshed some wine into a cup, taking a long drink before he met her defiant glare. He inspected the cut on his arm then took another drink before he put the cup back on the table. He strode toward her, catching her chin between his thumb and forefinger none too gently. He half expected her to look away, but her eyes narrowed and—though he didn't think it possible—her chin rose slightly higher.

"Beware young master," Morven grumbled. "She's not to be trusted."

Kyran nodded, yet still held her gaze, pleased that the fear he'd witnessed earlier had vanished. "Morven," he began with an amused smile, "I would like you to meet the witch who saved my life."

The moment they left Sayrid alone in a chamber several doors down from Aswyn's, her anxiousness increased tenfold. With no secret passageway to slip through, she remained trapped and at the warlord's mercy. She began to pace, wondering what would happen next. Would he demand she be punished? Surely, after what she'd done, there would be some sort of retribution. By the black lines on the fat saffron candle, an hour had passed, yet it felt as if she'd been there all day. Her belly grumbled and she wished for a chunk of Gwendolyn's delicious bread.

And what of Gwendolyn and Dafydd? Would they be punished for her foolishness? She should've never mentioned their names to the redheaded cohort of the king. As she paced, she remembered the coin in her shoe. She sat on the cot and removed it, wondering if she could bribe the guard. She continued to plan her escape, when she heard the sound of a key in the lock.

She turned at the same time the heavy door opened. She expected to see the Viking giant or another one of the many rough-looking guards, but the king had come, dressed now in brown chausses and a clean, cream-colored tunic. A small bandage around his wrist peeked out from under the sleeve. The wide belt cinched around his hips accentuated the breadth of his shoulders. When she met his bold gaze, she found it sensually enticing.

"Why have you come back and"—he hesitated as his gaze raked over her—"why are you disguised as a child?" He appeared to inspect the snug fit of her bodice. "Isn't that uncomfortable . . . to bind them so tightly?"

She wondered if the clenching of his jaw was caused by her silence or the throbbing of his shoulder and arm. Unconsciously, she cradled her own right arm. She would have fled if possible, but pride held her fast, caused her to match his dauntless stare as he came closer. Her heart beat a little more rapidly and her mouth grew uncomfortably dry, as it had before in his presence.

For the first time she noticed a small scar on his cheek, below his left eye, and another on his forehead above his temple. For a breath of a moment, he appeared as he had when she first saw him, a brutal warrior capable of dispatching the most fearsome warriors to their deaths. His hands were large and tanned, his palms heavily calloused with several healing blisters—the sign of a man well accustomed to the weight of a sword and a shield.

Had she not been told of his highborn nobility, she would have seen him only as a soldier—a warrior most likely trained from childhood to do battle. No sooner had she thought it, than she saw him as a boy—proud, yet beaten and battered, shoved to the ground by a large Norseman, who hollered for him to get up and fight like a man.

"There's no need to be frightened. I won't—"

"I'm not frightened," she lied.

His smile turned from gentle to arrogant. "No? Perhaps you speak too quickly."

He walked past her and peered out the narrow arrow-slit

window, and 'twas then that she noticed the tiny beads of perspiration on his forehead—the way he braced himself against the ledge. She felt his fatigue—she was tired herself and, like him, refused to acknowledge it.

"Though small, this is one of the few chambers that face the sea." He took a deep breath of salty fresh air, then turned and faced her. "Do you know who I am?"

She quickly moistened her lips, unaware that it made her mouth even more irresistible. "Aye, you are Kyran, the warlord who killed King Aswyn and captured Dragon's Head."

Though she tried to meet his gaze, she failed, sensing he took it as a small victory. He came closer—close enough for her to feel the warmth of his breath near her ear. "You know of me, yet I know very little of you. That, my little witch, is an unfair advantage."

"Unfair?" she repeated, raising her chin. His gaze instantly fused with hers, causing a jolt of excitement to course through her chest and lodge in her lower belly. "You have the advantage, my lord, not I. When I had the advantage in the forest, I relented and tended to your needs. 'Tis unfair to hold me against my will without an explanation. 'Tis because of me you are still alive. And now, because of you, I'm a prisoner."

A slight smile tugged at his firm mouth. She tried not to notice how his eyes were made even more striking by his dark brows. "I vaguely remember being robbed whilst I lay wounded, and then today you tried to take a lock of my hair with mine own dagger. Why?"

"To trade for other, more important things."

"Such as?" he countered.

"Such as . . . as food and cloth to make clothing for my people," she stammered. She would have turned away to fill a goblet with watered wine to ease her dry throat, but he caught her arm. The moment he touched her, her shoulder began to ache and she was very nearly overcome with the desire to sleep. Many times she had seen men fight for days without rest, and now she wondered how they endured it.

She pulled her arm free and clutched her hands before her, hoping he would not see them tremble. "If confinement is to be my punishment, then I will accept my fate, asking that I be allowed to do so in solitude."

His soft laughter didn't obscure the fatigue in his voice—in his being. "A woman by the name of Gwendolyn has inquired about your welfare. What would you have me tell her?"

Sayrid's head snapped up, but she sensed 'twas best to remain quiet lest she draw her dear friend into her predicament.

"Are you related to her? A daughter mayhap?"

A strange pain tightened around Sayrid's heart. She had no family, and, worse, she had no memory of family. "I'm not," she said firmly. "I'm responsible for mine own actions. To punish Gwendolyn or Dafydd would be unfair."

"That's the second time you've accused me of being unfair." He pressed his thumb and forefinger to the bridge of his nose and closed his eyes, but only for a breath of a moment. When next he looked at her, his expression appeared guarded. "Dafydd and Gwendolyn have pledged fealty to me, yet I am curious why family to them is allowed to roam the forest, is apparently a skilled archer, and appears and disappears at will."

He reached out and dragged the back of his knuckles down her cheek. As if he felt her anxiety, something flickered in the depth of his eyes—stilled his touch for several confusing moments. "You are real enough, so there is only one explanation that makes sense."

She tried not to look at him as if he had gone mad, but knew by the change in his expression that she'd failed. "I don't know what you're speaking about, my lord."

This time when he smiled his features softened. "I think you do. And that's why I'm curious." He went to the door and opened it, motioning for her to follow. Two guards were standing in the hall, but he waved them away. "Follow me. This room is small and dark."

He lifted the pitcher, wrinkling his nose. "And I've no stomach for watered wine."

She hesitated. "Where?"

He glanced over his shoulder, apparently not used to having his commands questioned. "Stay then."

He would have closed the door, but she hurried out and followed him to his bedchamber, swallowing nervously when he asked two village women to forgo their cleaning and leave. Once they left, he closed the door and leaned back against it. "My friend Morven is convinced that you're a spy—sent by Oddrum."

"I am not," she replied defiantly. "Oddrum is . . . was Aswyn's ally, and, like Aswyn, he has little love for his people. His kind is unworthy of my allegiance."

"I see. And what of me? Am I also unworthy?"

"Are you Welsh?" she challenged.

His soft laughter startled her. "If I were to say yes, would you believe me?"

"Nay, not even if you swore it. You're a Norseman. Though I've heard rumors that say you killed King Arcas, I sense there is something corrupt, that mayhap you pretend to be the opposite of who and what you really are. I believe you've fooled the people, but soon they will learn that you've been sent to rule them as if they were sheep—no better and, so far, no worse than the warlords you dispatched to their deaths." She lifted a defiant brow. "Are we to call you Master or King?"

Much to her surprise the warrior placed his left hand on his chest. "Your words cut. I am kinder than Aswyn, and more just than Arcas, and will in due time prove it."

He gave her no time to respond, turning to fill two goblets with wine. He held one out to her. "Would you believe me if I told you that because of my loyal service to a demon, I earned his trust, which in the end allowed me the right to avenge my family and reclaim my birthright?"

"Birthright?" she scoffed, taking a badly needed drink. "Because King Arcas condoned it, does not make it so. You called him demon, yet it is you who lives whilst he rots in his grave. I have heard it said it takes a demon to dispatch a demon." She glared at him over the rim of the goblet. "Dragon's Head is Welsh, destined to be ruled by a Welshman. Others have tried." She took another sip. "And, as you know, have failed. In due time, so shall you fail."

The warlord took a swallow of wine, apparently unaffected by her rebellious words. "Is this your prediction as a sorceress?"

She held out her arms and shrugged. "What you see is what I am."

He grinned, letting his eyes slowly drift down her length, causing an anxious fluttering in her breast . . . and lower. "Your friend, Gwendolyn, has told me that you were a slave to Aswyn. Is this true or is it a story contrived to make me feel pity for you and your lost virginity? She also said you heal the sick. But that I know, as I have experienced it."

Sayrid's anger at being thought a whore lived a short life, quickly replaced with dread for the welfare of her friend. Poor Gwendolyn must have been tortured to divulge such things. Sayrid swallowed hard but controlled her emotions well, a ploy she learned while enslaved. "She would say anything if she thought 'twould ease my plight. As I would to ease hers. I will tell you everything you wish to hear when she and Dafydd are released with your promise of no retribution."

"Ease your plight? Retribution?" he repeated with a sly grin. "Though your eyes deny it, methinks I hear fear in your voice.

Do you fear me, witch?"

"Nay, my lord. Not you as the man. Yet, I must confess, I fear your intentions toward my friends and the people of Dragon's Head."

Again he laughed, but it lacked any real humor. "What know you of my intentions? Methinks *I* do not even know what they are at this moment." He continued his careful scrutiny. " 'Tis well known that Welsh women are capable warriors. I know this because of many things, but mostly because a female archer sank a broadhead in my shoulder from the parapet whilst I battled Aswyn. Since the arrow did not pierce my heart, methinks she missed her mark."

He took another drink of wine. "In the forest another archer dispatched mine enemy to his death. I wonder. . . ." He paused and stared at her for several moments. "Perhaps the archer wasn't one of Aswyn's warriors, but a slave seeking her freedom by doing a deed to please her master. And, at the river, a slave who missed her mark a second time?"

His doubtful expression angered her when she shouldn't have cared. "Aye. 'Twas my arrow that killed your opponent at the river, though I must confess, my lord, 'twas you I had in my sights. The wind grew unfavorable, so do not feel overly indebted to me. Nay, had the gods been with me, your men would have found your corpse."

"The arrow embedded in my shoulder had been tainted with juice from laurel-wood berries. Though 'tis a favorite and easily acquired poison, only a few have the wisdom to purge it from a wound and those few are held in high esteem by the people. Gwendolyn holds you in high esteem."

"As I do her," Sayrid countered.

He took another swallow of his wine, his eyes twinkling over the rim. When finally he put the goblet down, she felt as if he could see through her—read her thoughts. She hadn't experienced this type of vulnerability since she'd been Aswyn's slave, and she refused to feel it now. Though she wanted to meet his gaze, he'd unnerved her, and she feared he'd see it in her eyes. In self-defense, she quickly turned her attention to her goblet, finishing the last of her wine.

She steeled herself when he came closer, reached out and grasped her hand. A startled gasp escaped her lips before she could stop it. Where his fingers lay upon her skin, it tingled, not painfully as she first expected, but pleasurably, exciting her in a way she had never felt before. Liquid heat coursed through her body, pooling at the junction between her legs, roiling as water tumbling over a fallen log. She yanked her fingers free.

"Stop that," she demanded breathlessly. But he caught her hand in his again more forcefully.

"Stop what?" he asked softly, placing his calloused palm over her hand. "I see fear in your eyes, Sayrid. I will ask you again, are you afraid of me or of the strange things that pass between us whenever we are together?"

"I—I told you. I'm not afraid of you," she repeated. She tried in vain to pull free—couldn't resist when he dragged her up against his chest. As soon as their bodies touched, hers reacted, thrusting her breasts upward, pressing them and her hips intimately closer to him. He responded as well, his warm hand inching down her back, over her buttocks where his fingers tightened a little before they pressed her even closer to his instant arousal. Gently, he nipped at her lips, teasing her mouth with his tongue until she instinctively opened, kissing him back the moment his mouth covered hers.

Sayrid unconsciously moaned as visions of Aswyn bedding his whores sprang to her mind—torrid memories of their sweat-dampened, naked bodies entwined in corporeal pleasure. Shaken by the wave of lust that washed over her, she closed her eyes, mortified with the knowledge that had they not been dressed and standing they surely would have joined together then and there. Gathering every ounce of control she could muster, she shoved him back, grunting with the effort. The moment they weren't touching, the visions disappeared, leaving in their wake an ebbing desire to run back into his arms and couple with her enemy.

"You are no better than Aswyn," she whispered breathlessly. Slowly, still stunned by what had passed between them, she met Kyran's eyes, startled to see a glimmer of the same confusion flickering in their depths.

" 'Tis rumored," he began, and she felt certain that he sounded as if he'd been running, "that when a woman finds her life-mate, there's no power on earth that will keep them apart." He sloshed more wine into his goblet and looked at her. "But, for certain women, there's more than just the power that binds her to a male. When together, the two lovers think the same thoughts; they experience the same pleasure and suffer the same pain." He stared at her for several long moments before he drained the cup. "These women who feel such things are called by the name of sorceress." He gave her an arrogant smile. "The men who feel such things are called fools."

Again her anger flared. Infuriating man, to have so many opinions on so many topics. She felt as if she were getting a headache with the effort to keep up with him. "You think it foolish to be bound to a woman?"

His eyes twinkled. "Aye. Why settle for one when there are so many?"

She scoffed. "You speak like a true warrior—taking what you want regardless of who is hurt or dishonored."

This time he laughed. "Think you it is dishonorable to couple with a man?"

Sayrid took a calming breath and smoothed the apron over her gown, refusing to look at him, refusing to be drawn into his confusing verbal melee. "If you wish to repay my kindness for saving your life, you'll let me go."

His smile faded slightly. "Leave? Nay, my little sorceress. I cannot. You must allow me the opportunity to prove you wrong. I insist you stay and witness with your own eyes the difference between Aswyn and myself."

"I must decline, and ask again that you allow me to leave . . . to spare yourself an impossible task."

This time he smiled quickly and humor twinkled again in the depth of his stunning eyes. "Then if not to impress upon you my virtues, then to repay you for a kindness done in my time of need." He held up his hand before she could speak. "I insist. A woman will come with garments more suitable a lady. Later we will eat—"

"There is no need. These garments suit me well." She met his gaze when he turned. "Nor do I desire to sup with you and yours. It seems whilst in your presence, I've lost my appetite."

He shrugged, wincing as he kneaded his right shoulder. "Alas, my little sorceress, you may accept my invitation as my prisoner or as my guest. The choice is yours."

He went to the door, stepped out and pulled it closed behind him, leaving her alone in the room. She wrapped her arms around herself to try and quiet the tremulous feeling still stirring inside. His subtle warning didn't go unnoticed. She took a long deep breath and began to pace, grateful that he'd left before she embarrassed herself and threw herself back into his embrace. What had happened to her? How could she think him different?

"Fool," she muttered angrily as she took a deadly looking dagger from the shelf, blowing away the dust that marked its removal. Noble? Perhaps by birth, but definitely not in behavior. He had the charm of a starving hawk swooping down on any little creature that moved on the forest floor.

Certain she'd waited long enough, she raced to the bookcase and with trembling fingers pressed the hidden latch.

CHAPTER SIX

Kyran entered the great hall in search of the cook. He wanted something special prepared. He would show Sayrid a softer side, if he could manage it. After so many years as a warrior-slave, he'd almost forgotten how to behave as a nobleman should, but at the very least he would have an extravagant feast placed before her and they would dine quietly together in his chamber.

"Kyran," Bynor called, drawing him away from his musings. His friend sat at a table, holding a pretty young maid with jet-black hair and violet eyes. "Come, join us." Bynor whispered something in the woman's ear, helping her to her feet before he motioned Kyran over. Kyran felt the woman's gaze wash over him before she hurried away.

"Since you are up and walking around in only three days, rumors of magical mud must be true." Bynor grinned, but didn't give Kyran time to answer. "Of course, look at you. Other than a little fatigued, you look as if you could lead the men into battle with Oddrum on the morrow." He began to say more, but the maid came back and placed two tankards of ale on the table.

Kyran caught the maid's arm, somewhat disturbed when he felt her stiffen before he glimpsed a spark of anger in her eyes. For a moment he questioned whether it had really been there or if he had imagined it. "There is a young woman in my chamber. Prepare a scented bath and see to her comfort."

The maid gave Kyran a forced smile and nodded. "Aye, milord, but first you must let me go."

Unaware that he still held her captive, Kyran quickly released her, wondering why his fingers felt so cold.

Bynor pushed a tankard toward Kyran. "Ha. You are better and horny as well," Bynor said, his voice sounding hollow as he spoke into his tankard before taking a long drink of ale. "I always feel better after I've sated myself with a comely maid. Mayhap I should drink your ale"—he winked at Kyran—"whilst you follow that maid upstairs." Bynor raised a dark brow and motioned toward the departing maid. "If you weren't here, she would have been glad to have me."

Kyran grinned. "Do not underestimate your prowess with women, my stalwart friend. I remember a time or two that we could dispatch half a division to their deaths and bed nearly as many women in the same day." They laughed, clanked their tankards together and drank, nodding as if Kyran's exaggeration were true.

"So, tell me. What have you learned?" Kyran asked once their humor had waned.

Bynor's forehead knotted. "Did Cyric mention that a woman was murdered?"

"He did, and I would hear more about it if you have it."

"I've been asking the villagers, but the people of Dragon's Head are a tight-lipped bunch, sticking closely together like the legs of a frightened virgin."

"Your vocabulary hasn't improved, my friend."

Bynor nodded to the fine woolen tunic Kyran wore. "How we dress or speak matters little. We are soldiers, not diplomats. Forgive me if I offended your sense of decency." Bynor raised one dark brow. "However, before you chastise me, I remember a favorite saying of yours—"

Kyran shook his head in a silent warning to stop. "Have you

considered the woman might have been killed by a jealous lover?"

"Aye, but I would sleep better if I could find the culprit." Bynor feigned a shiver. "To think there is a murderer walking freely among us is unsettling. If you give the word, I will intensify my interrogations. Mayhap with the threat of punishment for keeping secrets, someone will have some information."

Kyran heaved a tired sigh. "These people have been sorely abused by old Aswyn, and they fear anything spoken to us could be used against them."

"Then we must win them over, heh?" Again Bynor's voice echoed in his cup a moment before he put it down on the table. "More ale," he hollered, banging his tankard playfully against the table.

"Aye, we should, and I think I know how to accomplish it." Kyran stood with a pleased smile. "Send some men out to hunt. We shall have a feast, as soon as it can be arranged. And ask Cyric to invite the entire village."

"Why not tonight?" Bynor asked with another grin. "Methinks I saw Morven ride in dragging three fat boars behind him."

Kyran shook his head. "I have something else to tend to. I will dine in my chamber tonight."

Bynor looked hopeful. "If that comely maid is still with her, I could join you."

"Not this time." Kyran nearly made it to the stairs when Cyric called his name. Turning, the look on Cyric's face appeared comical. "You look much like the cat who has sampled the cook's cream."

"I remember," Cyric said, his green eyes alive with excitement. "I know how the witch-woman comes and goes as she pleases."

"Well?" Kyran asked when Cyric started to pace as if he were deeply in thought.

"There are many tunnels and secret passageways throughout Dragon's Head. Though I know naught where they're located, I'm certain they exist. One is said to lead to a hidden chamber that is rich in precious stones and heavily protected by magic. Some think the spirit of the dragon that created Dragon's Head Castle protects it. In due time I shall—" He frowned as Kyran raced up the stairs. "Where are you going?"

Cyric glanced at Bynor, obviously disappointed. "He didn't let me finish."

Bynor stood up, walked over to Cyric and put his hand on Cyric's shoulder. "Do not vex yourself. I believe he will be very interested on the morrow. This eve he has much more important matters on his mind."

Bynor leaned a little closer so only Cyric could hear. "He has a willing wench waiting for him in his chamber; though I am certain he will be interested in magical treasure, treasures of the flesh come first."

Brynn turned the latch to the master's chamber as quietly as she could, and opened the heavy door just enough to see inside. She swore softly when the dagger in her apron pocket made a muffled clank as it struck the stone wall when she entered. A quick glance sent her temper to the brink, and had she not heard approaching footsteps she would have vented her anger more forcefully.

As quietly as she had entered she stepped out into the corridor, pulling the door closed. A moment later she hurried down the hall, slipping into another chamber before she was seen.

Kyran threw open the door to his bedchamber and found it empty. A quick search revealed nothing that looked like a hidden passageway. Furious, he strode to the head of the stairs and leaned over the balustrade, bellowing for Cyric.

Sayrid poured a bucket of cool water into the small tub she'd dragged out from under her cot. She added a cauldron of steaming water and swirled it around with her hand. The king's image appeared in the water, his eyes locking with hers for several moments until she hurried to the shelf and grabbed a small jar of dried lavender Derwyn had given to her to ward off unwanted visions. The moment she sprinkled it into the water his image disappeared.

But not his memory.

Distressed, she stripped and hastened to bathe, eager to wash away the primal hunger she'd felt for the man. Even as she scrubbed her skin pink, memories of how he looked, how he felt, the hard length of him pressing against her hips when they'd kissed, threatened to overwhelm her and send her flying back to the Dragon's Head and his bedchamber.

She took a wooden bowl and poured water over her breasts and back, closing her eyes and her mind to any thoughts except the cleansing feel of the hot water. Still, she floated back in time, to when they'd kissed in his chamber. The feel of him lingered—the roughness when he grabbed her buttocks and shoved her closer to his loins—the gentleness of his hands caressing her as they kissed.

By the gods, why is this happening? Silently cursing, she stood, wrapped herself in a long, soft cloth and stepped out of the tub, refusing to glance at the surface of the water lest she glimpse the object of her thoughts regardless of Derwyn's lavender.

Instead, she thought of Gwendolyn and Dafydd whilst she dried. She'd been worried that her friends had been taken as slaves and, regardless of the rain, had stopped by their home to see about their welfare and to give Rhonwyn the gift before fleeing into the safety of the forest.

" 'Tis true," Dafydd had said. "We were never his prisoners. We are free, granted this privilege by the new master. Fear not, Sayrid. Gwendolyn is here—has been the whole time. The king does not seem the kind of man who would punish us for your disobedience."

"Disobedience?" she muttered, returning to the present. Her forehead crinkled again with distrust while she sank down on a small stool to dry her hair in front of the fire. How could a warlord free his slaves and expect them to stay and do his bidding? Was not fear the basis of their loyalty? Yet had she not witnessed women cleaning, and men chopping wood and carrying chairs and other furnishings into the castle? Had she not seen Gwendolyn paid for the bread?

You may accept my invitation as my prisoner or as my guest. The choice is yours. The memory of the king's words served to reinforce her opinion. " 'Tis trickery," she muttered as she worked the tangles from her hair. "Free, indeed, but for how long? We are all prisoners, each and every one of us."

Her thoughts turned from her friends to the man they praised. As if he'd been summoned, his features appeared in the flames before her. Unlike the first time she had seen his image in the water, this time his firm mouth turned upward into a sensual smile which instantly sent a delightful quiver straight into her stomach.

She groaned, and then turned her back, refusing to give in to the urge to look upon the fire. When her hair dried, she braided it. Her pallet looked inviting, but she knew sleep would be elusive. She had to know why she felt such a strong attachment to this man. Could Aswyn be responsible? Had she been his slave too long? She had tended to him whilst he bedded his whores, and maybe that's the reason Kyran had so easily awakened her sexual curiosity. Or did Kyran awaken something stronger—something deeper, something even more primal?

Sighing, she slipped between the furs and closed her eyes. On the morrow she'd take the king's lock of hair to Derwyn. Maybe then she'd get some answers. The thought caused her to glance up at her medallion and then over to his. She wondered, if she touched it would she know how he fared? Her fingers itched to try, but she stubbornly refused and rolled to her side.

Sayrid slowly opened her eyes, shook away the last dregs of sleep. She stood naked near her little table. The object of her earlier dreams appeared to be resting in her bed. Confused, she cast a frantic glance at the door, trying to remember what happened—how he found her and why she let him in. Had he entered whilst she fetched more water? She tried to piece together the puzzle when his deep voice drew her gaze.

"Where are you going?" he asked, his expression hidden in the shadows. He held out his hand. The moment her fingers touched his, he pulled her down, forcing her to sit on the edge of the bed. "Do you fear me?"

"I—I do not know," she said, hating how weak and breathless her voice sounded. But she knew. She knew the moment he touched her—the instant his thumb stroked the back of her fingers—that she didn't fear him.

Nay, she wanted him. She tried to see into his eyes, but the moonlight that had drifted in through the opened door disappeared behind some clouds.

He pulled her closer, his glittering dark eyes fusing with hers. "What magic have you cast upon me, to make me want you as I have wanted no other?"

She thought to resist. But when his warm mouth captured hers, she returned his kiss. His kisses only heightened her arousal. He urged her closer, folding her in his arms as he rolled and pinned her beneath his hard muscular body. Kyran's flesh felt warm beneath her cold fingers as she traced the outline of the magnificent dragon tattooed on his chest. Like the eyes of the dragon, Kyran's gaze turned wildly primal, almost frightening, causing the fingers of her other hand to close around the hilt of her stolen dagger.

He teased her lips until they parted, then his tongue plundered her mouth. He kissed a path down her neck until finally his teeth scraped lightly over the peak of her breast, and then he drew the nipple into his hot, demanding mouth, drawing upon it until she burned to have him do the same with the other.

She moaned, as it felt like lightning arcing through her body. The feel of the furs against her bare skin was almost as stimulating as his hard body covering hers—his hardened shaft pressing against her thigh. Consumed by desire, she yielded when he placed his knee between her legs, spreading her. She arched up to meet him as he gathered her into his arms. And when he whispered her name, the double-edged dagger slipped soundlessly from her grasp.

Sayrid sat up in her bed, her chest rising and falling with each anguish-filled breath. A quick glance around her cottage told her that all she'd felt—all she'd experienced—had only been an erotic dream. Slowly she rose and with shaky fingers touched a taper to a candle, staring at the flames as her heartbeat slowed to normal. She glanced at her pallet, not at all surprised to see the dagger nestled in the fur. She picked it up and placed it on the table before walking to the door and throwing it open. She stood for a long time, letting the predawn breeze cool her sweat-dampened skin.

Dark clouds squatted on top of the mountains, and the air smelled again of rain. Still shaken, she closed the door and leaned back against it, unsure if she were relieved or disappointed that it had only been a dream.

Thunder rumbled in the distance. Kyran woke with a start, drenched in sweat and with a need for a woman so great 'twas nearly painful. He'd dreamt of women before, but never with such clarity. Nor had he ever felt the voraciousness of a rutting beast that he felt for Sayrid. He cursed aloud for not tending to his needs earlier. After he'd gotten over his anger of her deception and her escape, he'd gone in search of a willing woman, and twice he returned alone to this chamber—and for what? To awaken in primal agony? There were plenty of agreeable wenches hiding in the shadows of the old fortress.

Yet, even now, he doubted any would satisfy him—for just a few hours ago, he had touched and tasted perfection. Though he longed to sleep, the more he thought about his dream and Sayrid, the more restless he became. He swore under his breath and stood. He went to the balcony, brushed aside the skins and threw open the doors, mindless of the pounding rain. A cool breeze misted his heated body as he gazed out over the darkened, fog-shrouded forest, wondering where his enchantress slept and if she'd given him more than a fleeting thought.

He sensed she had.

Once again lightning flashed, causing the forest to look even more ominous. Thunder rumbled, but this time it sounded as if it filled the room, reverberating from the walls rather than the sky. He dragged his fingers through his hair, forcing himself back to reality, away from the woman in his dreams. As if by magic, the rain stopped, and the beginning of the new day grew peaceful.

Kyran studied the skies, frowning. After a few moments, he splashed some water on his face, then dressed and went in search of his friend, Bynor. Surely winning some of his captain's hard-earned coins in a game of chance would chase away any thoughts of Sayrid.

Kyran found Bynor sitting at a long wooden table in the great hall, heavily in his cups, with several of his men in the same condition. Game pieces were scattered over the table next to their tankards of ale. By the looks of them, they'd been playing and drinking all night. Once they saw their leader approaching, they rose, swaying a little, and saluted him, each placing his fist over his heart, two leaning heavily on each other. "My lord," Bynor said formally.

"As you were," Kyran ordered. Before he could ask to join, Bynor turned to the others and told them to seek their beds. "Has Cyric gone to bed?"

Bynor gave a bark of laughter. "Aye, hours ago. Why?"

"He remembered a secret passageway earlier, but we failed to find it."

"Aye, and sorely disappointed he was that he'd let you down. Shall I send for him?" Bynor yawned and stretched.

"Nay. Methinks you should seek your pallet instead. 'Tis nearly dawn."

Bynor shrugged. "Dawn? Are you certain?"

"Aye, I'm sure. 'Tis why I suggested you should go to bed."

"I'll have plenty of time to sleep when I'm dead." Bynor motioned for Kyran to sit and waved over the same pretty, dark-haired maid with the violet eyes, who sat on Bynor's knee and smoothed her hand down his cheek, accepting his kiss and returning it with the same vigor.

Kyran recognized the woman immediately—remembered her to be the one who stared at him, asking to be released. Looking at her now, her seductive smile, had he not first laid eyes on Sayrid, he would have thought her quite appealing. Yet he felt something amiss—something in her manner that didn't fit the way she dressed or the way she giggled when Bynor's hand inched up her thigh.

"Ale for the king," Bynor ordered, planting a quick kiss on her cheek before he pushed her to her feet, missing the angry lifting of the woman's dark brow. She met Kyran's appreciative gaze with one more pleasant, especially when Kyran reached out, clasped her hand and turned it over, rubbing his thumb against her calloused palm. Again her hand felt cold, his fingers icy. The moment he released her she snatched it back, clutching it to her breast. She stared at him and left, casting one more glance over her shoulder.

"I saw her first," Bynor began with an amused gleam in his eyes when Kyran turned his attention back to his friend. "Besides, you have a woman, and a beautiful, mysterious one at that. There is much curiosity among the men. They want to know if the witch put a love spell on you."

Kyran shook his head. "I can see a few days away from fighting have turned them from warriors to gossips."

Bynor laughed. "What is more important than the pleasures of the flesh, heh?" His eyes danced with mischief when he picked up a single wooden die. "The night is old, but the day is young. What say you to finding a couple of women?"

"I have a better idea," Kyran said with a lazy grin. He reached into the pouch on his belt and withdrew two silver coins. "What say you to a game or two of chance before practice begins?"

Sayrid nocked her arrow, raising the bow to take aim on the unsuspecting piglet that had wandered away from his wild and terrifying mother. She hesitated a moment, certain she'd heard a strange sound coming from over the rise. Be it the piglet's mother, the risk of being attacked outweighed her recently acquired craving for roasted pig.

Slowly, she lowered her bow, detached the arrow and slipped

it back into the quiver. The sound came again, frightening the piglet away. Had her ears deceived her? Did she hear men grunting and the sounds of wood striking wood? Curious, she crept through the thick trees and shrubs surrounding a small meadow.

Staying low to the ground to keep from being seen, she spread the foliage. Morven and Kyran, both naked from the waist up, circled each other, armed with long wooden staffs. Quickly it became apparent that they were engaged in a fierce competition of some sort.

Sayrid massaged her shoulder. No wonder it ached. Kyran, the foolish man, had not given it time to completely heal, and there he fought, in a meadow, testing his strength against Morven—more an ill-tempered bear than a man. She gave a disgusted shake of her head, yet didn't immediately move away. The more she watched the two men fight, the more fascinated she became.

Morven, for his size, moved quickly, his blows forceful, and by the ache in her shoulder, punishing as well. Kyran moved with fluid motion, dodging and retaliating with brutal strikes of his own. With each blow he dealt, pain reverberated down her shoulder and settled in her fingers.

If she had to judge, she would have said they were evenly matched. That is, until Morven swung low, knocking Kyran off his feet and onto his back. She frowned, expecting him to stay down and use the moment's reprieve to catch his breath. But, much to her surprise, he leapt upright in a single motion, and spun, giving a battle cry that scared the birds from the trees in a frenzy of flapping wings.

Why would a king push himself so hard? she wondered. Surely four thousand men could protect their ruler and her people from any of the neighboring kingdoms. And why would he risk further injury? Hadn't he suffered enough? She narrowed her gaze. Morven certainly didn't seem to hold back. She winced when Kyran hit the ground once more, and this time seemed slow getting up.

She watched for several more moments, finding herself silently cheering for the king. Each time he landed a good blow, she felt like clapping. But such strikes were growing fewer with each passing moment. When he took a fair blow to the ribs and fell to his knees, she suddenly clutched her side, aware for the first time that this type of training wasn't meant for the weak or softhearted. Mercy wasn't asked or offered. It took determination and fortitude to withstand such punishment.

Much to her horror, Morven raised his staff as if to strike the fatal blow, then tipped back his head and laughed, extending his hand to help his exhausted master to his feet. "Come, weakling, let me help you back to your sick bed. I'll find a pretty wench to nurse your bruises."

Sayrid slowly let out the breath she'd been holding. She was much relieved, yet strangely annoyed. Just the mention of a woman being sent to Kyran's bed filled her with feelings she'd never experienced. She instantly disliked the thought of him being with another woman, yet she'd convinced herself that she wanted no more of his lusty advances. King or no, he acted more the horny soldier than the well-bred noble.

She'd learned as a slave that men, especially soldiers, sated their primal cravings on any willing wench—anyplace and, most definitely, anytime they got the urge. Some with more than one woman. So why did it offend her to hear Morven suggest his master make use of one of the castle whores? Pity the poor woman.

Disgusted with herself for watching so long, she crept back the way she'd come, retrieved her bow and quiver, and left the men, secretly hoping the new king would insist on continuing their foolish game and Morven would beat him senseless.

★　★　★　★　★

Kyran didn't know how he knew, but he felt Sayrid's watchful gaze upon him. He frowned, dodging a sweep of Morven's staff and landing a hefty blow to his wooly friend's back. Thinking Morven would take a moment to recover, Kyran turned slightly to see if he could find her hiding place—grunting when Morven struck him in the ribs, knocking the air from his lungs.

Blocking yet another thrust, Kyran forced his attention back to the mock battle, angry with himself for being so easily distracted. Regardless of her alluring beauty, he'd let no woman distract him from what had to be done. And, right now, all he wanted was to beat Morven at his favorite game. Kyran held onto that thought until something rustled in the bushes. He turned and caught sight of a doe just before Morven's staff knocked the air from his lungs yet again.

Once practice ended, Kyran saddled the gray stallion he'd received as a reward from Arcas for battles past and rode into the forest. The animal was surefooted and of a pleasing temperament, and responded well to Kyran's commands. As they rode, Kyran thought of the past. Try as he might, he could not remember his mother's or father's face—just fire and smoldering thatch, screams and moans, and the rocky face of Dragon's Head shrouded by smoke as his captors dragged him away from it shortly after the binding ceremony ended.

It proved difficult to think of himself bound to a woman of whom he knew naught. Had she survived the chaos? Could Sayrid be Jenalyn? Refusing to dwell on the dark days of his past, he rode to the lake, dismounted and hobbled the stallion to allow the beast to graze on the lush grass. Kyran took a deep, cleansing breath. It felt good to be outside the stone walls, away from so many people. He looked forward to fishing and even more forward to eating his catch.

With his saddlebags over his shoulder, he took his dagger and cut a narrow branch from a nearby birch. Sitting on a fallen log, he tied a long piece of string to the tip, and to the string he fastened a bronze hook Dafydd had made for him. He lifted his gaze from admiring the hook and froze.

On the far side of the pool stood a naked woman. Not just any woman, but Sayrid. Be she a witch or sorceress, she'd managed to cast a spell on him the moment his lips grazed hers. Watching her now, his thoughts of fishing were forgotten.

Long, copper-colored hair cascaded down her pale shoulders, curling over her breasts and brushing the tops of her hips. Her lower body nearly obscured from his view by the waist-high reeds, she appeared to test the water with her bare toes before she waded out to take a swim.

Kyran quietly put down his pole and rested his forearms on his knees while he watched. She dived under and glided toward the small waterfall that tumbled over a rocky crest. While she washed her hair in the falls, he took the opportunity to move behind a brace of trees where he quickly shed his clothes.

He took pains to move slowly so as not to draw her attention. Before he entered the water, he unsheathed his dagger and stabbed the weapon into a protruding root near the water's edge, just in case he needed to reach it quickly. He eased into the cold, clear water, took a deep breath and disappeared under the smooth surface.

CHAPTER SEVEN

Sayrid came out from under the falls, wiping the water out of her eyes. She would have leaned back and floated, but a shape moved beneath the surface. 'Twas too large to be a fish, so she quickly decided to forgo her swim and started to swim toward her clothes.

A moment later, she felt an arm come around her waist from behind and pull her against a very hard chest. She screamed, but a hand came over her mouth. When she twisted to look, she stared into a pair of eyes so blue she almost wished she had a gown the same vivid color.

"You," she gasped, her voice muffled by his palm. When he removed his hand, she intensified her struggles.

"Shussh," Kyran said, smiling.

"Release me," she gasped again, trying to catch her breath and gain her balance. Much to her surprise, he let her go. She shoved away, treading water at the same time she turned to see if he followed. Though the water felt cool, heat rose up her neck and settled into her cheeks. She cast a frantic glance over her shoulder toward the bank, then turned back to glare at him when she heard his soft laughter.

" 'Tis a fair distance. Dare you try to escape me again?" He swam slowly around her, and she knew that the moment she would try to get away, he would capture her again. Could she resist if he persisted? He'd only held her for a moment and already her insides tingled.

"Your hair acts as a veil and keeps from me that which I long to see." His eyes glittered brighter than the sunlight on the ripples.

She drew a quick, deep breath and dove to escape, but he caught her hand. She was off balance, and water ran into her eyes and nose before she could surface. Coughing too hard to try again, she allowed him to pull her closer. More deep laughter caused the tingling to spread lower and grow warmer.

"Silly woman, think I would let one so beautiful drown?" He stared into her eyes. "I remember thinking when I caught you in my chamber that you were afraid of me. It seems I was mistaken. I see no fear, only defiance."

He released her, but continued to circle, foiling any chance of escape. The infuriating man swam like a fish.

"I saw you from yonder bank. Your bath made the water look inviting." He reached over and moved a strand of wet hair from her cheek. "Tell me, sweet witch. How did you escape the confines of my chamber—and since we have the time to converse—where are my ring, my dagger and my amulet?"

"Though you have me at a disadvantage again, my lord, I beg mercy. I ask you to remember that 'twas I who saved your life and took away your pain. Those things are the price I require for such services."

She tried again to slip away, but he blocked her. "Think you I would harm the sprite who came to my rescue? Nay, sweet witch, nor would I force myself upon her." He paused and smiled. "Unless she so desired."

Her arms started to feel heavy, growing tired as she worked to stay afloat. He leaned a little closer and would have stolen a kiss, but she pulled up her feet and pushed off his chest. She swam with all her might—long, strong strokes. She had no need to look back to know if he pursued, for the sound of splashing and controlled breathing confirmed it.

Donna MacQuigg

When his hand closed over her ankle, she tried to kick free, but he dragged her under. His hands moved up her thigh, to her buttocks, searing every inch of her skin before they stopped on her waist and he hoisted her upward, her torso out of the water, where he held her for a moment before he let her sink back into the lake's warmth. Finally, her feet touched the bottom. Furious, she tried to scratch his face. He quickly caught her wrists and forced them behind her back. He pressed her to his hard body, the water lapping around his waist. She silently groaned at the jolt of desire that passed between them. Her nipples instantly hardened and for several moments she thought she'd die of shame from her body's reaction.

Kyran drew in a short breath the moment they touched—the shock of her pressed so intimately close to his manhood ran rampant through his body. He'd been a long time without a woman, and he attributed his instant arousal to that fact. Had this enchantress been one of Aswyn's wenches he would have sated his need then and there, but Sayrid was different—perhaps even destined to be his mate. Though he didn't understand it, 'twas clear she had the power to jumble his thoughts and make him lose control. He hungered for her, to taste her lips, to feel her skin against his, and more . . . something far more.

As if she heard his innermost thoughts, she stopped struggling. With a rebellious toss of wet hair, she glared up at him. Though he felt her tremble, her eyes narrowed, and her lips thinned with defiance. "I will not yield without a fight," she hissed.

Aye, he knew she wouldn't, and it made him want her even more. "Although I like a woman with fire in her eyes, I've no desire to fight you." His mind raced. If he kept her captive, he'd frighten her, yet he hated to let her go. "Methinks we could come up with a more peaceful solution. What say you?"

"There is nothing to resolve, my lord. You're a barbarian and

116

will always be a barbarian."

"Nay, you are wrong." He purposely tightened his hold, enjoying her hips pressed so firmly to his manhood. "It appears, my spirited witch, that you are again my prisoner." He bent his head to steal a kiss, but she turned away. Undaunted, he brushed his lips on her temple, then again on the sensitive spot below her ear, frowning at the amount of restraint it took to stop. Each time he held her, it became more difficult to let her go.

Had he any sense at all, he'd take her, willing or not, and learn what secrets she held that made his lust uncontrollable. Maybe once sated, he'd be satisfied and clearheaded, and he could get on with the difficult tasks ahead of him. Reluctantly, he released her wrists, but grabbed a handful of wet hair and forced her head back. He purposely let his warm breath caress her ear as he whispered, "One kiss, freely given."

She put her hands against his chest and shoved him back. He grinned at her determined expression. "One kiss for your freedom."

Much to his surprise, her eye flickered down to his mouth a brief moment before she looked up at him. "One?" she challenged, her chin quivering ever so slightly.

Fighting for control, he nodded. "One . . . freely given."

He watched the battle rage in her eyes a moment before her features softened. Matching his determined gaze, she touched her lips softly to his. Carnal passion, hot and potent, exploded inside of him.

Sayrid could barely keep her balance when Kyran's arms wrapped around her. When she tried to protest, he kissed her again, long and hard. At first, he'd been gentle, but then she sensed something in him snap like a brittle twig. Between his mouth devouring hers and the hard length of him pressing intimately against her hips, a fire boiled in her belly, and she knew if he persisted, she'd give in to her burning desire to couple with him. Liquid fire coursed through her, and, instead of pushing away, her arms came around his neck and she clung to him, answering his voracious kisses.

He groaned, cupped her bare bottom and drew her closer. Shamelessly she wrapped her legs around his waist, giving in to the swirling sensations in the pit of her stomach that coiled even more tightly with each torrid touch of his mouth and hands on her skin.

With each kiss, he hoisted her up a little higher, nipping at the sensitive spot on her neck below her ear. When he lifted her a little more, his gaze held hers a moment before he bent his head and closed his hot mouth over a taut nipple.

Goddess of the forest, what magic did this man possess that could drive her to madness? Tipping her head back in sweet agony, Sayrid moaned his name. A storm brewed between them as he teased both breasts with gentle nips and scrapes of his teeth. Lightning crackled and sparked though her brain when his persistent fingers probed her feminine folds. She squeezed her eyes tightly closed. She wanted to resist, but she arched against him.

Nearly mindless with the want of her, Kyran smiled, ready to lift her and place her on his shaft, when her eyes flew wide open.

A goddess one moment, a banshee the next.

She shoved him back with surprising force. The next instant, she rolled in the water and pushed off his chest with her feet, knocking him off balance. Water rushed into his mouth and nose. He recovered quickly and reached for her, but she'd already scrambled up the bank.

He watched her gather up her clothing before she disappeared into the dense foliage. Shrugging his stiff shoulder, he reluctantly accepted defeat, standing waist-deep in the water, wondering why he'd turned into a rutting animal. "Because you are," he muttered angrily. Frustrated, he dove then rolled to his back, floating and drawing in long, deep breaths to try and clear his head. Only then did he notice dark roiling storm clouds in the sky.

Lightning ignited the thunderheads at the same time Kyran closed his eyes, recalling what had transpired, reliving each hungry kiss, each torrid touch. Had his thoughts not been on Sayrid, he would have noticed the sun peeking between the waning clouds. A smile spread across his peaceful features, for now he knew what he wanted to know.

The maddening woman was a virgin.

Pleased beyond measure, he rested back and floated, paying no attention to a flock of ravens that few high overhead, circled once, then perched in the top of a towering oak tree. With only thoughts of Sayrid in his head, Kyran never noticed when one bird swooped to the ground behind a spiny hawthorn bush.

Brynn carefully stepped out from behind the bush and went to the water's edge where she knelt down. Much to her delight a small eel scurried under a rock near where the lake lapped at the bank. Brynn drew a circle in the glassy surface of the water, muttering a few well-chosen words, scrambling back when the water began to bubble. A moment later the eel erupted halfway into the air, twenty times its normal size.

Go and drown the man. Brynn's eyes never left the two round orbs that stared back at her. Once the eel slipped silently under the surface, Brynn sat wearily on a nearby rock, making no effort to hide behind the bush. Nay, she didn't care if the king caught a glimpse of her. Changing from bird to her normal form and casting a spell on the eel had drained her strength, but it hardly mattered. In a few moments he'd be dead.

Kyran basked in the cool water and the warm sun. It had been years since he'd enjoyed a swim as much as this, and he felt certain he had Sayrid to thank for it. He was just about to roll and swim to shore when he thought he felt something smooth slither under his back. A fractured second later, a large, black, slippery, snake-like beast wrapped around Kyran's waist and dragged him under. The water closed over his head, and no matter how hard he tried he couldn't grab any part of the thing that continued to hold him under. Only when the long body wrapped around Kyran for a second time did he get a look at its face.

An eel. He felt certain of it, but one of a size he'd never seen before. The next moment, Kyran's feet touched bottom. Using every ounce of his strength, he pushed upward, drawing a huge breath as soon as his face broke the surface. His relief was short lived, as water closed over his head again and the eel tightened his hold around Kyran's ribs.

Sayrid doubled over, gasping for breath, feeling as if her ribs were about to break. Stunned by the force of the pain, it took her several moments to realize that if nothing was harmful to her, it must be Kyran. Drawing in a shaky breath, she ran back to the lake only to find no sign of the king. The next instant, the air was forced from her lungs again, and at the same time a giant beast broke the surface. Held fast in its snake-like body, Kyran fought to reach the eel's huge head, grabbing its lower jaw and forcing its mouth open as wide as he could.

Gasping for breath, Sayrid nocked her bow, still fighting against the urge to close her eyes and succumb to the darkness that beckoned. Her arms felt heavy and her vision started to blur, but she managed to take aim.

His strength failing, Kyran ignored the pain in his fingers from the eel's sharp, pointy teeth and continued to pry its jaws apart until he heard the bones of its mouth cracking. A heartbeat later, the beast gave a massive roar as a painted arrow pierced its skull. Too exhausted to care how the creature died, he shoved it away from him and slowly swam toward the bank. Once his fingers grasped the root where his knife was embedded, he felt much better and took a moment to rest and catch his breath. Nearly recovered, he swam back and dived, finding the dead eel.

A few moments later, Kyran slowly dragged himself out of the water and rolled to his back on the bank, where he gradually regained his strength. In his fist, he held the arrow he'd cut from the beast's brain.

Brynn couldn't believe her eyes. Upon catching a glimpse of Sayrid nocking her bow, she practically fell backwards off the rock as she scrambled to hide behind it. In shock, she watched Sayrid loose her arrow, which struck the giant eel directly in the head. "Curse her," Brynn squealed in fury, even more dismayed when she saw the king slowly swimming toward the shore. "Curse them both."

Careful not to be seen, she crept back to the cover of some thick bushes and young saplings where she felt safe enough to rest before she returned to Dragon's Head.

Sayrid rested on a flat rock and tossed several pebbles into the pool not far from her cottage. She'd come to fetch more water and gather reeds, but chose to linger in the peaceful forest a little longer. She thought about the creature—wondered who could've conjured up such a thing—when she suddenly felt cold, and Brynn's face appeared for a moment in the ripples of the pond.

A shudder slithered down Sayrid's spine as she remembered Kyran's near-death experience with the giant eel. 'Twas frightening to know that Brynn was capable of such evil. Refusing to think about it any longer, Sayrid concentrated on more pleasant things.

Visions of Kyran danced in her mind. His broad chest, the hard muscles of his shoulders and upper arms marked with battle scars and something more—a magnificent tattoo of a dragon. The same dragon she'd always believed to live in the bowels of the old castle.

Flaxen and bronze hair clinging to Kyran's wet skin—the sight of him had stimulated more than just her curiosity about his intentions toward her people. A mistake she could not afford to do again. She squeezed her eyes tightly together. What had happened to her? In his arms she had lost all desire to leave. More than that, she had lost the desire to remain chaste. She had wanted him to take her, to do with her what she had seen Aswyn do to his women. Thinking about the way he kissed her, an aching began in the center of her being, and she somehow knew that, if she had stayed, he would have soothed it.

She heaved a despondent sigh. Even now, knowing it to be wrong, she wished she'd let him join with her, just so the erotic feelings would relent. He'd kissed her with the hungry urgency of a savage warrior, yet his hold had softened to silken shackles. Could she dare hope to defeat such a foe if he proved to be her enemy?

She could never hope to defeat him, she confirmed bitterly as she dipped the bucket into the pool and waited for it to fill with water. Only when a jay called repeatedly to his mate did her tortured thoughts return to her task.

★ ★ ★ ★ ★

Maldwyn came into the great hall of Raven's Wings Castle and filled a goblet with wine before he took his usual place in an ornate chair near Oddrum's throne. "My lord," he muttered, tipping his head briefly out of respect. Though he cared little about Oddrum's welfare, he asked, "I trust you slept well?"

"Aye. And you, my old friend? Any more dreams?"

Maldwyn took a drink before he helped himself to some fruit on the table between their chairs. He looked at his king, seeing a man who, in all his years of service, never gave anything back to those who served him. 'Twas time to rectify that. 'Twas time to put his plan into motion. "I dreamt of a maiden. One of extraordinary beauty . . . and extraordinary power."

"Ha, you old fox," Oddrum said, laughing. "Still rutting at your age?" He plucked several grapes from the silver tray. "I care little about your nighttime trysts with some young sorceress. 'Tis the new king I want to speak of. Did you dream of him . . . this Kyran?"

"Patience, my lord." Maldwyn stared into his cup. A vision of Sayrid appeared, her features appearing smooth and unaffected by the deep red of the wine. Memories of his past crept into his mind—memories of his lust for Derwyn. Had she accepted his advances, Sayrid could have been his granddaughter—Cyric his grandson. They could have all been family—a very powerful family—powerful enough to have ruled all of Wales with the simple wave of the hand.

Mentally he cursed Derwyn and would have sent her a memento of his hate, but he knew she still had enough power to send it back to him, and what he would have done to her would be done to him tenfold. Nevertheless, he would have his revenge for being spurned. He would make sure the old sorceress lived long enough to see her granddaughter bound in marriage to him, and her grandson bound in marriage to Brynn. If that didn't kill the old bitch, he'd finish her off barehanded.

"You must hear me, as this maiden is the means by which to defeat this king and finally claim Dragon's Head."

Oddrum put down his goblet and leaned a little closer, his black brows drawing tightly together. "In your dream, did she divulge her name?"

He almost told him 'twas Sayrid, but caught himself in time. "Nay, she did not. She is young and naïve." Maldwyn heaved a long, loud sigh and decided to give Oddrum enough information to keep him interested. "I cannot be sure, but I suspect she's a relative of the one we all thought dead."

"Old Derwyn?"

"Aye. As of late, I've sensed she didn't die in the attack—that her skill as a sorceress kept her whereabouts secret. But she is old now, and her powers have weakened."

"And what of her relative—this woman you speak of. Is she also a sorceress?"

Maldwyn nodded. "Aye, the girl's power is strong—some of it inherited, some of it a gift from the Ancient Ones. I'm certain Aswyn had hoped to make use of her special powers, but died before he could make it happen."

Completely aware of the king's increasing impatience, the old man took a chunk of cheese and put it into his mouth, chewing for several moments. 'Twould be nice to cast a spell on Oddrum and be done with his interrogation, but when he was young and foolish he'd sworn a wizard's oath to never use magic on the king. After Maldwyn swallowed, he cleared his throat, staring out into space, pretending he'd forgotten their topic because it gave him a small measure of happiness to prick his sovereign by any means he could conjure up.

"Well," Oddrum growled.

Maldwyn inwardly smiled at the same time he feigned forgetfulness. "My lord?"

"The girl, you old fool. Tell me more about the girl."

Again Maldwyn dragged his hand down his long white bread, another thing he knew annoyed Oddrum. "Though she is a bright girl, capable of great powers, she is unaware just how powerful she is, or that her powers will manifest more each day and totally when she comes of age."

"And when will that happen?" asked Oddrum, taking another sip from his goblet. He took a chunk of cheese from the platter.

Maldwyn pursed his lips. "Soon, my lord, very soon this girl will become a woman. There is a man she is attracted to, but she refuses to admit it."

"What are you saying? She must couple before—"

"Aye, but not with any man. The man she lies with must be equally as gifted if she is to take full advantage of her power. 'Tis imperative she couple with her life-mate if her powers are to reach their full potential."

Oddrum frowned. "If she is the means by which I can defeat the new king, pray tell, where can we find her?"

"I fear you must travel to Dragon's Head. There is only one way to win the lady's hand and that is to kill her life-mate."

Oddrum nearly choked on his wine. "My peace-loving wizard encourages war?" He frowned, then smiled. "There is danger in murdering a life-mate. If he dies, so might the girl."

"True, but are you not living proof that one can survive the loss and still continue?"

Oddrum heaved a despondent sigh and for a moment Maldwyn felt a sting of pity for his king. "I've need of a new wife," Oddrum began, smiling arrogantly. "And, after hearing you speak of her beauty, my loins grow heavy with the want of her."

Maldwyn nodded. His king had a simple mind, usually thinking with what he kept tucked in his chausses. "In due time, my lord. 'Tis the new warlord we should fear—him and his army. All powerful warriors, trained from childhood to deal out death.

Where your army will fight to protect your kingdom, Dragon's Head's army is fighting to protect their families and their homes. Most have lived as slaves and have vowed never to do so again. 'Twill make them a much more formidable foe."

Oddrum gave an arrogant snort. "Fear naught, my old friend. We have many warriors and the gold to hire many mercenaries. Let him come with his powerful death-dealing army, and you and I shall watch their demise from two comfortable chairs on the balcony."

Maldwyn toyed with the end of his beard, frowning as if deeply in thought. Had Oddrum heard anything? Nay, likely not . . . only what he wanted to hear. "You must outnumber them. You must have at least two warriors to their one if you are to have a chance at success. You must attack—strike first if you are to kill the king and win the woman. To wait for him to come to us could mean your destruction."

Oddrum's smile faded. " 'Twill take days to prepare to march—weeks if I am to haul enough food to feed them all. And if we lay siege. . . ." Oddrum shook his head. "My stores are full—food for all. Perhaps we should make them come to us."

Maldwyn frowned, remembering his dream, wondering what Oddrum would do if he told him the truth—that the true king of Dragon's Head planned to marry Brynn to unite the two kingdoms. If they waited, a messenger might get through with the proposal and ruin his plans. Maldwyn took a long drink of wine. Over his dead body would he let that happen. Brynn, not Oddrum, would rule Dragon's Head. Maldwyn heaved a sigh. "War is our only course. Striking first is our only hope of victory. I feel it in my bones."

The moment Derwyn touched the lock of Kyran's hair, there was a glimmer in her eyes. And just when Sayrid thought Derwyn would divulge more information about the warrior, the old woman hobbled to the table and started to knead a lump of dough.

"There is a need for ye tae go tae Dragon's Head on the morrow and attend the feast," Derwyn replied.

Frustrated, Sayrid watched Derwyn work the bread as if it were an old enemy, never looking up whilst she ordered her to do the impossible. Derwyn's bread would grow moldy before Sayrid would willingly attend a feast at Dragon's Head.

Suddenly she felt Derwyn's firm gaze leave the bread and settle on her. Sayrid met Derwyn's eyes and knew the old woman had read her thoughts. "Why?" Sayrid asked, trying hard to be patient. "Why is it important that I go?"

"Because there is tae be a great feast. There will be plenty of food and music too. All who have stayed in the village have been invited. Gwendolyn and Dafydd. Rhonwyn too." Derwyn sprinkled a little more flour on the cloth covering the table. "Ye spend too much time alone in the forest. Ye should go and present yerself tae the new king."

"I don't like him. I like living alone in the forest." Memories of Kyran—his brutal, hungry kisses—flashed in her mind and caused her cup to rattle ever so slightly against the saucer. "I've no need—"

"Still ye do no' believe me, even though I have given ye cause. I wasna' sure before, but I am now. Yer destiny lies with him and with Dragon's Head, no' out here in the forest." Derwyn wiped her hands with a frayed cloth. "Heed my words, child. Even I canna' know everything afore 'tis time tae know. My powers are no' as strong as they used tae be. Soon, very soon, we will have the answers."

The old woman went to a shadowy corner and removed a deerskin coverlet that covered a trunk. The rusty hinges squeaked when she opened the lid and pulled out a cloth-covered garment. She quickly removed the cloth, exposing an elegant, diaphanous overgown of iris-blue, and placed it in Sayrid's arms along with a matching under-gown, thin golden circlet, wimple and soft kid slippers.

"They're beautiful. Where did you get them?" Sayrid asked in a voice barely over a whisper.

" 'Twas yer mother's and now 'tis yers."

"My mother's?" Sayrid cried, her mouth falling open. "You knew her?"

Derwyn nodded solemnly. "Aye, a kind soul. Ye remind me of her."

Sayrid put aside the clothing and stood, gently grabbing Derwyn's shoulders. "Tell me. Tell me everything you remember about her."

Derwyn's eyes glistened with unshed tears. "Soon, but there's no time today. On the morrow, the women will be hangin' their wash early in preparation for the festivities so ye'll no' be noticed. Take the gown tae Gwendolyn. She'll fit it tae ye and make it a bit more stylish." Derwyn put her knobby hand on Sayrid's cheek. "Be sure to wear yer amulet, and keep the other in yer pocket. But, before ye leave, give it back tae him."

"But—"

"Shush. 'Tis important ye do as I say."

Sayrid swallowed past the lump that had formed in her throat, fully aware that she'd get no more information from the old woman. She forced a smile, picked up the clothing and numbly turned toward the door.

"There's one more thing, my child." Derwyn's smile changed into a frown when Sayrid turned to meet the old woman's gaze. "Keep secret all that I've told ye. There is still much danger."

Sayrid lay in bed, but she couldn't sleep. Her mind raced with the happenings of the day, learning that Derwyn knew her mother. As kind as the old woman could be, she was also infuriatingly complex, tossing out little bits and pieces of information as if she were tossing crumbs of stale bread to the birds.

Shifting to her side, Sayrid heaved a despondent sigh as she stared into the waning fire. It popped and smoldered, spreading warmth across her face. She thought about the past days, almost wishing things had never changed—that old Aswyn still ruled Dragon's Head. At least when he did, she could sleep soundly and not dream of fierce, handsome warriors. Her gaze traveled up from the dying flames to the hearth where Kyran's amulet rested next to his ring. The smooth oval almandine in his ring twinkled harmlessly in the flickering light.

"I'm not a thief," she muttered, remembering Derwyn's insinuation. "And I shall prove it." In spite of the late hour and the rain, she hurriedly dressed. Donning a dark-green, woolen shawl which she used to cover her head, she picked up his ring and slipped it into her pocket. A few moments later she wondered at the wisdom of walking through the Mystical Forest in a storm.

CHAPTER EIGHT

Kyran awoke, groggy at first, but slowly regaining his bearings. Rain fell steadily outside, the pleasant sound of it pelting against the skins on the balcony. 'Twas mornings like this he favored the most—the cool air, the clean, fresh smell. He yawned and sat up, glancing at two small muddy footprints on the stone floor by the bedside table. He stood quickly, staring at the prints until something caught his attention.

There on the table sat his ring. He snatched it up, curling his fingers tightly over it, swearing under his breath as he searched the floor for more prints. Except for the mud next to the table, the floor showed no sign of anyone walking to the door or balcony. Once again, Sayrid had come and gone as if she'd vanished into thin air. Yet he knew the woman who haunted his dreams to be definitely flesh and blood.

"Cursed woman," he muttered, dragging his fingers through his tousled hair. He spent the next hour going over the walls in his chamber, looking under the bed, and pressing on nearly every stone and rocky protrusion in the room, feeling for anything out of the ordinary. Finally, he accepted failure, pressing his forehead on the cool stone in frustration.

Suddenly he jerked back and stared at the wall—certain he'd felt more than just cold rock. It had felt alive. He pressed his hand against it again, drawing it away with a muttered curse. He glanced at his fingers then touched his forehead, frowning. Had he not known better, he could have sworn that for a moment the rock had turned into scales, slithering lifelike beneath his touch.

By the time he dressed, the morning rain had gone, leaving the sun to dry the mud. He hesitated before he left the chamber, glancing around the cold grayish-green stone. Had he felt the walls move? Could it have actually been real?

"Fool," he muttered, annoyed he'd let his imagination run rampant, and even more annoyed that he'd been duped again by such a beautiful enchantress.

Sayrid leaned back against the stone in the passageway, barely able to keep from laughing out loud. "We've fooled him again, old one," she whispered, certain that if a dragon's spirit lurked within the old castle then he, too, would be grinning impishly. It had been worth the early-morning trek through the forest in the drizzling rain to spy on the king and watch his reaction when he awoke. She'd purposely left her footprints by the bedside table to further annoy him and had been rewarded with muttered oaths of revenge against her person.

"Silly man," she whispered as she slipped her shoes back on, mindless of the drying mud. Still smiling, she yawned. Sleep had been elusive, and what with traveling back and forth from her cottage twice in one night, she felt fatigued. Carefully, she made her way down the well-worn stone steps. She had only traveled a short way when she paused. To her left she knew there to be another hidden passageway—one that led to another stone staircase, only this one spiraled down into the bowels of the castle. At the bottom of the stairs there had been a rocky platform about as large as the interior of her cottage. She'd crept to the edge on her hands and knees, frightened nearly to death that she'd pitch over the edge into the dark abyss that appeared on two sides of the platform.

She'd been so terrified, she'd scrambled back, pressing herself against the wall—her fingers accidentally brushing against an ancient symbol carved into the stone. To her horror another door-size chunk of rock rotated open, exposing yet another steep stairway leading into pitch darkness. She'd refused to enter and hurried back the way she came.

Dare she explore this new chamber now? She wondered, certain that she'd grown more mature and wouldn't be so easily frightened. She stared at the solid rock hoping to remember which rock she'd pushed to reveal the hidden door leading to the spiral staircase. But no matter which stone she touched, nothing moved.

Aggravated that she couldn't remember, she leaned wearily against the wall, instantly reminded that she needed some rest. She descended the steps into the small oval chamber, and after she placed the candle on the shelf, she slipped unseen through the stone portal and into the thick trees and bushes of the forest of Dragon's Head.

"Kyran," Cyric called. "You cannot be thinking to go outside. Come and join us. 'Tis not fit for man or beast out there. Come, play a few games of dice with me and Bynor."

Kyran paused, frowning at a loud crack of thunder that brought more rain to pound on the heavy front doors even harder. Reluctantly, he crossed the short distance to where his friends sat and joined them, calling to a servant to bring them all a tankard of ale.

"Is that your ring I see?" Cyric asked, his eyes alive with humor. "Pray tell, did you have a magical visitor during the night?"

Kyran fought back the urge to wipe the teasing grin from his friend's face with his fist. "It appears so, does it not?" He grabbed the dice. "How high are the stakes?"

Bynor laughed and glanced at Cyric. "It seems our fierce

protector isn't in the mood to tell us how he recovered his lucky charm. Is she still abed in your chamber?"

Kyran's uninterested expression didn't change. "If she were, do you think I'd be playing a silly game with you two?" He tossed the dice to Bynor. "Where's Morven?"

"Who is to know? Nothing keeps him from hunting, not even the weather. I'm anxious to see what he'll do when winter comes."

Cyric tossed a silver coin on the stack, his high spirits apparently doused by Bynor's remark. "Do not keep us in suspense. Did you see Sayrid again, or did your ring appear whilst you slept?"

"By his frown, I'd say 'twas there this morn when he awoke." Bynor laughed. "I'd nearly forgotten the woman can appear and disappear as she pleases." The warrior rolled the dice, mumbling how, if it weren't for bad luck, he'd have none at all. "I checked on our men this afternoon after they practiced with Morven," Bynor said with a crooked smile, "and thought that I heard them say the wench who nearly killed you disguised herself as a child and attacked you yet again . . . a few days ago . . . with a broom no less?"

"Remind me to have a talk with Morven." Kyran took a drink from a heavily jeweled goblet while Cyric reached for a tankard of ale. "And," Kyran continued, "how many times must I tell you, she saved me in the forest. She did not try to kill me." He bit down hard to keep from telling them that she'd saved his life again, certain the arrow he removed from the giant eel had been one of Sayrid's.

"Aye, saved after she missed her target," Bynor added with a chuckle, his voice sounding even more comical as it echoed in his raised tankard. He placed it down on the table with a definite thud. "And what about the second part?"

Kyran's dark brows snapped together. "The second part?" he

asked, fully aware what his friend was getting at.

"Aye." Bynor's eyes were alive with mirth. "The broom attack."

"Need I eject you from this hall?" Kyran asked calmly, raising one questioning brow.

Bynor laughed again, rolled the dice and then swore under his breath.

"There has to be a secret passageway somewhere in your chamber." Cyric dragged his winnings to his side of the table, stacking the coins on those he'd already won. "A secret passageway that could put in danger all we've worked so hard for."

"If she knows of it, do others?" Bynor asked. "Methinks we should have done what I suggested before."

"And what was that?" Kyran asked, rolling the dice. "Eight." He motioned to Bynor. "Put in eight or forfeit."

Bynor counted out the coins from his stack and tossed them on the table before he took a turn with the dice. "When you were sick, I suggested to Cyric that we move you out of the master's chamber. I would've taken your place; being uninjured and able to move more quickly, I would've grabbed her before she escaped. Seven to you, Cyric."

Kyran gave a humorous laugh. "Your trick might have worked, but I doubt it. Think you I sleep so soundly that someone could enter my chamber and I wouldn't hear?"

"Of course not. I have never seen anyone sneak up on you."

"Nor have I," Cyric added. After he paid the debt, he rolled the dice. "Ha, I win," he nearly shouted. "Shall we play again?"

Kyran shook his head, his brows drawn together in thought. "There has to be another chamber outside the wall of my chamber—a place that leads to the forest—a place where she can hide until she feels safe enough to leave. 'Twould be impossible to come in through the front doors. There are too many guards."

"Suppose, if you will," Bynor added with a sly grin, "that all our jests on disappearing is true . . . that she can disappear or become invisible or change her appearance so much that she wouldn't be recognized. Wizards have done it before. If so, she could easily slip past our guards."

"I do not think that is possible," Cyric stated with a shake of his head. "Even if she could become, as you say, invisible or change her appearance, surely she cannot walk through solid rock or wood. The guards would notice if the door opened or if suddenly a portion of the wall moved." Cyric looked up at Kyran, and grinned. "My mother had a way of sneaking up on me when I least expected it. 'Twas most infuriating. Especially if I was doing something I shouldn't be doing."

"You both are mad." Kyran stood. "I'm going outside. There has to be another way into the castle, and I intend to find it."

"But it's raining . . . harder than before," Bynor complained.

Kyran took a long drink, and then put down the empty tankard. "Aye, but rain or no rain, I mean to find it, and I'll be waiting for her the next time she chooses to appear."

Carrying a fresh pitcher of wine, Brynn kept her gaze diverted as the redheaded warrior approached. 'Twas strange, she thought: each time he came close, she felt a warmth in the pit of her stomach, a feeling she'd never felt before.

"I'll take that," Cyric said, lifting the pitcher from her grasp.

" 'Tis no trouble," she murmured, cringing at the mewling sound of her voice. What magic did this man possess that could turn her into a simpering, gutless woman? She'd been taught the ways of a warrior by Maldwyn and knew enough spells and potions to bring all of the men in Dragon's Head to their knees. This slight show of compassion from a man confused her, left her feeling shy and hesitant.

Cyric's warm fingers brushed against hers, and she quickly

tucked her hand into her pocket, hoping he didn't notice her surprise. Troubled by her feelings of weakness, she turned and hurried toward the castle's kitchens.

Sayrid sat on the edge of her bed, preparing for a nice long nap. She took her medallion from around her neck and cradled it in her palm. Though the stone was slightly smaller, it had never glowed or shown any signs of life as Kyran's had. She stared at it, willing it to glow—disappointed when nothing happened.

A steady rain fell outside. Feeling chilled, she stood and placed her amulet next to the one on the mantel. It made a slight tinkling sound as the edges touched, but she paid it no mind. She bent and added another log to the smoldering coals, blowing softly until it ignited into flames. A jolt of light shot upwards from the two medallions, startling her so badly she jumped back and cried out in fear. She stared at the amulets and at the streams of red-gold light that shone more brightly than any light she'd ever seen before.

Fearfully, she grabbed the long stick she used as a poker. Moving as carefully as she could, she separated the two medallions, relieved when the streams of light retracted as if she'd doused a flame with water. She took a calming breath, only now aware that she'd been holding it. She slipped the poker under the chain of her amulet and lifted it off the mantel, catching it as it slid down the smooth staff. She expected it to be hot, but it felt cool. Slowly she turned it over in her palm, watching in amazement as a glowing, soft light in the center of the almandine slowly fizzled out.

Uncertain it would remain dormant, she quickly hung it in its usual place over her bed, far away from Kyran's. When her heartbeat returned to normal, she found a small piece of cloth and wrapped his medallion before she carried it outside and tucked it securely under a rock near her door. Satisfied there'd be no more unwanted encounters whilst she napped, she smugly dusted off her hands before she looked up. The flock of ravens had just returned and, after perching in the treetops, watched her curiously. The largest hopped from branch to branch until it perched much closer than the others. It cocked its head, its black gaze locking with hers in a most disturbing manner.

"Who or what are you?" she asked, surprised by the calmness of her voice when she felt so unnerved.

The big bird was soon joined by a smaller, sleeker one, but the first ignored the second. After a few moments the larger bird appeared to grow bored. It fluffed its feathers and began to preen, apparently unafraid as Sayrid slowly crept forward.

"Are you part of the prophecy?" Sayrid whispered, reaching out to see if she could touch it. She cried out in pain from a sharp peck of its powerful black beak that drew a small speck of blood. She snatched her hand back and clutched it to her breast under the watchful eye of the raven. The smaller raven squawked and took flight, followed by her mate. The others joined the leader and, together, the flock disappeared over the treetops.

Sayrid watched them depart for a moment more before she inspected the bite. Though not serious, it hurt and continued to ooze blood. Scolding herself for her foolishness, she went inside to wash the small wound.

Kyran raked his wet hair out of his eyes. Though moisture dripped from numerous mossy faults in the stones, he found no manmade cracks, no mortar missing, and no marks on the wet ground where an opened door might scrape across. He smoothed his hand over the stone, drawing back when it felt as if he'd cut his finger on a sharp rock. Although he felt pain, there wasn't any sign of an injury. As he rubbed his finger with his thumb he thought of Sayrid. Had she pricked her finger on a thorn and that's why his finger hurt?

"Cursed rain," he muttered, paying no particular attention when several moments later it stopped. Frustrated with his futile search, he went inside and climbed the stairs to his chamber to change into dry clothing, not at all surprised to see Cyric waiting for him. "If you've come to learn what I found out, you're wasting your time. I found nothing."

"A message came a few moments ago from the spies you sent to Oddrum's kingdom." Cyric's reddish brows knotted together. "Oddrum knows of Arcas' death, and is even more uneasy with Aswyn's. There are rumors he is gathering mercenaries to add to his army in preparation for war."

Kyran yanked off his wet tunic. "I'd expected as much. 'Tis why I sent a messenger ahead with your proposal." He filled a goblet with wine and took a long drink.

"You what?"

"When Oddrum reads with his own eyes our proposal and sees that we've come in peace, he will know that what we now hold is rightfully ours."

"But you've lost proof of that, Kyran. Without the amulet how will they believe us?"

"I will make them believe." Kyran shook his head in disgust, still preoccupied with Sayrid's disappearance as he tugged on clean leggings. "She was here in this room, yet no one saw her enter Dragon's Head or leave it."

"By the gods, Kyran," Cyric began a little desperately. "Oddrum is adding mercenaries to his army as we speak and you have nothing to say about it?"

"Have I ever let you down?" Kyran demanded, still angry and growing more so. "Need I remind you I am well trained in battle? I've years of experience—have maimed and killed more men than you have hairs on your head." He continued dressing, tugging a clean tunic over his head.

Cyric's expression grew sober. "Oddrum and his men, in

truth, are our people . . . our brothers. If I could, I would make peace with them, not war."

"Aye. You have told me many times. And I have told you I am a warrior, not a peacemaker." He held up his hand when Cyric started to interrupt. "For you and our people, I will do the best I can—pretend to be something I'm not—but know this, my friend. I'll be no man's slave ever again. I will succeed one way or the other."

Kyran turned away from Cyric. He filled another goblet with wine and held it out to his friend, refusing to remember the times he prayed for death during his training. " 'Tis because of Arcas I learned to be strong, obedient and determined."

He took a drink from his cup before he turned to study the ancient carvings in the stones over the hearth. "I'm troubled more by those who call themselves Welsh and secretly cast their lot in with foreigners in hopes of securing Dragon's Head for their own means."

"What say you?" Cyric complained. "Even among Welsh there are different tribes—tribes that fight between themselves like beasts over a fresh kill. Need I remind you that our parents' deaths were arranged by Aswyn and Arcas? I remember him bragging about it to his wife." Cyric's knuckles grew white where he gripped the goblet. "Were they not Welsh?"

Kyran glanced at the contents of his cup, unaware of the dark frown that marred his forehead. "There have been traitors since the time of the Ancient Ones. Even the old dragon rumored to have built this castle was betrayed. I swore a blood oath to return to Dragon's Head—to protect our people, and nothing short of my death will prevent that from happening."

He made a wide sweep with his arm. "Look about you, Cyric. This is not a Viking structure. It's not cast of wood and iron, but of rock and clay and earth." He traced several runes with the tip of his finger, frowning more when once again the stone felt alive. "Dragon's Head was built by the Ancient Ones, not carved by the sword of Thor."

"There are many who believe it to be created by the last living dragon, to protect his dying mate," Cyric added with a skeptical shake of his head.

Kyran turned and faced Cyric. "I know naught what to believe of its creation, only that it is destined to be ruled by a man with the heart of a dragon."

"Dragon's Head should be ruled by a strong man like you," Cyric confirmed with a woeful smile. He raised his cup. "To Dragon's Head."

Kyran's features softened. He touched his cup to Cyric's. "Aye, and to the true king." Both men drank. Kyran went over to his chest and found a dry, black-leather belt and fastened it around his waist. "By the power given to me by the gods, and the trust given to me by my friends and our people, I'll do everything I possibly can to prevent another war."

Kyran put his hand on Cyric's shoulder. "Come. Enough talk of Oddrum and war. 'Tis time to see what delights await us at the feast."

"Delights indeed," Cyric confirmed. "Morven went hunting early this morn. He seems to spend all his time in the forest these days, but he brought back four more fat boars and sent others to fetch four harts he killed as well. And, as I told you before, the cooks are magical. Not only are there several kinds of bread, they have baked pies filled with apples and berries, the crusts glazed with honey."

Kyran nodded, yet couldn't force a smile. "Tonight we will feast on succulent food, savor the taste of sweet wine, and forget our troubles. In a few days, I will take a hundred of our best warriors and make myself known to King Oddrum."

" 'Tis good that you brought this to me early," Gwendolyn said as she held the overgown for Sayrid to admire. "I just finished the alterations. Now, before you say anything, look at this." Gwendolyn laid the overgown over a chair and picked up the soft, lavender-colored kirtle that matched. They looked absolutely stunning together. At that same moment Rhonwyn stepped from behind the leather drape that separated the bedroom from the living area.

Sayrid had never seen her dressed in such finery—a soft yellow gown with a shorter, more golden overgown, gathered under her breasts to fall in soft, gentle folds to just below the knee. Rhonwyn's light-brown hair had been brushed to a high luster, both sides pulled back, braided, and then the braids coiled around the top of her head to resemble a crown. Instantly, Sayrid recognized the small, bronze-and-topaz brooch pinned on the girl's shoulder to be the one Cyric had given to her when she'd brought the bread.

"You look beautiful," Sayrid cried, hugging the young woman.

" 'Tis my wedding dress," Gwendolyn said proudly. "And easily made to fit. She's almost exactly my size when I was her age." She went to her daughter and kissed her cheek. "Go and tell your little sisters a bedtime story whilst I finish with Sayrid." Gwendolyn turned back to Sayrid. "Let us see if this gown needs any further alterations."

Sayrid shook her head. "Nay. Perhaps you should keep it safe—keep it in your chest for your daughters."

"Nonsense. All except for Rhonwyn are too young for such a gown. Besides, 'tis your gown. What harm could you do it?"

"I—I could spill wine on it."

"I'm surprised you didn't think to say that you could tear the hem dancing—"

"Not likely. I don't know how to dance." She heaved a long sigh. "I know how to set snares, find herbs and mushrooms and survive in the forest."

"Those things are helpful, but no longer necessary." Gwendolyn gathered up the gown. "Here, put this on."

Sayrid slipped her mother's gown over her head and smoothed the fabric. The bodice and cuffs had been embroidered with tiny silver birds and blue flowers that matched the shimmering material of the overgown. The square neck lay just a little lower than the square neck of the kirtle, exposing just enough ivory skin to be enticing yet modest.

The kirtle fell in gentle folds to the floor, barely touching the toe of the matching kid slippers. The long narrow sleeves ended in a point on the backs of her hands. The sheer, full sleeves of the overgown ended at the elbow and followed the folds of her gown to the floor.

While Gwendolyn fussed with the material, Sayrid had the strangest feeling. She saw a beautiful woman who'd been lost in the very far reaches of her mind—a woman with long, coppery-red hair—a laughing, happy woman. The harder Sayrid tried to visualize the woman's features, the more obscure they became. In the next instance Sayrid saw herself as a very little girl, holding hands with a tall handsome man and practicing dance steps before a huge stone hearth much like the one in the great hall of Dragon's Head. His eyes were very blue and his teeth appeared very white beneath a dark-red beard.

"Sayrid, are you going to answer me or not?" Gwendolyn asked.

Drawn back to the present, Sayrid shook her head not sure what to say since she didn't hear Gwendolyn's question. "I—I think it's too low. I don't want men staring at me all night."

Gwendolyn laughed. "That is exactly what we want for both you and Rhonwyn. You are of age now, Sayrid. Perhaps you will find a husband tonight."

Sayrid gaped at her. "I've no need of a husband." She tugged at the bodice, trying to pull it up a little higher. But it didn't budge.

Gwendolyn took a step away to look at Sayrid. "You're more beautiful than I imagined." She moved Sayrid to a stool and pushed her down before she began to run a brush though her young friend's thick, curly hair. An hour later, Gwendolyn stood back and admired her work. "No one will recognize you this eve," she said proudly. "And, with your amulet around your neck, you look like a queen. In this light, the stone seems to have come alive."

Sayrid accepted the polished brass plate Gwendolyn handed her to see her reflection. A gasp caught in her throat. Gwendolyn had managed to weave tiny bluish-purple flowers throughout the braid she'd wound atop Sayrid's head, and to this she'd added the circlet. Much to her astonishment, the almandine appeared to glow ever so softly.

"I would prefer to watch from afar," Sayrid managed to say as she adjusted the soft material under her chin to better conceal the amulet. Rising from the stool, she went to her old gown and removed Kyran's amulet, tucking it into the deep pocket of her mother's dress.

"What is that?"

"M-my dagger," Sayrid lied.

"Is it really necessary to arm yourself?" Gwendolyn asked.

"Aye. What if Kyran recognizes me and tries to kiss me again?" The last slipped out and she instantly regretted her mistake, feeling the heat of a blush rise up her neck. In truth she was beginning to enjoy his kisses, but certainly didn't want the whole village to know.

Gwendolyn's eyes brightened. "Again? He has kissed you before?"

"Gwendolyn, please. The children will hear you." Sayrid gave her friend a firm look.

"Never mind the children. I'm sure they are sleeping. Now, before I burst with curiosity, you must tell me what happened."

By the time Sayrid had finished with her story, Gwendolyn's expression had changed three times. First she'd been astonished, and Sayrid felt certain that if her friend owned a dagger she would have thrust it in the new king's heart. Lastly, Gwendolyn's frown changed to that of a scheming woman.

"I think I know why you feel it's necessary to carry a weapon. 'Tis simple," the older woman said after several quiet moments. "Methinks he was as gentle as he knows how to be. He's much more a warrior than nobleman. However, dressed as you are tonight, I'm sure he will remember to treat you accordingly and you'll have no need for a dagger."

"Accordingly?" Sayrid repeated, grateful she'd made the decision to leave out the part where the giant eel had tried to drown Kyran.

"More tenderly," Gwendolyn corrected. "At first, most men are somewhat overbearing. But, in time, once they realize the woman they love loves them back, they become more tender."

"Love?" Sayrid cried incredulously. "More tender?" she repeated, growing annoyed with her friend's silly little smile. "If what you say is true, then I pray to the gods that he's still too weak from his wounds to attend."

"A man is never too weak to share himself with the woman he desires. From what you said, he was well enough in the lake—"

"Swear you'll not repeat that to anyone," Sayrid pleaded.

Again Gwendolyn's laughter filled the small cottage. "Methinks you say one thing and wish for another." Gwendolyn cupped Sayrid's cheek. "There is a rosy blush upon your face. Methinks you desire him, and, from what you have told me, I'm positive he desires you."

Sayrid scoffed. "I do not desire him. And if he desires me, he will be sorely disappointed."

"Are you daft?" Gwendolyn said, giggling. "If the king desires you, you could become his wife and together you could rule Dragon's Head."

"I refuse to marry a Norseman, no matter his status—regardless of his promises to treat the people fairly. He is Norse and cannot be trusted." *Especially with my heart,* she added silently.

"Think long and hard on this, my sweet friend. Would it not be better to share the throne than to never have a say in uniting your people?" Gwendolyn pushed Sayrid toward the door. "Think about what I've said. There have been rumors that Brynn is quickly becoming a favorite in the castle. We both know what she's capable of. Would you prefer to have her as queen?"

Gwendolyn ushered Sayrid to the door, calling for Rhonwyn. "Go now, both of you, and hurry lest they close the gates."

"I should be so fortunate," Sayrid muttered to her friend. She turned to say more, but Rhonwyn's mother had already closed the door. Lifting the material of her long skirt, she glanced at the sky through the tall oak trees while Rhonwyn hurried ahead. The sun squatted on the mountaintops, but 'twas not the thin fingers of dark clouds that caused Sayrid to shiver. 'Twas the solitary raven that perched upon the tallest branch.

"Come, Sayrid," Rhonwyn called. "We're sure to have a wonderful time."

CHAPTER NINE

Bynor took another drink before he dragged the back of his hand across his mouth. "That, my friends, is good ale."

Cyric glanced at Bynor, then shook his head in disbelief before speaking to Kyran. "I suppose that explains why he's had three of them and the feast has yet to begin."

Kyran smiled. He'd fought beside Bynor many times and knew him to be loyal and trustworthy. He also knew Bynor could hold more drink than most and still be able to rise early for battle practice. A cupbearer came, and their tankards and goblets were refilled.

Kyran's thoughts turned from the amount of ale his friends drank to those of Sayrid. He'd never wanted another woman as badly as he wanted her. And, instead of taking what he wanted, he'd made a silly bargain with her.

He unconsciously placed his hand against his blue woolen tunic, feeling again her soft breasts pressed against his chest.

"The witch, Sayrid, is late and holding up our supper." Bynor's words sounded slightly slurred.

"You invited her?" Cyric asked.

"The entire village was invited," Bynor interjected. "Surely she'd know of it."

"Aye," Kyran answered, slightly confused why Cyric's smile faded. "Look Cyric. Is that not the maid you pointed out to me the other day? Gwendolyn's daughter?"

Cyric grinned. "Aye. Her name is Rhonwyn."

146

"And a beauty she is. She appears to be looking for you." Kyran took a drink, anxious as a boy about to experience his first time with a woman, waiting to see if Sayrid would come.

A servant hurried to refill his cup and, in his haste to please his king, spilled some drink on Kyran's hand. Had Kyran not been distracted, he would've noticed when Sayrid had entered the great hall, as many of his men's heads turned toward her.

"By the gods, she's a beauty. Is she not?" Bynor murmured, lightly punching Kyran's shoulder. "Behold, could this vision be our future queen?"

Kyran's head jerked up at the same time he felt Cyric's fingers close on his arm. "Is she the witch . . . I—I mean . . . the woman who saved your life?" Cyric asked.

"Aye, she is." Kyran tried to stand, but Cyric's grip tightened, preventing it.

"Kyran, a word if you please. 'Tis urgent."

"Later, my friend. Go to Rhonwyn before she's snatched up by another." Kyran stood, unaware of Cyric's stunned expression. He easily shrugged away from Cyric's hold, unwilling to be detained any longer. The moment he saw Sayrid, it felt as if the breath had been knocked from his lungs. The woman had to be magical, to look so beautiful in the simplest of gowns.

In three long strides he arrived at the foot of the steps which descended into the hall. She stopped on the last step, and he sensed it gave her a small measure of superiority to look down upon him. He smiled, pleased by her high-spiritedness.

"My lord," she said, a little breathlessly. Had it been from her descent or did she lust for him as he did for her? He hoped the latter.

"My lady," he responded in kind, giving her a respectful nod of his head. Out of the corner of his eye, he saw Cyric approach Rhonwyn and bow deeply before kissing the back of her hand. For a breath of a moment, Kyran thought to do the same—to be more of a gentleman—but he feared if he kissed Sayrid's hand, he'd be unable to stop from pulling her into his arms and smothering her protests with kisses. He offered his arm instead.

Much to his relief, she placed her hand lightly on his sleeve, as regal as a queen, causing the muscle of his forearm to jump in response. She would've fooled him with her cool demeanor had he not seen the slight trembling of her fingers—felt the heat that coursed up his arm and spread across his chest. By the gods, did she feel the attraction too? "What magic do you possess that you can turn from nymph to nobility? The change is astounding."

"I wish I could say the same about you, my lord. But it seems no matter how you dress, you're still a barbaric Norseman."

Kyran laughed. "Ah, you took time to sharpen your tongue as well as bathe and dress." He gave her a sideways glance, pleased beyond words that even though her fingers still trembled, she yet found ways to wound him.

" 'Tis my curse, my lord. I am sharp-witted by nature."

Her answer satisfied him, as did the way she walked beside him to the table, nodding a polite acknowledgement to Bynor, Cyric, and Rhonwyn as they bowed deeply, Bynor staying down until Cyric dragged him up. Kyran couldn't be sure, but he thought he noticed the two women exchange bemused glances.

While Kyran had greeted Sayrid, Morven had arrived and stayed seated, refusing to offer any sign of a truce. His arms remained folded over his chest, and his scowl appeared so dark, Kyran, himself, felt tempted to flee. The moment Sayrid took a seat on the bench, Cyric filled her goblet from the pitcher of wine on the table.

" 'Tis a pleasure to meet you . . . formally," Cyric said with a slight smile that appeared more than strained to Kyran. Did his friend still blame her for his injuries? Kyran frowned. Cyric seemed to be staring at Sayrid with unrestrained interest—an

148

annoying interest unwarranted with the attractive young woman seated by his side. Kyran made a mental note to speak with the young woman—to arrange that she go to Cyric's chamber later that night, and pay her if necessary.

" 'Tis time to have the food served," Kyran ordered.

"Aye," Cyric answered quickly, waving over an older man who'd been standing by the scullery. The moment he finished speaking with the man, Cyric turned, whispered a few words to Rhonwyn, and then directed his attention back to Sayrid. "Lady Sayrid. Have you always lived near Dragon's Head?"

"I was born here," Sayrid answered before taking a sip of wine.

"As was I," Rhonwyn added cheerfully.

"And I," Cyric replied. "As were all of us, except for Morven, of course."

Kyran watched quietly as Sayrid's gaze fastened on Cyric's for several moments. By her expression, he sensed she didn't believe Cyric's claim.

Long trestle tables practically filled the great hall. The clanking of tankards and goblets, as well as men and women's voices, resounded from the wooden beams above while platters of food were carried in, preventing any further conversation. Four roasted boars with apples in their mouths, four stuffed geese and four haunches of venison were carried in; they were all quickly carved and the platters emptied, almost before they touched the table.

Village women dressed in crisp white aprons and wimples carried platters piled high with food. Wooden tubs of creamy butter were passed around as were jams made from blackberries and wild currants. Round loaves of crusty bread were torn in half and shared among the men, often tossed to a warrior's friend at the other end of the table over a roar of boisterous laughter.

Sayrid had never seen so many warriors sitting on benches in one place. No wonder Aswyn's soldiers fell, obviously outnumbered. Even more unsettling, many of her people sat among them, conversing, laughing and sharing trenchers as if they welcomed the intruders.

Another loaf of bread sailed through the air, surprising Rhonwyn as well.

Barbaric Norsemen, Sayrid reconfirmed with a disgusted shake of her head.

"My men have not eaten all day," said Kyran, his breath warm against her ear. She shrugged, trying to hide the fact that he'd practically read her mind. She glanced across the table where Cyric sat to the right of the man she knew as Bynor. Both Bynor and Cyric wore dark-reddish-brown, knee-length tunics, edged in a thick golden-leaf border.

Rhonwyn sat on Cyric's right, close enough where the two could converse without being overheard. Rhonwyn's long slim fingers gently touched the brooch, making Sayrid wonder what Cyric had whispered. Something about Cyric seemed familiar, but she contributed it to their earlier meeting when she'd brought Gwendolyn's bread. Morven the giant, barely fitting next to Bynor, appeared as a huge bear at feeding time trying to act human.

"Do not feel that you must excuse their behavior, my lord." She sighed as if bored. "They are only doing what they've seen done."

Although all three of the men watched her, 'twas Cyric's stare that felt the heaviest. She looked at him for several moments then turned her attention to her wine, disturbed by the intensity of his gaze. Perhaps he still blamed her for Kyran's illness. Were she Rhonwyn, she'd elbow him in the ribs.

"Your meaning?" Kyran asked, drawing her attention away from Cyric.

She turned. A mistake, she knew, but she had to look at him sometime during the meal, didn't she? Clad in a dark-blue knee-length tunic, a little of his cream-colored undershirt could be seen at the embroidered neck, and the tip of cream-colored sleeves showed under the tunic's cuffs. A thin, black belt secured his tunic at the waist. Dark-brown leggings, bound just below the knee by the narrow leather straps of his boots, made him appear more the warrior than the lord of a great manor.

Her mouth grew dry, and, before she answered, she reached for her wine. His hand came gently—more tenderly—down on hers, his touch awakening a swarm of cursed butterflies to tickle her insides. Better the flutter than the burn, she thought miserably.

"I would hear your implication first," Kyran added, apparently still vexed by her statement. She expected to hear impatience in his tone and see anger in his expression, surprised when he only arched one dark brow.

" 'Tis simple. They are Norse. Manners are not a desirable quality sought by Vikings. They are more prone to pillaging, rape and taking what isn't theirs."

Cyric nearly choked on his wine, reaching for a cloth to cover his mouth. Humor danced in his green eyes. "My sentiments precisely, my lady."

Unafraid, Sayrid met Morven's dark gaze for several moments before he turned his eyes on Cyric. The moment Kyran removed his hand, she picked up her goblet and took a few sips of sweet, spiced wine to replenish her dwindling courage while she continued to observe as platters were scraped of every last scrap. It appeared to her that there'd be precious little left, and hunger gnawed at her insides—though she'd never admit it to these strangers around her.

Had this been a feast given by Aswyn, he and his cohorts would have been served first, and any who dared to complain sent from the table hungry. She would've made a comment pertaining to it had not several servants arrived with more platters of roasted meat, and several dozen loaves of fresh, warm bread.

Kyran filled their shared trencher with choice pieces of pork, a good helping of boiled turnips and scallions, and a chunk of bread. Too hungry to care that she hadn't been given an eating dagger, she picked up a large piece of meat with her fingers and took a bite—feeling her face heat with color as Kyran moved a square cloth, exposing a small dagger and spoon.

"We barbarians prefer to use utensils, and if you place that cloth in your lap, it will protect your clothing from spills."

When she turned to glare at him, he nodded at her bodice where a tiny drop of gravy spotted her gown. Fuming, she snatched up the cloth and quickly wiped it away, convinced he'd purposely hidden her spoon and dagger to embarrass her.

"Kyran says you saved his life in the forest," Bynor said with a skeptical grin.

"Aye," Cyric added, taking a drink. "Morven thinks you a witch. Kyran thinks you a healer." He grinned, apparently over his fixation with her appearance. In fact, he appeared most cheerful. "What say you?"

Sayrid swallowed. "I say I am Welsh."

Morven gave a disgusted grunt, reached across the table and tore a haunch of pork from the carcass, taking a huge bite, heedless of the grease and juice that dribbled down his beard. She stared at him for a moment before she stabbed a small scallion, caring little if she'd said something which angered the bear. He'd find out another use for an eating dagger if he dared leave his bench to assault her.

"So, if you're Welsh, how is it you can appear and disappear at will?" Cyric asked, lifting his brows in amusement. He turned his attention toward Rhonwyn. "And what say you, my sweet.

Can you appear and disappear as well?"

Rhonwyn giggled and shook her head. "No, my lord. I cannot."

Cyric turned to Sayrid. "I'm Welsh, yet possess no such power. However, I seem to recall my mother having special powers."

Sayrid smiled, studying the young man with hair near the color of her own. "If I could disappear at will, my lord, I wouldn't be here now, would I?" She turned to look at Kyran. "Your lord must have been delusional . . . from his injuries, of course."

Bynor laughed out loud, apparently unaffected by the look Kyran gave him.

"On the contrary," Cyric continued, and she suddenly thought him to be more like a dog with a bone than the gentleman she first found him to be when she'd come into the castle with the bread. "I saw with mine own eyes proof that you'd been in Kyran's chamber, yet guards stood both at the door and below the balcony. And when Kyran awoke when we returned after supping, he said you'd been there."

Out of the corner of her eye, she saw Kyran shake his head at Cyric, trying to stop him as if he knew what she'd say.

"Again, it is as I said. Your lord is—"

"Delusional," Kyran finished impatiently. "Eat more, Cyric, and converse less. Your food grows cold."

Regardless of Kyran's status as king, Sayrid expected Cyric to take offense at his order, but apparently they were very good friends. Cyric grinned and took another bite, clearly enjoying himself more than when they'd first started. She glanced at the trencher, inwardly wincing that it appeared as if she'd eaten more than the king, especially after warning him she'd have no appetite if forced to sup with him.

'Twas too late to worry now. When he went to stab a piece of turnip, she stabbed it first, raising her chin a tiny bit in triumph as she popped it in her mouth. His soft chuckle served only to remind her of his nearness—a nearness she'd almost forgotten. A nearness that could make her fear him and her reaction to him, and it came quickly back and settled in her belly.

" 'Tis good to see our king so much better," Bynor said. "Regardless of who or what helped. Right, Cyric?"

"Aye. I am much relieved."

Nibbling some bread, Sayrid listened to the men as they discussed the building of new houses for the multitude of soldiers who still slept in tents. She held her tongue when she longed to ask questions, choosing to pretend interest in her food rather than carry on a conversation with these men and, in doing so, lengthen the time she'd have to spend in their company.

She glanced at Rhonwyn and doubted the pretty young woman shared her feelings or her urgency to leave. Rhonwyn seemed content to sit next to Cyric and share bits of conversation as they shared bites of food. The sooner the meal ended, the sooner Sayrid could seek the safety of Gwendolyn's cottage, change into her own clothing, and escape back into the forest. Rhonwyn would have to fend for herself. Not that she needed protection. Sayrid doubted Cyric would leave her side, nor did he appear to be the type who would take advantage of Rhonwyn's sweet innocence.

Sayrid swallowed and reached for her wine, contemplating her departure. What if Kyran followed? How would she escape? Again she took several sips to fortify her courage. Large wine skins were carried in and pitchers and cups refilled. After the meat and vegetable platters were removed, pickled eggs and honey-glazed, baked apples stuffed with raisins, oats and pine nuts were carried in with mincemeat pies and fruit-filled tarts— all practically devoured before they had time to cool.

Kyran chose two large apples, brimming over with the scrumptious stuffing, before the platter was passed to Cyric and Bynor. Once they helped themselves, Morven grumbled something under his breath, passing the platter on to another man farther down the long table. Curious why he didn't partake of the honeyed treats, Sayrid wanted to ask, but then thought better of it. Hadn't Derwyn warned her to stay away from the giant Norseman?

"He believes honey will take his manhood," Kyran whispered close to her ear.

She nearly choked on the bite she'd just swallowed. She looked up to meet his eyes, noticing the humor dancing in their depths.

"In truth?" she asked, matching his cautious tone.

Kyran grinned and nodded. "He was attacked by a swarm of bees one day whilst out on patrol. There wasn't a place on his body that escaped a sting. Lucky for us, we were near a small village filled with many young women who wanted to help. For two days, he could barely stand and, for two more, could not walk without help."

Bynor leaned over the table, interrupting their conversation. "Nor could he—"

Sayrid jumped the moment a huge dagger sank deeply into the wooden table by Bynor's trencher, barely missing his fingers. Bynor jumped back, clutching a crust of bread as if to protect it as well as his hand.

Morven's knuckles shown white where his fingers curled around the hilt. "What say you?" the big man growled at Bynor. "If you have something important to say, speak up so we can all hear. Otherwise shut your trap."

Bynor's smile slipped, and he visibly swallowed before he nodded at Morven. "Calm down, my wooly friend. I was just telling the lady that her people know how to prepare a fine meal." He turned to Sayrid with a pleading expression. "Is that not right, my lady?"

Sayrid looked at Bynor and then at Morven before she looked back at Bynor. "I'm afraid I didn't hear exactly what was said, nor was I certain you were speaking to me." She blinked innocently. If these fools wanted to kill each other at the table, who was she to stop them?

"More wine," Kyran called to the cupbearers. The moment Morven's hand slipped from the dagger, the king reached across and pulled it free. He admired the hilt for a moment, then offered it to Morven. "Is this new?"

Morven's scowl deepened before he answered. "Aye, 'twas among those lost in the battle."

"Aye, lost." Cyric smiled. "Morven found it in the chest of one of Aswyn's men. I believe the poor man threw himself upon it rather than face Morven in hand-to-hand combat."

Rhonwyn giggled at his jest. Morven scoffed, but to Sayrid the Viking seemed pleased that an opponent would rather commit suicide than face him. Morven shoved away from the table, stood and jammed the large dagger back into its leather scabbard on his belt. "I've better things to do than sit and listen to foolish chatter." He tossed a glance over his shoulder at Kyran. "Any who wish to discuss my prowess should remember that 'tis I who will be wielding the staff at tomorrow's practice."

The moment Morven left, Cyric burst into laughter, soon joined by Bynor and, lastly, Kyran. "I swear," Cyric said to Bynor, barely able to catch breath. "You should have seen the look on your face when Morven stabbed the table."

Bynor shook his head as if he couldn't believe what had just transpired. He chuckled again, held up his hand and wiggled his fingers. "I have met many a fierce warrior on the battlefield and have not felt the fear I experienced just moments ago. I've heard losing a finger is quite painful."

" 'Tis foolish to provoke him," Kyran said with a knowledge-able nod. "Mark my words. He will remember this on the morrow and challenge you before your men so that you cannot refuse. I suggest, before that happens, you send several of your best men to challenge him ahead of time and pray to the gods they wear him down some."

"Several? Methinks I should send fifty." Again male laughter mingled with the rest of the voices in the room.

Sayrid watched and listened, still wary, but finding that she enjoyed their easy banter. Certain they were too busy teasing each other to notice, she carefully slipped her eating dagger into the pocket of her gown. Scanning the huge hall, she noticed several of the village men join with some warriors and move aside many of the tables. Soon the sound of cheerful music floated up and over the din of couples talking and laughing. Cyric rose from his chair and escorted Rhonwyn to the center of the room. She'd just begun to relax when Kyran stood, grasped her elbow and pulled her up.

"My lord?" she gasped, taken by surprise. She fought against the urge to tug free, but her skin began to tingle pleasantly where his fingers tightened on her arm, halting her desire to leave.

"A dance before you depart," Kyran said, nodding toward Cyric and Rhonwyn who, along with several other couples, had already begun to twirl arm in arm to the lively music. Kyran gently, yet forcefully pushed Sayrid toward them.

"I—I don't know how," she stammered, resisting as best she could without drawing attention to herself.

" 'Tis like walking in a circle, only faster, and whilst holding hands."

She stopped and frowned. "Walking in a circle," she repeated skeptically. "It takes much more than that."

She silently fumed when he grinned before he spoke. "Then

you do know. I thought as much."

Sayrid jerked her arm free at the same time he let her go, causing her to nearly stumble into the dancers. He caught her hand before she made a spectacle of herself.

"See what you nearly caused me to do?" she hissed, having no choice but to follow him as he joined the others.

"Me?" He raised one dark brow and that irritating twinkle appeared in his vibrant eyes. " 'Twas your own fault. You should stop fighting, relax and, in doing so, learn to enjoy yourself." He twirled her around, held her hand high so she could pass under their arms and come around on the other side, whispering in her ear. "There, see? 'Tis like swordplay. Precise and controlled."

"Had I a sword, my lord, I'd soon teach you the meaning of precise and controlled."

"Aye, I'm certain. However, it seems the only weapon you carry is the dagger in your pocket. I'm beginning to believe you're prone to thievery, but no matter. Should you decide to use it, 'tis far too puny to teach any man control." He leaned a little closer, his thumb caressing the back of her hand. "I assure you, I'm using a great deal of control at this moment."

It felt as if sparks from a burning log skittered across her hand, up her arm and down her spine. By the gods, why did she yearn to throw herself into his arms and let him carry her up the stairs to his bedchamber? Love? Certainly not—'twas nothing like that. 'Twas lust—a primal attraction all living things experience.

She glanced quickly around, wondering if he sensed her thoughts or if any of the others could tell how badly she wanted him. She caught a glimpse of Cyric and Rhonwyn. Rhonwyn's face glowed with happiness, making it easy to see she had deep feelings for Cyric. The couple greeted her as they passed by, both of them nodding.

Certain they knew, Sayrid inwardly groaned. "All eyes are

upon us and that silly smile of yours."

"I'm smiling for several reasons," he began, "but mostly because I'm enjoying myself. I've not danced in many years. And I've certainly not danced with one so beautiful or desirable." Again he twirled her around and then drew her into the center of the circle where all the dancers raised their clasped hands before they backed away, bowing to each other. "Everyone seems to be enjoying the dance except you. Perhaps your mind is on other things, such as my amulet, so much like the one carefully concealed between your breasts."

She stared at him, wondering again if he could read her thoughts. She let go of his hand to link arms with the girl in front of her, twirled once, then linked arms with Kyran and began the steps all over again. Although she wanted to deny it, each time they touched she felt her heart pound against her breast, a feeling unlike anything she felt when she touched the other dancers.

The king appeared to be enjoying the dance as much as the others, laughing when one of the men said something she couldn't quite hear. The music finally ended and all the dancers bowed one last time before they strolled away, leaving Sayrid standing in the middle of the room holding Kyran's hand.

"Come," Kyran said, and this time she let him escort her to the stairs, until she realized his intent. She put her foot against the first step, effectively stopping their ascent.

"I will not be your whore," she said firmly even though her body would have willingly complied.

" 'Tis not what I want either," he said softly, his eyes searching hers for several moments. She couldn't look away, couldn't pull her hand from his gentle grasp. She felt as if they were alone in a room with a hundred other people. She saw herself in his arms, pressing intimately close, her breasts crushed against his chest, their hips touching while his mouth ravished hers.

159

When next he spoke, she didn't hear his words. Frightened that she'd act out her fantasy, she forced her eyes from his and instantly everything went back to normal.

"Did you hear me?" Kyran asked. "I would have you live here, in Dragon's Head. I will arrange for Rhonwyn to be your companion if you so wish it. I'll have a chamber readied for you both. But first there is much we should discuss . . . in private."

The huge doors in the great hall opened. From the smell and sounds, she knew a storm had arrived sometime during the dancing. She glared at him, blaming him and her overindulgence of wine for her alarming behavior. "I've no need of your charity. I have a home."

"I'm sure, and a fine home too, hidden in the forest with all the wild things." He smiled, and she saw something primitive flicker in his eyes. "There are many who fear the forest at night, especially when it rains. But not you. Yet I sense you fear me. Why? Think you I could hurt someone as beautiful as you?"

She raised her chin defiantly. "I told you, my lord. I do not fear you. Nor am I easily won over with flattery," she replied tightly, wondering why she felt the need to challenge him. After all, she loved Dragon's Head. She felt as if the spirit of the beast who had created the old castle belonged, in some small way, to her—was there for her to love and protect, so she would, in turn, be loved and protected.

Truth be told, she longed to make it her home, longed to be Kyran's woman. But right now, standing this close, her thoughts were jumbled, her senses filled with Kyran's touch, how his warm breath lightly touched her cheek, the way his thumb grazed the back of her fingers. The woodsy scent of him.

"I am as confused by what passes between us as you are. What harm could it do to explore it?" he asked.

She scoffed, toying with her cuff, refusing to say more lest she slip and unintentionally let him know the depth of her craving. She raised her head, glancing at the lined candle squatted on the wall sconce, still refusing to believe, yet hearing again Derwyn's voice: *Yer destiny lies with him and with Dragon's Head.*

"The hour grows late," she said in a voice so soft she barely recognized it as her own. She cast a glance at the open door, wishing he let her go so she could leave—to go out into the cooling rain. Perhaps if she did it would wash away her torrid thoughts.

"Aye," he agreed, yet he continued to grasp her hand. "I say again. Why not stay the night, here, where it's warm and dry and you're protected from the storm?"

His words didn't immediately penetrate her thoughts. She'd focused on the warmth of his hand. Did he feel it now? she wondered—this barely controllable urge to be with him, kiss him and have him hold and kiss her?

"Protected?" she repeated before she realized it. She looked from her hand to his eyes where the twinkle had returned and intensified. "Trapped is perhaps a better word, my lord."

He fell silent for several moments. She would have left, but the floor seemed to swell and sharply ebb, tossing her none too gently into Kyran's arms. He held her firmly, the frown on his tanned features a testament to his own surprise. But he took advantage of their situation, held her tighter and kissed her. The kiss was short but thorough, leaving her shaky and weak, and badly in need of more. Had he not had hold of her, she felt certain she would've floated to the floor, then wondered if it would move again and pitch her back into his arms—almost hoping it would.

Gathering her strength and courage, she pushed away and felt suddenly cold—colder when she took a cautious step back, glancing at the floor and the placement of her feet. She halfway expected the stones to move, but they remained solid. With shaky fingers she retrieved Kyran's amulet from her pocket and held it in her outstretched palm.

The king raised one skeptical brow. "What? No one would give you anything for it?"

She gave an impatient sigh. "Nothing of any value," she countered. "Take it. I no longer want to be burdened with it."

"My little sorceress has a conscience?" He took it and placed it around his neck. The stone brightened as if his touch awakened something powerful deep inside, and then she felt her own amulet vibrate against her heated skin as if in response.

"Perhaps the next time, you'll accept my offer?"

Still stunned by what had just transpired, her mouth gaped open. She watched Kyran turn toward the others, sensing it was the very last thing he wanted to do. Vexed by his abrupt dismissal, she grabbed a fistful of skirt and, muttering her displeasure under her breath, quickly climbed the stairs to the door. She'd only just placed her hand upon the latch when she thought she heard a very deep, very soft growl. Fighting the urge to look to see whence it came, she threw open the door and fled.

Brynn had stayed to the shadows, keeping well out of sight but able to watch the festivities. A memory flicked in the dark depths of her mind—a memory of happier days—of a time before her brother became king. Searching the faces of the dancers, her gaze fell upon Cyric and the young woman with whom he danced, the pair of them laughing and having a pleasant time.

"Rhonwyn." Brynn gave the woman only a fleeting glance. Nay, 'twas Cyric who fascinated her. The more Brynn watched him with Rhonwyn, the more jealous she became.

CHAPTER TEN

Kyran returned to his place across from Cyric. "Where's Bynor?" he asked before he sat down and reached for his goblet, angry with himself for letting Sayrid leave. Would he forever play this game when around her? She knew how to prick his pride and make him say things he didn't mean. Cursed woman.

Cyric grinned. "He left with a comely maiden . . . a raven-haired beauty with the most unusual eyes."

"He's a smart man. I thought you would've stayed with the comely maiden from the village." Kyran took a long drink of wine, feeling Cyric's gaze upon him as heavy as if it were a wet woolen cloak. Kyran dragged the back of his hand across his mouth. "What are you staring at?" he growled, forgetting he wore his amulet.

"The gods have answered my prayers," Cyric said. He also took a drink, pausing for a long time. "Sayrid gave it back to you?"

"Aye. Seems she thought it a burden."

"If she only knew its importance." Cyric shook his head. "You don't remember her, do you?" he asked.

Kyran refilled his goblet before he pushed away from the table and threw himself into one of the two leather-padded chairs closest to the fire. "If you speak of the girl, she's Gwendolyn's daughter, and quite a beauty, too."

"I speak not of Rhonwyn, but of Jenalyn . . . my sister," Cyric said, following. He sat down, heaved a sigh and stared into his cup. "You don't remember her, do you?" He lifted his gaze and met Kyran's. "You were bound to her, and yet you don't remember?"

Kyran looked away, angry, but not at Cyric—at himself. If Sayrid were Cyric's sister 'twould explain much—especially their forceful attraction to one another. "At the binding ceremony I was eight winters old, she barely four. I've little memory of anything after the feast. All I remember are the warriors who attacked and dragged us away, and the cries and screams of our people as they were butchered."

He leaned his head back against the chair and stared into the fire, reliving that terrible day. He felt certain Cyric's sister couldn't have survived. She had been too small, too young to know the danger or to seek a place to hide. When Cyric remained silent, he felt obliged to add, "The past is best left in the past, my friend."

Both men were quiet for a long time until Cyric cleared his throat. "I remember my mother," he stated softly. "She was kind and beautiful . . . and gifted. Sayrid reminds me of her. The same eyes, the same smile, and, because of it, I'm compelled to believe she could be the sister I thought dead— that perhaps by the grace of the gods she survived."

Kyran frowned. "Need I remind you her name is Sayrid, not Jenalyn? We searched every face among the survivors, remember? Had your sister or any of our families survived, we would have found them whilst we marched to Arcas' kingdom."

Another long silence fell over Cyric, giving Kyran hope that the subject of the ceremony and the amulet would be dropped. He had the cursed thing back—a symbol for all to see that the Protector had returned to shield the people of Dragon's Head. He inwardly scoffed. He was no Protector. He was a trained killer—a barbarian, his status lower than that of the executioner chosen to punish the wicked.

His head hurt, either from too much wine or the confusing thoughts lurking in the back of his mind. Should he voice his concerns about Sayrid—the strange feelings that pass between them every time they touched? And what of the old castle? If he said he felt a spirit of an ancient beast residing within it, would Cyric think him mad?

Cyric heaved a long sigh, drawing Kyran away from his troubling thoughts. Cyric leaned his forearms on his knees, clasping his fingers together before fixing his gaze on the lively fire. "Suppose Sayrid wasn't—"

"Cyric, for the love of the gods."

"Just listen for a moment," Cyric said. "Suppose Jenalyn survived—and I truly believe she did—and someone changed her name to protect her. Not all the people were killed." He motioned to the now near-empty hall. "Less than an hour past, this room was filled with our people. Many survived, Kyran. Perhaps a family like Rhonwyn's found her and cared for her?" Cyric raked his fingers through his hair in frustration. "They could have raised her as their own—afraid to reveal her true identity?"

Kyran met Cyric's steady gaze. Sayrid's amulet flashed before his eyes—a slightly different, slightly smaller version of his own. He lifted his medallion and turned it over. The back looked as if a smaller one could fit easily inside the intricate, rope-shaped edge. Yet how could he be sure it belonged to her? Hadn't she proved to him she was a thief? "If Sayrid is your sister, why didn't she say so tonight? Why does she stay hidden in the forest? Why hasn't she come forward to greet her brother and welcome him home?"

Annoyed, Kyran tossed the rest of his wine down his throat and stood. "Jenalyn is dead and gone and you must not torture yourself with thoughts that Sayrid, the sorceress, is your sister."

"But—"

Kyran shook his head. "I'll hear no more tonight. Tell me about Rhonwyn and how you came to favor her."

"I've no need to tell you. I doubt you would understand anything concerning love," Cyric stated, apparently annoyed. "And what difference does it make? I've agreed to marry another not of my choosing."

Kyran heaved an impatient sigh, paused as if to speak, then thought better of it before he left to go to his chamber, grabbing a pitcher of wine on his way. Once inside his bedchamber, he leaned back against the door, closing his eyes for a moment against the flood of thoughts that clouded his mind. Earlier, he'd felt the floor move, heard a deep rolling growl as if some beast had been roused from sleep. How? he wondered, raking his fingers through his hair. Again, he closed his eyes in hopes to call Sayrid to him—that she too would remember their kiss and the heat that had nearly consumed them both.

"Nonsense," he muttered, shaking the memory from his mind as he removed his amulet and dropped it on the bedside table. "No man can make a woman come to him by sheer will."

Annoyed that he even thought to try, he slammed the pitcher of wine down on the table and went directly to the shelves, more determined than ever to find the hidden passageway. As good a place to start as any, he grabbed the side of the shelving and, using every ounce of his strength, ripped it away from the wall, startled when he exposed a small, rusty square of iron mesh. He dragged his fingers over it, searching for anything that could be pulled or pushed.

Sayrid scrambled back, falling down several mossy steps and landing hard on her buttocks when Kyran destroyed the shelf that allowed her to watch his every move. Her fall had spilled the wax of her stubby candle, snuffing the flame. Engulfed in darkness and panting with fear, she quickly got to her feet, snatched up her skirts and began to descend the steps as fast as she could without pitching over the edge.

With sounds of wood splintering, she held out her hands, following the stones, hoping to find one of the many tunnels. However, without a candle to light the way, she decided it best to keep to the familiar steps and leave the castle entirely to seek safety in the forest. She could not explain why she came or why she refused to leave when she saw him enter. All she knew was that she experienced a longing—as if he had called to her—and she felt helpless to resist.

She had just entered the lower landing and reached for the latch to the thick, concealed door, when she cast a quick glance over her shoulder. Shadows flickered eerily on the stones leading up to the second story, and she knew if she didn't act quickly she'd be discovered. Her fingers closed over the rope that would loosen the wooden latch, but when she yanked it, nothing happened. "Now is not the time for games, great one," she muttered angrily. "Have I not been true to you?"

She looked back toward the way she'd come, tugging harder. "Then be true to me," she pleaded. As if the old castle understood, the latch clicked and the heavy stone door slowly slid ajar. A fierce storm raged, pelting her with large, angry droplets of rain. Lifting her arms to shield her face, Sayrid slipped through before the door had completely opened then turned and shoved it closed.

Drenched, she took a deep breath of clean, cool air and leaned back against the door, taking a few moments to catch her breath while her heart resumed its normal pace. Mindless of the lightning that split the night's sky, she gathered up her rain-dampened skirts and headed toward the forest.

Kyran stepped off the last step, holding the candle high to get a better look at the small chamber that appeared before him. A small circular room with no way out except for the way he'd come. He turned slowly, searching for anything out of the ordinary—anything that might show him another way out. His gaze landed on a small length of thick hemp lying on the dust-covered floor several yards away. Bending down on one knee, he brought the candle closer before he tested the rope to see if it were lodged in the dirt or in the stone.

A gust of warm wind whooshed down from the steps, instantly dousing his candle—a wind so warm it made the hair on the back of Kyran's neck tingle.

"Not now, old dragon," he said between clenched teeth as he groped around in the dark, his fingers searching for the rope. In the next moment he found it and pulled hard, not at all surprised as a portion of the wall slowly ground opened. 'Twas raining, but, by the sounds of the storm, it was moving away.

A streak of lightning flickered weakly across the sky, exposing trampled ferns. On closer inspection, there was a tiny path leading into the forest. Mostly hidden by ferns and covered in grass and moss, 'twas difficult to follow in the dark, but he hurried along, thankful the worst of the storm had passed. Only when he came to a rocky formation did he stop. Barely discernable in the dark, the path divided into three different directions.

A gust of wind tousled Kyran's wet hair, and by the loud clap of thunder, he knew the storm had returned with a vengeance.

"Cursed woman. Think you I'm so easily defeated?" he growled over the wind and increasing rain as dark clouds covered what was left of the moon. "I swear on the spirit of the dragon, I'll find you if it's the last thing I do."

Dressed as a servant, Brynn had been watching Sayrid all night from the opening to the scullery, knew the moment she'd left, as well as when the king ascended the stairs with a full pitcher of wine. Perhaps if he got drunk enough, she could thrust her dagger in his heart and have Sayrid take the blame.

She cast another cautious glance over her shoulder to make sure she was alone in the long corridor—her lover passed out drunk in his chamber. She had been about to sneak into the king's chamber when she heard the sounds of wood splintering, then of stone grinding. When it grew silent she slowly turned the latch to the king's chamber and quietly stepped inside. The room was empty. She reached into her pocket and retrieved a short, narrow candle, touching it to the stumpy, half-melted candle in the iron sconce.

Shadows flickered on the stone walls from the dying fire. Brynn glanced around. The large wooden shelf where Aswyn had kept his plunder had been ripped from the wall. She stood in the center of the room and closed her eyes as Maldwyn had taught her—clearing her mind—she saw the king in a fit of rage—saw him searching and then saw him watch in stunned amazement as a portion of the rock wall opened.

She cursed cheerfully and hurried to the wall, grazing her fingers over the latch, jumping back when it opened. She peered into the darkness, holding her candle high. She smiled—satisfied she'd discovered the way to murder the king without anyone knowing.

Feeling quite pleased, she spotted, on the bedside table, a medallion she hadn't seen before—a beautiful piece adorned with an almandine in the center. Holding it high, she admired the intricate carvings before she slipped it into the small pouch on her belt. She went to the hidden opening, slowly descending the ancient stone steps, down to the circular room.

A moment of panic settled in her breast before she noticed the hemp and the footprints in the dust. 'Twas only a moment more before she stepped outside, pausing to take a long breath of fresh air. With the amulet carefully hidden, she hurried through the forest, pausing only when she came to a small clearing where a flock of ravens roosted. She scanned the birds, who watched her intently, locking eyes with one large male. The bird flew down and landed on her shoulder.

"Take this to Maldwyn," Brynn stated. She took the little leather pouch and tied it securely before she offered it to the bird. The raven took the end of the strap in its beak then took flight.

Calling on all her power and strength, Brynn closed her eyes and imagined flying.

Recovered from her hasty escape, Sayrid made her way carefully down the path toward her cottage, muttering under her breath the entire distance. How had he found the passageway? Had she not been careful? And how dare he dismiss her? Had it not been for her, he would still be sick or dead. And love? Foolish words spoken by her friend who knew nothing about the man. Love, indeed. 'Twas as she thought. Simply a male and female attraction—one she could easily resist.

And now that she'd returned all his possessions, there were no more reasons to go to Dragon's Head. Good. No more trips in this miserable weather. If the gods were good to her, she could avoid seeing the king or any of his men for a very long time. The moment she finished with her mental tirade, she knew it was all a lie. She wondered when her disdain had turned to desire, her attraction to need—refusing to admit she might have fallen in love.

"Love?" she muttered. "Never."

Had she not been so angry, she would have noticed the long shadow stretching out over the path ahead. She thought she heard the flapping of wings, and glanced over her shoulder, but clouds had covered the moon and all she saw was darkness.

Her foot caught on a protruding root, tripping her. She landed on her knees, but stood quickly, trying to inspect her gown for damage—relieved when there was none. As if by magic, the clouds moved away from the moon, and that's when she noticed the shadow. Fear crawled spider-like up her spine as she bent and grabbed a broken limb to use as a weapon.

It sounded as if someone or something hid in the bushes. Glancing at the small branch she held, she quickly tossed it aside and chose a bigger one, thinking it would work better if what stalked her was a wild boar or bear. Something flew past her head. She ducked and would have started to run, but strong, warm fingers closed over her upper arm.

She stiffened, ready to fight, but her whole body felt warm. "How—"

"Hush," he said as he pulled her closer under a tall oak where the ground was dry. "Does it matter how I knew, or only that I did, and now I'm here?" He cupped her face then kissed her. Sparks came alive in the pit of her stomach. "You can drop the branch. 'Twas I who threw a stick over your head."

"Knave," she hissed, trying with no success to tug her arm from his firm grasp.

"Tonight I saw you as you entered the hall and I have never seen any so beautiful." He kissed her again, more forcefully.

"I would finish what we began at the lake," he murmured near her ear, sending tiny shivers of delight down her spine. He pressed her back against the trunk of the huge oak, his hands causing her skin to tingle even through her clothing.

Slowly, his eyes twinkling in the moonlight, he removed the golden circlet, hung it from a low branch with the sheer wimple, and began to loosen her hair. She shivered again. When he finished, he sank his fingers into the silken mass, holding her still as his mouth claimed hers a second time, tormenting her, driving her wild with need.

"Nay," she moaned, fighting the urge to tear at his clothing, to spread her palms against his skin. "Leave me alone. I don't want you to touch me."

He drew back, his gaze smoldering with passion. "Liar. A thief and a liar. Shame." He smiled a moment before his warm, soft lips brushed a path to her neck and then back up to the sensitive place near her ear. When he lifted his head, she stared into his dancing eyes, wondering what magic he had, to cast her so easily under his spell. "Tell me again to leave—that you don't want what I can give you?"

She couldn't answer—couldn't deny what he said was true— that she'd already begun to throb down low in her belly—it started the moment he pressed her close to his body. Her knees grew weak with the realization that she could so easily be seduced. His pulled her into his arms. This time after he kissed her, his tongue toyed with her lips until they parted, and, the moment they did, he plundered every recess of her mouth until she did the same to him.

"Sayrid," he whispered near her ear as he placed a kiss on her temple. "Yield to me."

She felt no shame when he eased the diaphanous overgown over her head, then loosened the ties of her kirtle. When it would have slipped from her shoulders, she caught it, and held it protectively over her breasts. His big hands covered hers as he gently took them away. The gown slipped off her breast, caressing her hips before it fell to the ground—exposing her amulet.

He did not take her into his arms as she had thought he would. Instead, he smiled and cupped the amulet in the palm of his hand. " 'Tis as it should be," he said, causing even more confusion to flood her senses.

He released the amulet and loosened the ties that held up her undergarments. They floated to the ground. Moonlight bathed her body, and she stood before him naked and exposed, yet felt more powerful than she had ever felt before. She looked at him, growing bolder by the moment. Slowly she stepped out of the pool of clothing, and then, as he had done to her, she began to undress him, encouraged by his steady gaze.

When she reached up to lift his tunic over his head, his warm hands closed over her breasts and she paused to accept a ravenous kiss. With each item of his clothing she removed, she became more and more shameless. When she undid the laces of his shirt and pushed it off his broad shoulders, she could not draw her gaze away. In the muted light, the scars she had seen before vanished. He lifted her in his arms, pressing her back against the tree, taking her nipple into his hot mouth, drawing on it until she moaned, before he teased the other in the same sensually torturous manner.

The bark against her skin no longer felt rough, but like the smoothest velvet. He bent his head, kissing a trail from between her breasts, over the smooth plain of her abdomen to the soft mound of curls at the junction of her legs. He spread her legs, ignoring her whispered protest, persistent yet gentle. She wanted him to stop, but lost the ability to speak—could only feel the touch of his fingers, the heat of his mouth between her legs.

"Yield to me," he repeated, and this time when he stood she kissed him with the same hunger. Her fingers glided lightly over his chest, caressing his skin as he had done to her, brushing lightly over the scar, tracing the dragon. He sucked in his breath when she bent her head and circled the nipples on his chest with her tongue then nipped and scraped them lightly with her teeth.

His hands sank back into her hair, lifting her face to his at the same time he pulled her away from the tree. His breath felt hot against her neck. His palms brushed against her shoulders, slipped around to her back until he cupped her buttocks. When he lifted her, she wrapped her legs around his hips, the throbbing between her legs nearly driving her mad.

Slowly, purposely, he entered her, covering her startled moan with a hungry kiss. He stilled, whispering soothing words. She

173

tried to move, but he held her trapped, kissing her softly on the cheek, then once more on the mouth.

"I have changed my mind," she whispered a little desperately. "I do not think coupling is a good thing. 'Tis painful."

"Hush, my little witch. Your maidenhead is breeched. Let me show you that coupling is, indeed, a good thing."

When she looked into his eyes, they were bright with humor. "I am well pleased that you are a maiden of virtue."

"Was," she corrected, shifting her weight—surprised to find that such a small movement sent a jolt of pleasure through her body, reviving her appetite for more. He kissed her hungrily, moving his mouth over hers until the heat began again. Slowly, gently, he rekindled the flames, touching and teasing, until she writhed against him. She tightened her legs around his waist and rocked her hips to match his thrusts. She thought the throbbing would subside, but it intensified as he moved within her, gentle at first, but then harder and faster.

Kyran closed his eyes in pure carnal pleasure. She was wet, her sheath so tight he fought to control himself, to give her a small amount of pleasure before he spilled himself like a rutting buck. He groaned against her hair when her body tightened around his shaft, pulsating with her first climax. She arched her back, and he watched her looked upward—following her gaze. A million stars swirled above them, calling to him to join her there—and he did, roaring with the intensity of his release.

She collapsed against him, burying her head in the crook of his neck, her long soft hair acting like a cloak and warming them both. He held her, his forearm supporting her weight while he listened to her rapid breathing until it grew calm and steady. She did not resist when he took her arms from around his neck and placed her gently on her feet, tucking a strand of her hair behind her ear.

He bent down and gathered up their damp clothing, tugging on his braies. He kissed the tip of her nose before he picked up her clothing and helped her dress. "I know not what spell you have placed upon me," he began as he turned her and tied the laces of her gown. He moved aside her hair and brushed his lips against her neck. "But 'twould please me if you came back to Dragon's Head."

Sayrid looked at him. He knelt to tie the laces of his boots, and then reached for his belt, but she'd tossed it several feet away. The moment he turned his back, she slipped silently into some bushes, continuing swiftly and silently until she was well away. When she heard him curse, she nearly faltered and quickly crouched behind a large jagged rock. How easy it would be to return to him; but she could not. The feelings he conjured up were too confusing. Using the moonlight, she ran down the path to her cottage, aware that storm clouds were gathering again.

The cool air of the night washed over Kyran as he returned to Dragon's Head. His temper at having lost Sayrid again had diminished, and the moon had slowly reappeared, full and high, aiding his decision to walk around the castle's perimeter in search of more hidden openings. He went around the tower wall, frowning at the open stone portal that he distinctly remembered closing.

Cautiously he stepped inside and searched until he found a long, discarded taper. Perhaps he hadn't seen it before in his haste to follow Sayrid. He glanced at the floor which appeared the same, covered with decades of dust and fresh footprints. He closed the door and reopened it to be certain it would. To be sure he'd be able to find it again, he stepped outside and closed it behind him, placing several small stones in a straight line next to the castle wall.

A stick snapped behind him. He turned, but saw nothing. He continued around the wall, occasionally brushing his hand against the rough stones and rocks, hoping to find something out of the ordinary—perhaps another hidden opening.

In the moonlight, he caught a glimpse of a bird—a large, dark bird that landed on the parapet above, slowly tucking its wings against its body. Strange, he thought. Most birds roosted at night. He'd no sooner renewed his search when he heard a raspy voice call his name.

At first, Brynn had envied the soldiers Maldwyn had sent to watch over her—envied their raven forms. But he'd also sent a spell that taught her his secret. Brynn liked being a bird. It gave her many things her human form could not. Freedom to fly above the village, to glide upward on the air currents to perch on the tallest turret of Dragon's Head. Freedom to wander from branch to branch where she could observe and learn without drawing too much attention.

She smiled inwardly, fluffing her satin-black feathers. Occasionally she was even tossed a bite of bread. If a raven could laugh, she would have, many times. She remembered Sayrid's expression as she stared at Brynn in her bird-form. No doubt Sayrid wondered why a bird followed her. 'Twas most amusing when one of her guards had bitten Sayrid, for Brynn longed to do that and more to the bitch, and would, once she'd dispatched the king.

She sat on the parapet and fluffed her feathers again, watching Kyran in his futile search, surprised when she heard someone call his name.

"Who goes there?" Kyran asked cautiously, his fingers grasping air where his dagger should have been. He'd forgone wearing a weapon to the table hoping to appear less the warrior and more the noble gentleman. "Fool," he muttered softly, glancing around for something he could use to protect himself if needed.

"Fear not, my lord. . . ." An old, withered woman hobbled from behind a hawthorn bush. She wore dark clothing, walked with a crooked staff, and kept a dark tattered shawl over her head, obscuring her features. "I've come tae tell ye yer fortune."

Kyran couldn't see past the shadows covering the woman's face. "Be gone, old woman. I'm not in the mood to hear it. If you've need of food or shelter, go to—"

"Then ye've no interest in the girl, Sayrid? No' a wee bit curious why yer drawn tae her and she tae ye?"

"How do you know her?" he asked, his brows snapping together. He knew naught what to make of the bent and crippled woman, but her words gave him reason to pause. A bony hand slipped out from under the shawl, palm up.

"Coin first, fortune after."

Kyran gave an annoyed laugh. "What if I tell you I have no coins?"

"Ye'd force me tae say ye are a liar."

Reluctantly, Kyran pulled a copper coin from the small purse on his belt and pressed it in the old woman's palm. "Be you witch or a sorceress?"

"Is it important? Come with me and ye shall find out." The woman turned and hobbled toward the forest. " 'Tis cold and damp out here. No' a good place to hear one's fortune." She turned, and in the muted light from the moon he caught a glimpse of a toothless smile. He cautiously followed her down the shadowy path, wondering why they'd stopped when, as if by itself, a vine-covered door opened from the side of a knoll, spilling warm yellow light over them.

Somewhere from behind and higher as if from a tree, he heard the flapping of wings but paid no attention. Ducking his head, Kyran entered, unwilling to let the old woman out of his sight until he could discover how she knew Sayrid.

"Come in and sit down," the old woman said, smiling. "I've been waitin' tae meet ye."

High from her perch in the top of an oak tree, Brynn watched carefully—her dark eyes darting from Kyran to the old woman he followed inside the cave. Suddenly her breath caught in her throat, and she made a high, bird-like squeal. *Derwyn, you old witch,* she muttered silently as light from the hidden cottage washed over the old sorceresses' face. *At last, I've found you.*

"Do ye like honey in yer tea?" Derwyn asked as she placed a cup before the handsome young man. He appeared fit, with shoulders so broad they barely squeezed though her little door. By his size and his scars, a warrior for sure. Although she would never show it, she felt a pang of sympathy for him.

"Tea?" the young man repeated. "I've come to learn what you know of Sayrid, not to sit and have tea."

"You young people are always in a hurry." Ignoring his scowl, Derwyn filled the cups. "There was a time when I could boil water using my powers." She heaved a tired sigh. "But no more. I'm gettin' old, my powers grow weaker with every day that passes, and that is why I thought it best we meet."

She hobbled to the table and sat down. Again he frowned, but added a drizzle of honey to his tea. "I am called Derwyn."

A dark brow arched skeptically. "How do you know who I am?"

She gave a cackle of laughter. "Aye." Derwyn narrowed her gaze. "I know much about ye . . . from touchin' a bit of yer hair I got from Sayrid . . . and from holding yer amulet. Small things, but things that tell me what kind of man ye are."

The warlord took a sip of tea. "And what kind of man am I?"

"Fearless," Derwyn said with a firm nod. "And that is why I will tell ye all ye need to know." She took a sip of tea before she pushed the cup aside. "Sayrid is my granddaughter, but 'afore ye ask me any questions, drink yer tea and listen well, fer I'm about tae reveal the details of the ancient prophecy."

CHAPTER ELEVEN

'Twas nearly midnight when Kyran used the hidden passageway to enter the castle. "She's mad," he muttered, but deep down inside he knew differently. No one could make up the story Derwyn had told and tell it with such vivid detail. Not a living soul could have relived that terrible day without being there. The old woman had confirmed Cyric's belief. Sayrid was Cyric's sister Jenalyn and Kyran's life-mate. Neither Kyran nor Sayrid had a choice, as the decree had been sealed by the Ancient Ones—at the sacred altar built near the waterfall—before Aswyn had torn it down. To deny it would only bring death and destruction to both of them.

After he'd listened to many other stories, he'd left the old woman's cottage with a thousand thoughts battling each other in his head. It felt as if he'd been given too much information too quickly, yet knew it had to be done, because he and Sayrid were running out of time. He'd done as he was told and listened to every word the old sorceress had spoken. Though he'd never believed in the old ways, he came away believing.

He steadily climbed the stone steps to his chamber, leaving the candle on a rusty sconce before he opened the rocky portal. Once inside, he leaned back against the wall, surveying with regret the damage he'd done. The shelf would have to be replaced to keep others from his discovery.

Ye are the guardian of the people—the Protector—their only hope for peace. Derwyn's parting words rested heavily on his shoulders, but had not completely surprised him. He'd known from the day they made him a slave, he'd return and avenge his family—that he would die to keep his and Cyric's secret. As he'd grown older and stronger, he had also grown more confident that nothing would get in his way—nothing would stop him from this quest. No matter the price, he would make certain the true king—a Welsh king—would rule Dragon's Head.

But now he knew the price he'd have to pay.

Kyran went to the hearth. After tossing some kindling on the dying coals, he knelt and blew softly to encourage the flames. 'Twas becoming cold at night—fall had arrived, and the harvest would soon be ready. Still kneeling, he added two small logs, staring into the fire. He'd promised Cyric he'd be ready to go to Oddrum, but after hearing what the old witch had said, he doubted the intelligence of their plan. Could he get an evil man to see the wisdom of Cyric's proposal? A proposal that would bind his friend to an evil woman for the rest of his life? For all of Cyric's attributes, he would not be able to withstand such a life. Even as a slave, he'd been sheltered—a household servant in charge of Arcas' accounts.

Heaving a tired sigh, Kyran rose and yanked off his tunic and tossed it on the bed. He went to the table where he'd left the pitcher of wine and sloshed some into a pewter goblet, drinking it down. *Ye and Sayrid are life-mates, bound to each other, yer promise sealed with yer amulets.* He refilled his goblet then looked at the table, noticing at once that his medallion was gone.

Cursing under his breath, he pressed his thumb and forefinger to the bridge of his nose, willing his anger away—only now aware that each time he'd become angry, the weather turned foul.

"Not again, Sayrid," he muttered through clenched teeth.

Thunder rumbled in the distance, forcing him to take a calming breath. "Not when I need it the most."

Clad in a black velvet robe, Brynn sat on the soft fur rug before the fire, her legs tucked under her body, staring into the cavorting flames. A glossy black raven preened on a wooden perch in the chamber, stopping occasionally to watch his mistress.

Memories, like the sparks that occasionally flew from the log, skittered across Brynn's mind, igniting brief moments of her past. She saw herself as a child, happy and carefree, but the sweet feeling the memory brought didn't last long. She closed her eyes and saw herself older, weeping at her parents' burial, turning to her older brother for love and support, finding him cold and uncaring. How she wanted to be like him—so brave, so strong. But she also remembered wishing he'd notice her—show her the slightest sign that he loved her as much as she loved him.

Seeking approval, she turned to Maldwyn, and became his apprentice, learning everything she could from the kind and gentle wizard—who, she learned over the years, wasn't as kind and gentle as he pretended to be. He insisted she learn everything, even his darkest, most frightening spells.

Then, one day, her brother came and, without an explanation, sent her to Aswyn. Aswyn proved to be even more evil than her brother and Maldwyn, making promises he never kept. She had endured his wet kisses and groping hands, blocking out all thoughts except those of becoming queen. Only as queen could she finally be the feminine equal of her brother.

Brynn opened her burning eyes, refusing to cry. She heaved a tired sigh. What had happened to that carefree child? She had sacrificed far more than her maidenhead to be accepted by her brother. She lifted the brush and began to drag it through her hair. Two long years she'd been away from her home—her

182

people, and for what? Aswyn had filled her head with impotent promises, taken her innocence, and laughed when she asked him to make her his wife. Soon, he would say, soon.

And she had believed him.

She had believed. All her hopes had died the day an army of slaves led by a traitor destroyed her life.

"Curse him," she muttered, shaking her head. If only her aim had been a little better, a little more to the left. Mayhap if she'd killed him and had been able to deposit his body at Aswyn's feet, she'd have won his favor. As queen, she could have convinced Aswyn to attack her brother and take back her childhood home.

Her musings turned from those of her brother to her teacher, Maldwyn, and the many spells she'd learned under his tutelage. Although they had infrequent visits, she missed the old man— longed to confide in him, to tell him about her feelings of failure, and to confess that she wanted to rule her kingdom without the interference of a mate. Surely Maldwyn would understand. He himself had never married. She remembered him saying that he'd loved a woman once, but that she'd spurned him.

As selfish as he was, Maldwyn had never judged her when she confided her silly childhood secrets. 'Twas he who comforted her when she'd skin a knee. 'Twas he who had sent the ravens to watch over her. She glanced at the bird—the captain over the others. It watched her, almost as if he were ready to hear her confession.

She put her brush aside and thought about the warlord who had crushed all her dreams. She saw his image clearly in the flames. How handsome he looked in his oyster-colored tunic, a beautiful yet fierce dragon adorning his chest. She could have enjoyed being his woman—so much so, she felt a jealous pang stab into her chest. As her eyes grew darker, her thoughts turned to his woman—Sayrid.

Sayrid didn't deserve to be queen. Kyran was too much the warrior for a little mouse like her. But Brynn sensed that something had recently changed—that Sayrid had changed—acquired more power without the knowledge to channel it. Brynn scoffed. She knew instantly who would help her do so. "Derwyn, you old witch. I should have sought you out myself and finished what Aswyn had tried to do so many years ago."

Brynn narrowed her eyes with hate, silently thanking the gods and Maldwyn for her ability to change into a raven and take flight—to have the foresight to follow the king and find the cave where the old sorceress lived. Brynn had grown stronger these past two years, too. But was she strong enough to test her skills?

Brynn methodically gathered several saffron candles and placed them in a circle on the floor, saving the largest for the center where she made a place to sit. She took two, small, leafy twigs from a leather pouch.

"Foolish old woman. Think you the only one with the gift?" she murmured as she prepared for the ceremony. The small flames danced and cavorted in the breeze from the narrow arrow slit in the room, but she hardly noticed. Instead, she closed her eyes and began a low guttural incantation, pinching a sprig of blackberry bush between the two middle fingers and thumbs of both hands. Slowly she began to rock, her head gyrating as she murmured ancient words, so lost in her spell she never heard the rumble of thunder or the low, angry growl that emanated from the walls.

Derwyn woke, groggy at first, but then sat up quickly as she felt a deathly chill. She looked at her door. Long fingers of red fog oozed from under it, curling upward, crawling up the rocky walls and ceiling, inching toward Derwyn's bed.

"Be gone," Derwyn ordered, rising to fetch her staff. Holding it out before her she whispered ancient words. The fog began to writhe as if in pain, retreating the way it came. "Be gone, you evil thing, and back tenfold to her who sent you."

A blast of wind swept through the arrow slit, doused the candles and knocked them over, spilling hot wax on the floor and onto the thin material of Brynn's nightgown and slippers. Stifling an angry scream, she frantically brushed at the wax at the same time her bird flapped his wings and squawked in protest.

The wind grew stronger, heaving her across the room, slamming her against the stone. Her long black hair swirled around, slapping her cheeks and stinging her eyes as she slowly slid down and landed on the floor. When the wind calmed, she slowly stood and stared at the spot where the blackberry sprig had curled and shriveled. In a fit of rage, she ground it into dust with her foot.

"Bitch," she hissed, inspecting the reddening skin on her thigh and a place on her ankle. "Think you this will stop me?"

She gave a dry, humorless laugh, then went to the perch and quieted her pet. The raven stepped onto her outstretched hand, took several steps up her arm then hopped to sit upon her shoulder. Brynn went to the bedside table and opened a narrow drawer, retrieving a small piece of parchment. Taking a narrow reed she held it in the fire until it blackened, then with the burnt end scribbled a message about Derwyn on the parchment before she folded it into a very small square and tied it to the raven's leg.

"To Maldwyn," she prompted as the bird flew out into the night sky. She watched it disappear then changed her ruined gown and went to her bed, drawing back the fur cover and slipping beneath it. She tucked her arm under her head, forcing her mind to think of more pleasant things. In the morning, she would start the wheels of her new plan turning, and this time she wouldn't fail—this time she would have the help of the most powerful wizard in the land—Maldwyn.

Certain she'd chased away the evil, Derwyn tossed several fat logs on the smoldering coals. After a jab with a charred stick, the flames revived and licked hungrily at the dry wood, bathing the small room in soft, warm light. Derwyn stared into the flames, pausing to warm her cold hands for several moments before she took a small pouch from the mantel and opened it. She threw a pinch of white powder into the flames, watching while it sparked and hissed for several moments. "Show me her teacher."

Faintly at first, an old man's features appeared in the flames. "Maldwyn," Derwyn whispered, obviously disappointed. "I had hoped you were dead."

She wrapped her arms more tightly around her frail body, warming herself before the fire till the chill had passed. She glanced around her little home—a home no longer safe. In the next day or two, she'd pack a few of her most prized possessions and make the tedious trek to the castle. She'd enjoy visiting the village, but, more importantly, 'twas time she introduced herself to her grandson and moved back into Dragon's Head.

Morven dropped a black-clad warrior at Kyran's feet before he reached for the pitcher of wine and drank his fill. By the man's glassy eyes and white lips, Kyran knew he was dead. The broken shaft of an arrow piercing the man's heart confirmed it.

"A gift, for me?" Kyran said sarcastically.

Morven scoffed. "A man now. A bird when I shot him."

Kyran's smile faded. "What kind of bird?"

"A black bird. I grew hungry whilst hunting. A flock of ravens roosted in the trees so I took aim." Morven nodded toward the dead man. "That's what hit the ground."

King Oddrum drummed his long tanned fingers on the intricately carved wooden arm of his thickly padded throne, angry that the news of his uncle's death had taken months to reach him. Even after the messenger explained that his leg wound kept him from making the long journey, the man received a verbal reprimand and was ordered from the hall. The news of Arcas' death shook Oddrum and ruined his plans to ask his uncle to send his army to assist with the war. Maldwyn sat on an equally elaborate chair across from the king, his left hand stroking his long white beard, his right hand holding the dagger delivered by the messenger.

"Well?" the king asked impatiently, hoping for better news than what he'd just received. "See you anything—the face of the man?"

"Arcas' blade, but not his in truth. 'Twas taken from another many years ago—a man who resided in Dragon's Head." Maldwyn slowly took his fingers and outlined the serpent design on the blade's hilt. His eyes opened wide. "I see King Arcas. He is bloodied and on his knees, sweat drenched and defeated."

"Who killed my uncle? I demand to know," Oddrum ground out through clenched teeth, half-rising out of his chair.

Again Maldwyn closed his eyes, this time gently rocking back and forth, muttering an ancient chant, the words barely audible to King Oddrum's ears. "There is much pain," the old man whined, acting as if he felt it himself. "Much death . . . fire and smoke . . . 'tis difficult to breathe."

Oddrum took a quick swallow of wine, annoyed that Maldwyn only gave him bits and pieces—wheezing like an old cat choking on a fur ball. Of course he felt pain and saw blood. King Arcas had been murdered—his throat slit, and, by the gods, if the old wizard didn't tell him who'd killed his uncle, he'd be doing more than wheezing, he'd be bleeding.

As if Maldwyn sensed Oddrum's thoughts, the sorcerer's eyes flew open. " 'Tis the young warrior I dreamt of . . . only he's not dressed as a king, but as a common soldier, wearing rags, without the protection of armor."

"A slave?" Oddrum nearly shouted, standing. "The man's a slave?" Oddrum rounded on the old wizard, placing his hands on the arms of the chair, trapping Maldwyn with his violet stare. "What of Arcas' army?"

"Dead . . . most of his soldiers dead."

"What of his sons—my cousins?"

"One dead—the other dying." Maldwyn shrank back, clutching the dagger with one hand, his throat with the other. "M-mutiny, my lord. Their own slaves betrayed them. Those few who offered support were slaughtered with them."

"Slaves?" Oddrum roared, grabbing the old man by the shoulders and giving him a firm shake. "This man . . . this man, Kyran . . . is he a slave?"

Maldwyn seemed to shrink even more. "Aye, my lord. To Arcas he was a slave. To the people of Dragon's Head he is their liberator . . . their Protector."

Oddrum moved away and motioned to one of the two soldiers who stood at the door. "Go, and tell my commander to send a messenger to my sister. I would know the number of my enemy's army before we march on Dragon's Head." The king angrily raked his fingers through his dark hair. "I've no desire to continue our game. You may retire to your chamber, old man."

Maldwyn sat in his favorite high-backed chair in his chamber. He'd beaten the king once and could have easily beat him a second time, but it wasn't wise or in the best interest of his health to humiliate Oddrum a second time. Nay, his sovereign was a stubborn, arrogant man. So much so, he wouldn't listen to reason. Aswyn and Oddrum were two peas in a pod, and yet Oddrum refused to believe that the man called Kyran—the slave taken as a child, years before—had beaten Aswyn at his own game of warfare.

The fire felt warm. Clad in his soft slippers and comfortable robe, he felt quite relaxed. He yawned, catching his breath when two large ravens landed on his windowsill, poked aside the deer-hide shutter and let himself in.

Blinking his surprise, Maldwyn ducked when the bird flew over his head to roost on the back of his chair before dropping a folded note and pouch into the wizard's lap. "Well, well," Maldwyn murmured. "What have we here, my friends?"

After he'd read Brynn's missive, he carefully untied the pouch, shaking the contents onto his lap.

"By the gods," he gasped, lifting the amulet to admire it more closely. He cast a quick glance around before looking at it again. Certain it was what he thought it to be, he slipped the amulet back into the pouch before he stood. He hurried to the chest at the foot of his bed. Casting one more cautious glance around his small chamber, he dug down under his many robes and safely tucked the pouch under his clothing.

Rising to his feet, Maldwyn plucked several fat grapes from the dish on his bedside table and held them out for the bird. "I'm sorry to learn you've lost a friend," he crooned to the bird, stroking the sleek black feathers. "You've had a long flight and deserve a reward."

Yawning, the old wizard pulled back his soft fur coverlet, kicked off his comfortable slippers and slipped into bed. "On the morrow, you shall take a message to your mistress. But, for now, take yourselves out to yonder oak tree. 'Tis sheltered by the castle. We all need our rest. I sense that we'll have a long journey ahead of us."

★ ★ ★ ★ ★

"My lord."

Cyric turned from checking the girth on his horse. The young woman he'd seen recently with Bynor hurried outside. The early morning sunlight gleamed brilliantly on her long black braid, and she carried what appeared to be a skin of wine.

"My lord," she called again, catching Cyric's full attention. He returned her smile. She appeared to take a calming breath, hesitating a moment before she walked toward him, her head held high. Could she possibly be nervous? Though the thought made him hold his smile a little longer, it displeased him that she still felt fear toward him and the others who'd captured Dragon's Head.

She held out the skin. "I thought that you might take this with you . . . should you get thirsty on your ride."

For a moment he wondered how she knew he'd decided to take a ride—to go into the forest for some peace and quiet, since he'd told no one and had only made the decision a little while ago. His fingers briefly touched hers when he took the wine. A simple touch, but unsettling.

"Thank you," he said. He smiled again from the surprise he saw flickering in her eyes. The woman seemed to appeal to Bynor and, upon meeting her, Cyric could see why. Her wide, violet eyes appeared to hold a touch of mystery. She bowed her head—out of respect, he guessed—then returned to the scullery. Though Cyric never noticed while he mounted his horse, a few moments later a large black raven circled once then perched on a nearby tree.

Cyric took a long deep breath. The fragrant smell of pine, tinged with salty sea air, filled his senses, replenished his strength and conjured up old, nearly forgotten memories. He remembered bits and pieces of the binding ceremony—his shy little sister peeking out from behind their mother's skirts—

Kyran trying to act like one of the older children, standing straight and tall, frowning when Cyric found it impossible not to giggle.

"We were all just children," Cyric muttered, leaning to pat the palfrey on the neck. Try as he might, he could not remember much more—just fire and smoldering thatch, screams and moans, and the rocky face of Dragon's Head shrouded by smoke as their captors dragged them away.

Refusing to dwell on those dark days, Cyric glanced at the sun hovering over the distant horizon, and gave thanks that he was finally home with his best friend and a legion of loyal men. No longer could the Vikings and former slaves who traveled with them be considered their enemies. They had become like them, in search of a better place—a place to call home.

As he followed a narrow river deeper into the forest, he couldn't shake the feeling that Jennalyn had somehow survived and was the beautiful young woman he'd met at the feast. He could see by Kyran's actions that he was attracted to her, which made him even more suspicious. Cyric frowned, remembering the girl who'd brought him the wine—how her fingers trembled when he took the skin. For a moment he wondered if his people would ever learn to trust him.

He guided the gelding around a fallen log, trying to find fault with his theory about Sayrid and Kyran. He wondered if he'd made the right decision—to keep his identity a secret. Soon, Kyran would go to Oddrum—not to kill him, but to seek an alliance—a marriage to ensure peace. 'Twas known that Oddrum had a beautiful sister—a sister rumored to be as cunning as the king himself.

His thoughts turned to Rhonwyn, deepening his frown even more. In the short time he'd known her, he'd grown to care for her; he knew that if his position allowed, he would ask her to be his wife. Once again, his mind wandered to Oddrum, and he wondered if love could grow from a forced marriage. He wondered if his intended bride was tall or short, fair or dark haired, and if she'd have a sweet manner or violent temper.

He had hoped to surprise Oddrum, had hoped that Kyran could arrive on his doorstep with his proposal. But a clever spy could betray them and send word to Oddrum, no matter how many guards watched the roads and paths around Dragon's Head. So, Kyran insisted they send a messenger ahead in the hopes that Oddrum's sister would learn of the proposal and convince her brother to accept.

As Cyric rode deeper into the forest, he thought of the female archer who had wounded Kyran. They had never found her, even though many a search had been conducted. Perhaps she had escaped and had, by now, reported in great detail the taking of Dragon's Head. So be it. Perhaps by doing so, Oddrum would think twice before attacking.

Tired of thinking about war and secret proposals, Cyric rode until he came to where the river widened and spilled over some flat rocks, forming a deep tempting pool surrounded with ferns, reeds and smatterings of wild flowers. He dismounted and, with a long rope, tied the gelding to a willow, allowing the palfrey freedom to graze on the plentiful grass.

Dragonflies skittered across the glassy surface of the lake, sending tiny ripples toward the bank. He lifted the flap of his saddlebag and withdrew a long, narrow leather pouch. He found a shady spot under a tall birch tree and sat, leaning against it.

Brynn had watched Cyric ride through the gates of Dragon's Head, confused by the rush of feelings that had coursed through her. She frowned. The men she preferred were battle-hardened warriors, not good with accounts. It wasn't like her to act on impulse or to even consider anyone's needs but her own. She clutched her fingers together, remembering how they'd tingled the moment Cyric's had brushed against them. He didn't have that hungry look in his eyes like most men.

'Twas what disturbed her the most, that he hadn't noticed her at all. He only had eyes for that bitch, Rhonwyn. For a moment, she almost felt remorse for what she'd done as she hurried to the tree where the raven preened himself for several moments, apparently not too interested that she'd come. "You have word from Maldwyn?"

The bird squawked, then flew to another branch and then to another, leading Brynn deeper into the forest.

"Well?" she asked impatiently. "Stop your antics and—" She ducked as the bird swooped down, barely missing her head, and landed at her feet. "How dare you," she hissed and would have kicked it had it not magically changed into its human form.

"Maldwyn," Brynn gasped. She threw herself into the old man's arms. " 'Tis so good to see you. I've missed you so much."

Maldwyn hugged Brynn, then grasped her by the shoulders and held her at arm's length. Foolish wench, he thought, hiding his disgust. How dare she become pregnant when so much was at stake? A man's visage appeared before him. A warrior with dark, curly hair and eyes the color of the sky—a reckless, fearless warrior named Bynor. Maldwyn released her, wiping his fingers on his dark robe. "I have come because what I have learned is of utmost importance and I dared not trust anyone but myself to divulge it." He nodded at Brynn's worried look. "It concerns your brother and his plans to attack Dragon's Head."

"Let him come," she said with a defiant toss of her head. "I hope he kills all of them."

Maldwyn gave a disgusted snort. She meant it—he knew it by the evil gleam in her eyes. She had no feeling for any of them, especially the father of her child. "Nay, little one. There is one who cannot die."

"All men can die, my lord. Even powerful, magical men."

He nodded, only slightly bemused at her insinuation. Had she sensed his repugnance? "Methinks you speak of the one called Kyran?"

"You should know, my lord. After all, you're reading my thoughts, are you not?" Again a flicker of defiance flamed to life in the depths of her violet eyes.

"At times. At other times, it has become most difficult. You're learning all too well my secrets." He heaved a sigh. "I did not come all this way to anger you. And I care little of what happens to this Kyran. It is the true king, the one called Cyric, whose life is important to me . . . to us."

Maldwyn's smile faded as the color drained from his apprentice's face. "What is it?" he asked, his hawkish gray brows snapping tightly together. He grabbed her arm none too gently. "Tell me, Brynn, what have you done?"

Sayrid carefully spread the ferns, watching Cyric dismount. She'd just finished gathering some wild herbs. Although her good sense told her to leave and seek out her cottage, she watched, curious to see what he was about. He sat on the grass, tipping his head slightly as if listening to the sounds of the forest. A jay called to his mate, and a squirrel chattered from a branch high in an oak tree, causing him to look upwards. Oddly, he smiled, and she wondered if it had been many years since he could wander alone and enjoy listening to the sounds of such simple things.

He pulled something long and narrow from a leather bag. 'Twas a flute. Moments later soft, sweet music floated over her—a tune she knew—but from where?

Disturbed by the rush of emotion the music brought, she brushed away a tear, staring at the tiny drop of moisture on her fingertip. A tear? She shook her head in disbelief. She never cried. Yet, even as she denied it, the overwhelming urge to weep came over her.

Mesmerized, she listened and closed her eyes. A woman's face floated in the darkness of her mind—a happy woman with a gentle smile. And she saw herself as a child again, holding a cloth doll while her mother braided her hair as they sat before a cheerful fire. As the music played, Sayrid remembered more. Her eyes flew open. Stunned, she stumbled back, not caring if she rustled any leaves or snagged her sleeve upon a spiny hawthorn. Once far enough away to not draw Cyric's attention, she began to run.

Sayrid didn't stop running until she found herself before the vine-covered door of Derwyn's cottage. Too upset to notice the raven watching from the treetop, she threw the door open, stepped inside and leaned back against the wooden planks, her chest rising and falling with each ragged breath.

"Sayrid, child, come in," Derwyn stated with a worried frown. Wispy white hair peeked out from under her dark shawl. Noticing a bundle tied to a stick, Sayrid presumed Derwyn planned to take a journey. "Tell me, what's troublin' ye?"

"One of the warriors . . . ," Sayrid began breathlessly. "One of Kyran's friends . . . he came to the forest with a flute and he played a tune." Sayrid pressed her cold fingers to her forehead. "I knew the tune, but I'm certain 'twas the first time I've heard it."

"Aye, and I can see it upset ye." Derwyn reached to comfort Sayrid, but she drew back.

"While I listened, I—I remembered." Sayrid stared at Derwyn, watching as the old woman's kind smile faded. "I remember everything—my parents—my family—my name."

Derwyn caught Sayrid's cold hand and urged her toward the

stool near the table. "Sit, and I'll make us a cup of tea while we talk."

Sayrid snatched her hand back. "I don't want tea. I want the truth. You knew. All this time you knew."

Derwyn's old shoulders slumped a little more and her faded blue eyes filled with tears. "Tell me what you remember," Derwyn said, her manner and speech more refined than Sayrid had ever witnessed before.

"This man's tune made me feel like crying." Sayrid watched Derwyn as she filled a small pot with dry tea leaves before adding boiling water from the kettle over the fire. Derwyn carried the steeping tea to the table and fetched two cups.

"I hid in the ferns. At first I thought I should leave, but then he began to play, and I—I couldn't leave. I closed my eyes and became a child again. I saw . . . your face and those of my mother and father and another child. A young boy, older than me, but not by many winters."

"Cyric," Derwyn said softly. "Cyric is your brother, and I. . . ." Derwyn stared into the chipped teacup. "I am your grandmother, hiding here, pretending to be older than I really am—to stay alive and watch over you."

Derwyn heaved a tired sigh. "You must believe me, child, when I tell you that I thought him dead—had no sense of him, till just a little bit ago." Derwyn's eyes filled with tears again. "I'm old. With each passing day, as your powers grow stronger, my powers grow weaker. Had I known he lived, I would have told you. I was just about to go to Dragon's Head and tell him our story. Come with me."

"You—you can't expect me to believe that," Sayrid said hotly. She pushed away the cup and stood. "I've spoken with this man. If I were Jenalyn—his sister—wouldn't he have approached me?"

"I do not know," Derwyn said softly. "Methinks his memories

are as elusive as yours." Derwyn looked up at Sayrid. "Please, sit down, and I will tell you what I know."

Sayrid slowly sank back down.

"You and Cyric are only two winters apart, children of Maude and Euan. Your name was changed to protect you."

"There must be a mistake. Llewellyn was my mother's name." A long forgotten memory flickered to life in Sayrid's mind. She saw a boy running with her through a flower-sprinkled field, laughing, calling her Jenalyn.

"No, child. Llewellyn was a kind woman—a slave in the castle who kept watch over you for me. Your mother's real name was Maude. She and your father were murdered by Aswyn when he attacked our family at the binding feast. You were barely four winters. I thought Cyric had died and his little body burned with theirs."

More pictures formed in her head. She saw herself standing before the high priest, promising to hold herself for her future husband—turning to smile at a boy whose face she couldn't remember. "If what you say happened, why didn't Aswyn kill me too?"

"You were so young, and grew tired quickly. After the binding ceremony, I took you back to the castle, to stay with me for the night."

"Nay!" she cried, shaking her head. "I would remember that if it had happened."

"Aswyn must have made a pact with Arcas—Oddrum's uncle. On the night they attacked, they set a torch to your father's crops. When the men, including the castle guards, were busy fighting the fire to keep us all from starving, Aswyn hit me with a club. By the time I awoke, you'd been snatched away." Tears filled Derwyn's eyes. "Gwendolyn found me wandering in the forest half-dead, and nursed me back to health. She told me Aswyn had taken Dragon's Head, and she had Dafydd turn this

197

old cave into my home. At first I thought you were dead too, but then I learned you'd been spared. Aswyn kept you under lock and key for seven years; no matter how hard I tried, I could not find a way to free you."

Another forgotten memory caused fresh tears to burn the back of Sayrid's eyes—a memory of a dank chamber containing nothing but a cot and a few pieces of clothing in a small chest. There was a smell like burning logs, but mostly she remembered how cold and lonely she felt, wondering why her mother and father hadn't come for her. 'Twas only at night that she felt safe—grew warmer and fell asleep to a gentle, comforting rocking of her cot—wondering how a wooden cot perched on a stone floor could move. At the same time, she had her answer and nearly voiced it, but Derwyn began to speak again.

"Listen to me, child. All I have said is true. Your father and mother were murdered, but not by Vikings. Your uncle killed them."

"You lie," Sayrid said in a breathless whisper. She tried to think, tried to comprehend Derwyn's story. Aswyn had been her uncle? She felt the old woman's knobby fingers touch her gently on the shoulder.

"Nay, I do not lie. Aswyn was my son, your mother's brother." Derwyn stepped before Sayrid and cupped her cheeks with a sad smile. "Open your eyes and your mind to the truth. Feel what little power I have left and draw the truth from it. Draw my thoughts into your own and open your heart. You know that I could never lie to you. Sometimes our minds play tricks—to protect us from terrible memories, and I suspect that's what happened to you. But you're of age, now. 'Tis why you're remembering."

"I—I don't believe you," Sayrid cried, pressing her fingertips to her throbbing temples.

"You must." When Derwyn had Sayrid's full attention, she

slowly removed the shawl and cap, exposing a very ugly scar on the back of her head where hair no longer grew. When next she spoke, her voice flooded with anguish. "I am your grandmother, child. My own son nearly killed me to take you and make you his slave."

Derwyn slowly replaced the cap and dabbed at her eyes. "I am your grandmother," she repeated. "Your mother and Aswyn were my children. He grew jealous of her husband the king."

Sayrid fought the urge to run from the cave and seek refuge in her own little cottage. The sight of the terrible scar and the thought of the wound the old woman must have suffered twisted her stomach into a tight knot.

Derwyn covered her cold hands with her warm ones. "You have been seeing and feeling things as of late. Strange things. Sometimes they come to you in your sleep in the form of dreams, but now you see these things whilst you are awake."

Sayrid swallowed hard and nodded.

" 'Tis a gift passed down from me to your mother, now to you. But you're different. In you, the gift is much stronger. That's why you will survive no matter what is destined to happen. You're strong, Sayrid, and thank the gods for it. The night of the attack we were celebrating the binding of you and your intended life-mate."

"My life-mate?" Sayrid repeated, her mind swimming with everything she'd heard.

"Aye, the amulets. The one you have and the one you gave back to Kyran. They're connected, forged as one then separated, one given to you and one given to your life-mate. You are grown and ready to accept your place as one of us—as a seer and healer. We must go slowly, so you can learn how to use your powers wisely. To rush it will only corrupt the purity of the gift."

Derwyn rose and gently lifted Sayrid's amulet out from under her dress to rest openly upon her breast. "I know that this is a lot to hear and to believe, but there is more."

Derwyn took a shaky breath. "This man, Kyran. You love him?"

Sayrid shook her head in denial. "Nay . . . aye . . . I—I don't know what I feel."

"You think it lust, but it isn't." Derwyn met her startled gaze. "Kyran is your life-mate."

Derwyn nodded. " 'Tis good that you love him. Now the prophecy is near complete. I feared he would die before it would be fulfilled."

"Die?" A painful knot twisted at Sayrid's insides. "But he is the king, and you said the king would live to—"

Derwyn shook her head. "He is not the king. Cyric . . . your brother is the true king of Dragon's Head, and will live to rule our people. Kyran is a loyal friend who pretended to be king to protect your brother. He is destined to die for Cyric."

"Then they lied . . . lied to me . . . to all our people?"

"Aye, to keep your brother from harm."

Sayrid grabbed Derwyn by the shoulders. "Tell me. Tell me why he has to die?"

Tears flooded her grandmother's eyes. "I cannot. To do so may jeopardize our chance for peace."

"Peace?" Sayrid cried. "At what cost?"

"One life for thousands." Derwyn reached up to cup her cheek, but Sayrid turned away.

"Nay," Sayrid said in a deathly calm voice. She went to the door and threw it open.

Derwyn followed her out, stopping in the doorway. "He will not die in vain. 'Twill be the first time we will live in peace since the days of the dragons."

"And do I die also?" Sayrid asked, taking several steps back. "Are you keeping that from me as well?"

"Nay, my child. You are much stronger than most who are bound to each other. You will grieve, but you won't die."

Sayrid gave a bitter laugh. "I'll only wish I had. Isn't that right, grandmother?" She turned and walked away.

"Sayrid, please . . . 'tis the prophecy handed down from the beginning of time. We cannot fail the Ancient Ones—we cannot fail the spirit of the dragon."

Chapter Twelve

Derwyn's plea for Sayrid to return carried out over the treetops, but Sayrid paid them no mind. She began to run, unmindful of the low branches that snagged her hair and clothing and scratched her face. At last she came to the river and the place where it slowed and formed a smooth pool.

Gasping in deep breaths to ease the ache in her throat, she fell to her knees and stared at her reflection, remembering how she had writhed beneath Kyran's touch—how completely he had satisfied her, and how deeply she had satisfied him—how deeply she had loved him. Why hadn't she known it was love? Why hadn't she agreed to go back with him to Dragon's Head?

"Fool," she cried. For a few precious moments in Derwyn's cottage—while she'd told the story of their binding, Sayrid had begun to hope she would be his woman, bear his children and call him husband. But her hopes had been shattered by the old woman's prediction—the fulfillment of the prophecy.

Sayrid splashed cold water on her face, squeezing her eyes against the pictures in her mind—terrifying pictures of how her beloved would die.

"May the gods forgive me," she sobbed as she hunted for the plants and herbs she needed. "I cannot let Oddrum take him from me."

She had just finished filling her pockets when she turned, surprised to see that Cyric's horse had wandered this far. She held out her hand and, whispering words of comfort, easily caught the animal. The moment her fingers touched the reins, a frightening vision appeared. Her brother lay on his side on the grass where she'd seen him playing the flute. By his motionless body was a skin, the cork missing and the grass yellowed where the wine had spilled.

"Nay," Sayrid moaned. A stick snapped behind her. Before she could react, a bear-like hand closed over her nose and mouth, suffocating her. White spots formed before her eyes, and her lungs ached for a decent breath of air. In an effort to free herself from her captor, she called on the last of her dwindling strength and dug her nails into the back of his hand and kicked her feet, but with no effect. Growing even more lightheaded, she felt herself hurled to the ground, thankful for the abundance of fallen leaves to break her fall. Drawing in great gulps of air, the fog in her head quickly cleared. She struggled to her hands and knees. "You," she gasped, more angry than frightened. "How did you find me?"

Morven leaned his staff against the trunk of the tree, and glared at her. Dressed in fur and dark leather, he blended well with the forest. No wonder she didn't see him, the big brute.

"Think you are the only one who knows their way about in the forest?" He gave a shake of his shaggy head, his narrow gaze filled with disgust. "Where is he?" Morven demanded, grabbing her arm in a painful grasp. She narrowed her gaze, wishing he'd let her be. Something happened—a spark of sensation that felt hot. The next instant Morven let go and stared at his hand. "Where is Cyric," he repeated, taking a step away from her.

Confused by his reaction, she pointed into the trees. "There . . . he's over there. He's ill, and I fear he's been poisoned."

Grumbling like an old bear that had been rousted from his den, Morven grabbed the reins of Cyric's horse. "How do you know this?" Morven asked, towering over her.

Donna MacQuigg

"A vision when I touched his horse."

Morven grabbed her and none too gently plopped her on the horse's back. "Go to him, but remember I will follow."

Sayrid gathered up the horse's reins and turned him toward the clearing. Ducking down by the palfrey's neck, Sayrid urged the horse into a run, dodging low branches and jumping fallen logs. Hot tears burned her eyes when they slid to a stop in the clearing, and Sayrid jumped down and ran to help her brother, unaware as two ravens roosted in the very top of a tall birch.

With shaky fingers, she touched her brother's cheek, relieved to feel it still warm. She snatched up the skin and held it to her nose, instantly recognizing the smell. Sayrid frantically looked around, hoping to find the plants that would halt the effects of the poison. Rising, she ran to edge of the pool and searched through the heavy growth of ferns until she spotted the pale, milky-green plant she wanted. Pulling it up by the roots, she quickly washed away the mud, then pulled a large flat leaf from another plant and placed the other plant in the center where she began to mash the bulbous roots into a paste, adding a little water until she felt it would slide down Cyric's throat without much difficulty.

She knelt by his side, lifting him slightly so that his head rested in her lap. She forced his clenched jaw open and dribbled her concoction into his mouth, hoping he was strong enough to swallow. A moment later, he coughed but managed to take some more. Slowly his eyes fluttered open.

"Sayrid?" Her brother's eyes closed again, but she could tell he felt better.

"Aye," she said softly, moving a lock of red hair from his forehead. She studied his features, trying to remember something about him as her brother, but only saw a man she barely knew—a man she wasn't certain she could love if his rise in power meant the fall of her beloved. Sadness once again

204

threatened her composure.

"W-what happened?" he asked, trying to sit up. Once upright, he rested his arm on his knees, his forehead on his arm.

"First you must finish the cure," she said, urging him to take the last of her milk-colored potion. He did as she asked, then coughed again, apparently not pleased with the bitter taste.

"How did you find me?"

"Your music." She stood, her feelings still too raw to be overly friendly. "Can you stand?" she asked.

"I think so," he murmured softly, accepting her hand. His fingers closed over hers, filling her head with a dozen new memories. She helped him to his feet and then onto the horse's back. Still suffering the effects of the poison, he clutched the pommel to keep his balance. "What happened to me?" he asked again.

Sayrid picked up the skin and capped it, instantly seeing Brynn. "Someone poisoned your wine."

" 'Twas given to me . . . a young woman . . . a maid brought it to me before I left the castle."

"Aye," Sayrid said, absently. "She only pretends to be a maid." She gathered up the horse's reins and began to walk toward Dragon's Head, her thoughts on the poison she would make to take Oddrum's life.

Mayhap she would make enough for Brynn. Sayrid held her breath, narrowing her gaze and concentrating on the where-abouts of her enemy, but she sensed Brynn had left Dragon's Head.

Maldwyn frowned as he added another log to the flames, seeing Sayrid's image dance in the fire. Sayrid—a powerful sorceress— granddaughter to Derwyn. Though he felt gratitude toward the young woman who had saved the king's life, he hated her and her growing powers at the same time—hated that she reminded him of Derwyn when she was young and had made his blood boil with desire. Feeling the chill of the autumn eve, he dusted off his hands and glanced over at the fur pallet he'd made in his bedchamber for Brynn, to keep her hidden from Oddrum. 'Twould bode ill for both of them if Oddrum learned of their plan.

He strode to where she lay and held his hands over her prone body. Foolish girl, she slept soundly as if she didn't have a care in the world, unaware that she carried a child. Perhaps if he hurried Oddrum along with the war, and insisted upon an immediate marriage, he could convince Cyric the child was his.

Maldwyn's frown slowly turned into a smile. If he couldn't rule Dragon's Head through Brynn—if she grew too defiant—he could certainly manipulate a little child. The old wizard heaved a tired sigh and sought his own bed, content for now to wait.

Sayrid paused at the entrance to the bailey, holding the reins of Cyric's horse. Morven stood next to her, his features unreadable. Torches burned in their holders, casting cavorting shadows along the rough stone wall. Her brother slumped over the animal's neck, still weak from being poisoned. A guard called for her to wait. Moments later she found herself surrounded by armed, angry warriors. The reins were taken from her slack fingers and her brother taken from the horse before the animal was led away.

"Do not harm her," Cyric said in a raspy voice as two men laid him upon the ground. "She saved my life. Tell them, Morven. Tell them she saved my life."

"What is happening here?" Bynor pushed his way through the men, kneeling by Cyric before he looked up at her. "What have you done?" he demanded.

Sayrid lifted her chin, casting the giant a quick glance, frowning when he remained silent. "I've brought him back from death's doors," she said, pleased that her voice sounded strong and confident. She ignored the muttered oaths and accusations of his men, matching Bynor's stabbing gaze. "There's a woman among you—an evil woman. Her name is Brynn. She has jet-colored hair and violet eyes. Exact your revenge on her, not me."

Bynor's frown deepened, and, after speaking softly with Cyric, he stood and told four men to take his friend into the castle. They moved to do as ordered, but Morven hoisted Cyric up over his shoulder and carried him up the steps into Dragon's Head.

Bynor waited until he and Sayrid were alone before he grabbed her arm painfully. "How do you know it was Brynn?"

"She was Aswyn's whore and the witch who tried to kill Kyran."

"You lie. Can you prove 'twas not you who poisoned Cyric and wounded Kyran?"

As if he heard her silent cry for help, Kyran appeared and physically removed Bynor's fingers from her arm. "I can prove it. This woman, known as Sayrid to us, is truly Jenalyn and sister to Cyric."

Sayrid knew not how long she waited, but it mattered little to her. She felt as if her heart had been ripped from her chest, leaving her empty and hopeless. She'd removed her vine-like overgown and hidden it beneath the bed for safekeeping. Feeling exposed and vulnerable, she smoothed the skirt of her worn russet gown, wishing she had something better. Any other time, she would have slipped unnoticed through one of the many hidden passageways, but not tonight. Mayhap never again, because every moment that passed reminded her of the prophecy, and, if she had it in her power, she'd spend them with Kyran.

Unlike most of the other spacious chambers encased in solid rock, this one faced the forest. One of the few with an opening to the outside world, she leaned over and took a long deep breath of the fresh air, mingled with the pungent scent of the forest and the salty smell of the sea. More confusing memories danced in the shadows of her mind, ebbing closer, but seemingly forever out of her reach.

In the far distance, she caught sight of a small woman carrying a little bundle of her possessions. Derwyn. The old woman stopped, lifted her hand and waved, but Sayrid didn't return it. Still confused and angry, she blinked back bittersweet tears. She had a family. A grandmother and a brother. So why did she feel so terrible?

"Reyna," Sayrid whispered, somewhat startled that she knew who would knock on her door before she saw the person's face. Yet, even with this knowledge, her nerves were on edge, and she jumped when Reyna knocked again. "Enter."

Reyna gave a curt nod, then walked to the hearth and added several logs to the cheerful flames. "The master wishes a scented bath for you, and some clothing."

Sayrid returned the woman's smile. "You are Clywd's wife, are you not?"

"Aye, I am," the woman answered, pausing to share a smile before she went to a large chest against the far wall and opened it. "And I am so very pleased to serve you, Lady Sayrid."

Sayrid's fair brows snapped together while Reyna looked through the clothing in the trunk. "Are you also a prisoner?"

Reyna laughed. "Nay, and neither are you." Reyna stood and punched her fists on her ample hips. "There is nothing in there but some old bedding. Nothing fit for our new queen."

"Queen?" Sayrid would have liked to continue their conversation, but a knock came on the door and a guard stepped inside and bowed stiffly, while two men carried in another large trunk.

"My Lord Kyran sends word that you may choose anything out of this trunk you wish."

"I've no need—"

"Tell the king we accept," Reyna said before Sayrid could finish. At Reyna's direction, the warriors placed the trunk against the wall, next to the other one. As soon as they left, two more men carried in a large wooden tub and placed it before the hearth. A line of young boys formed in the room and out into the corridor, and handing buckets to one another, the tub was soon filled with steaming, hot water. Another young girl, whom Sayrid recognized as Reyna's daughter, carried in a pile of drying cloths and, after smiling at Sayrid, hurried out of the chamber with the other children.

All too soon Reyna had Sayrid dressed in an elegant willow-green kirtle made from a material she'd never seen before. The round neck and long, tight-fitting sleeves were embroidered with tiny topaz and amethysts. The gown fit well, hugging the slight swell of her hips and falling in folds to the floor. It seemed to shimmer each time she took a step. When Reyna came with the overgown, Sayrid felt reluctant to accept it.

Done in a richer greenish-blue, it had a fitted bodice that laced at the sides with golden cord. It cascaded over her hips and ended a foot above the hem of her gown. The V-neck was decorated with an intricate, ancient rune design accented with more tiny topaz and amethysts. A matching pattern had been embroidered around the long flared sleeves that ended at the elbows, and were lined with an even darker hue of the shimmering material.

Over this, Reyna tied a low-slung jewel-studded, leather girdle around her hips. Much to Sayrid's surprise, the belt had a small jeweled sheath in which nested an undersized, double-edged dagger with a dragon carved on the hilt. In the dragon's eye nested a tiny almandine.

Reyna insisted on weaving gold and ice-blue ribbons into Sayrid's long, thick braid, covering her head with a gossamer wimple in the same color as the kirtle. To this she added a simple gold circlet adorned with more tiny amethysts.

"You are truly beautiful," Reyna breathed as she took a step back. "Here, see for yourself."

Sayrid stared at her image. She actually looked like a queen, not a simple Welsh woman who had survived many winters in the forest. A small smile tugged at the corners of her mouth for several moments before she remembered who had supplied all these marvelous gifts, and wondered from whom they were taken. "Did Kyran—the king, tell you where he found these beautiful garments?"

Reyna's smile widened. "They have been here all along. Right under our noses."

"Do you know under what circumstance he came upon them? I do not remember Aswyn's concubines wearing such beautiful garments."

"I cannot say for sure, but they were hidden by one of the village women. Gwendolyn, I believe." Reyna went back to the trunk. " 'Tis full of gowns and jewels far more beautiful than any I have ever seen."

"Gwendolyn," Sayrid repeated, more confused than ever. A knock sounded on the door, and Sayrid knew it was Cyric before he stepped inside. 'Twas true, she thought. Her powers were growing stronger.

His smile comforted her. He was also richly dressed in a dark-blue tunic with bronze-colored cord on the cuffs and hem, matching his bronze-colored chausses. He wore a golden chain around his neck, but nothing too elaborate. By the half smile that still slanted across his handsome face, he appeared pleased. "Kyran sent me to escort you to the hall," he stated with a slight bow. He turned to Reyna. "You may leave us now," he said, his gaze never leaving Sayrid's.

The moment Reyna closed the door, Cyric grasped Sayrid's hands and gave them a firm squeeze. "I knew it," he said softly, excitement shining in his eyes. "I knew you had survived. I prayed each and every night for your safety, and now, thank the gods, I have you back, and we have our grandmother back, too. Come, Jena, we have a celebration to attend."

Calling upon every ounce of courage she had, Sayrid returned his smile. When he offered, she placed her hand on his arm and followed him out of the chamber. "It would please me if you called me Sayrid."

Although his smile slipped a little, she knew the moment she touched him that he loved her, and she felt loved. Yet he was still very much a stranger to her and she needed to get to know him better—to try and understand his reason for pretending to be nothing more than Kyran's friend. She took a calming breath and spoke her mind. "It grieves me that you've chosen to turn away from your obligation to rule our people and let our people believe that Kyran is their king."

She felt him hesitate a moment and knew that her words hurt him.

"I'm aware I've asked much of Kyran, but you must know I have not turned away from him or our people. There is much you don't know about him . . . us. There is still much danger. The woman who wounded him and tried to kill me has not been captured, though I have ordered every inch of this castle searched. On top of this, I'm trying my best to avoid a senseless war with her brother," he stated defensively. "Tonight we will tell the whole truth to those of our people who are closest to us, and I'm certain they will tell their friends, and, soon, very soon, we will tell everyone the truth."

Sayrid realized when she looked into his troubled eyes that

even though he'd met with Derwyn, her brother didn't know all the details. Cyric had no idea that in order for him to become king, Kyran would have to die. A sob caught in her throat, but she coughed softly to hide it. "Forgive me," she murmured, feeling his regret about the deception as if it were her own. "I have no right to accuse you of negligence when I have hidden in the forest these past years, accepting our people's charity."

"You had lost your memory, sister. How could you know your own importance? 'Tis the past that decides our future, Sayrid." Cyric patted her hand. "What matters is not how we lived these long years apart, but how we choose to spend the rest of our lives together, as brother and sister. You and Derwyn will no longer live in the forest. I have had spacious chambers prepared for you both." He stopped and smiled. "We shall be a family again."

"If you believe that, tell me why you would still marry Oddrum's sister? I will never be able to call her sister." Again she felt him tense, but he refused to look at her until she willed him to do so. "Knowing what you know, why would you make such a decision?"

"You are a powerful sorceress. Much more so than even our mother and grandmother, and I sense you will grow stronger yet, but there are some things you don't understand."

"Then explain them to me, brother," she pleaded. "Tell me why a king would marry a woman like Brynn?"

Cyric's reddish brows snapped tightly together. "Think you I want a woman like her? Nay. But I have no choice. There is no other way to convince Oddrum the tribes must make peace. It is best to keep our enemies close . . . very close. My marriage to Brynn will unite Wales and bring the tribes together as one."

Sayrid closed her eyes in frustration then met her brother's gaze. "Did our grandmother tell you to do this?"

"If you're asking if she agrees, then, aye, she does. However, the proposal has been part of the plan since the day Kyran battled Aswyn for Dragon's Head."

"Did she tell you about the prophecy?"

"I know I must unite the tribes—'tis why I have agreed to the marriage. I will make any sacrifice necessary to see that our people live in peace."

She wanted to respond—to tell him of an even greater sacrifice—the sacrifice of his friend's life, but they were nearly to the hall. She hesitated, drawing a concerned look from her brother. "A moment if you please."

"Certainly," he replied, his cautious smile reflecting his concern.

"Is it true? Kyran will leave for Oddrum's kingdom on the morrow?"

"Aye, at first light."

"Has he told you about me?" Sayrid asked cautiously.

"Aye. Many times. After Bynor and Morven found him in the forest, the day you cut a lock of his hair . . . he speaks of you constantly and has always stood firm that you are the woman who saved his life, and. . . ." He paused and gave her another one of his quick smiles. "And the one who tried to whack him with a broom."

She felt her heart lurch painfully.

Cyric's expression filled with compassion. "He also told me you are the woman he loves—the woman he is bound to, and when he returns he will ask my permission to marry you, although it is not required. You see, Sayrid, the binding ceremony is a marriage of sorts." He placed a chaste kiss on the back of her hand. "Do not fret. Among the many treasures kept for us, there is a gown for you and garments for Kyran that are fitting for a marriage ceremony." Smiling, he gently grasped her elbow and urged her on. "Come. I am most anxious to witness Kyran's expression when he sees you."

Kyran stood near the massive hearth with Morven and Bynor. Both Morven and Bynor wore oyster-colored tunics over peat-colored hose. Morven stood slightly behind the others, his hand resting on the hilt of a long, deadly curved dagger. The giant had his arms crossed over his massive chest, but turned and looked when she entered, his bushy brows nearly touching. On closer inspection of Morven, she noticed a barely visible hilt peeking out of each of his boots. Armed much more than the others, did he too expect some unforeseen danger to befall his young master?

"My eyesight is still a bit blurry from the aftereffects of the poison, but is that Rhonwyn I see standing with her parents?" Cyric asked as they finished the last few steps.

"Aye," she managed to say, pulling her hand from his. She would visit with her brother and her dearest friends later, after she'd calmed her jittery nerves—after she confronted Kyran. She'd tell him she knew about the proposal and plead with him to find another way to deliver it.

The moment her thoughts settled on Kyran, their eyes met, their thoughts mingled. She felt as if she couldn't move—as if they were alone in the great hall full of people—her people. Slowly he put down his goblet and left his men. She wanted to run to him, to throw herself into his arms and beg him to stay. But she instantly realized that it would be impossible. A strong sense of peace and security came over her—the feelings of the people around her—swirling together, washing softly over her, making her aware. Derwyn was right. The safety of her people must come first.

Blinking back tears, she accepted Kyran's hand, welcoming the sparks that shot up her arm—the tingling in the pit of her stomach. She smiled and sensed he knew she'd changed her mind about their relationship—that she would willingly accept him—would love him for eternity. By the mischievous sparkle in the depth of his eyes and the arrogant grin on his handsome face, she knew he wanted to skip the festivities and take her directly to his bed.

And she longed to let him do so.

"We cannot," she whispered, accepting a brush of his lips on her cheek. "However," she began, feeling the heat of a blush creep up her neck, "we can excuse ourselves before the evening is over."

His soft laughter brought even more warmth to her cheeks. She glanced at the colorful tapestries, depicting both Welsh heroes and powerful dragons, noticing a small flock of black ravens circling above their heads. She hesitated, drawing Kyran's attention. "The ravens." She nodded toward the tapestry. "They are not birds, but men—warriors under a spell of some sort sent to spy on us."

"Aye, I know. Morven killed one." Kyran covered her cold hand with his warm one. "I have alerted our men. They will be watching for them."

A young man played a happy tune on a small, hand-held harp as he strolled among many of the soldiers and their families. Kyran led Sayrid to the large fireplace where she accepted a goblet of mulled wine from one of the servants. She took a sip, trying to sort her thoughts—to think what she would say to him—what words she would use to speak of her new-found love. She closed her eyes and offered a swift prayer that her confession would not be unwanted.

Kyran lifted her hand. "Never," he said so softly only she could hear. "Never would I refuse you. 'Twould be easier to tear the heart from my chest."

Her eyes widened a moment before they filled with understanding. "You know what I'm thinking."

His grin was answer enough. "Not only can I hear most of your thoughts, my love, I see them in your eyes." He cupped her cheek. " 'Tis as it should be between life-mates."

" 'Tis happening so quickly, I—"

Kyran placed his finger gently on her lips. "I want you, Sayrid. I want you to agree to a marriage ceremony . . . soon . . . very soon, as the sun rises over Dragon's Head."

She started to tell him all the reasons they shouldn't marry so quickly when the floor moved and they both heard a very soft, very contented beastly yawn.

Sayrid felt the spark of excitement the moment the music ended. Both she and Kyran had stayed to share a dance, but now—now all she wanted was to be in his arms—feel him inside her. Whilst he spoke with Cyric and Bynor, she slipped away as planned and hurried up the steps, down the long corridor and into Kyran's chamber. Turning, she pressed her ear against the wood; when she heard his footsteps, she threw open the door and jumped into his waiting arms.

No words were spoken as he accepted her kisses, returning them with an ardor that matched her own. With her legs wrapped around his waist, he carried her over by the bed, took her arms from around his neck and placed her gently down on her feet. She gazed into his eyes, holding her breath as he lifted her amulet over her head and placed it on the bedside table.

She paid no attention as an orange-red glow spread through the room. All she saw was her beloved; all she felt were his fingers working to undo the laces of her gown. When he pushed the last of her garments off her shoulders, she shivered, but wasn't cold. His brows came together, but before she could tell him she shivered with anticipation, he left her, knelt by the fire and added two small logs. " 'Tis cold and damp at night without a fire."

She came to him while he knelt, and she brushed her fingers over his shoulders, feeling the heat spread through their bodies like the flames that spread over the logs. He turned, grasped her by the waist and kissed her belly, sending a jolt of desire straight to her woman's core. His hands left her waist to reach around and cup her buttocks, pulling her closer. He buried his face in the mound of red-gold curls at the junction of her legs, nipping and kissing until she thought she'd perish from his sensual touch.

Closing her eyes in carnal pleasure, she tipped her head back and moaned at the same time he spread her feminine folds, probing with his tongue, his other hand massaging the small of her back, using just enough pressure to keep her from stepping back. When at last, she felt as if she'd become a thousand tiny specks of light, his soft, contented sigh brought her back to reality. He whisked her up into his arms and carried her to the bed, dropping her on the fur-covered, goose-down mattress with a mischievous gleam twinkling in the smoky depths of his eyes.

She watched him with a lazy smile as he stripped, his shaft hard and fully engorged, ready to sheath himself inside her warmth. Before he could place his knee on the bed to climb in, she wrapped her fingers around his arousal, and, as he had pleasured her, so did she pleasure him. When she took the tip into her mouth, flicking it with her tongue, his fingers bit into her shoulders, and he gave a low, hungry growl. She would have pleasured him longer, but he shoved her back and covered her with his muscular body, trailing kisses down her throat, up her cheek to her mouth.

They kissed, tasting, tongues toying, and at the same time he spread her legs with his knee, entering her slowly when she would have taken him fully inside. Again, mischief sparkled in his eyes in contrast to his languid smile. When she raised her hips to take him deeper, he matched her movement, teasing her with only the tip, awakening another storm inside her.

Kyran gazed down at his beloved and smiled again, immeasurably pleased by her sensual response to each well-placed touch. With each subtle movement of her hips, her sweet torture drew him closer and closer to the brink, but he forced himself to hold back, to watch her climax. And she did, over and over. When he felt her pulsate against him, he could no longer hold back. He drove into her—his release so explosive, waves of pure pleasure coursed over him until he cared little if he were alive or dead—aware of only one thing.

He loved her more than life itself.

CHAPTER THIRTEEN

Sayrid knew the moment Kyran had left her bed. Though she didn't hear the messenger speak, she knew now that one had come; he had knocked softly upon the door and had given Kyran a small piece of parchment. Pretending to be asleep, she watched though half-closed eyes as he added another log to the dwindling fire, standing and staring at it for a long time. He appeared troubled, but she knew he would face the challenge ahead at any cost—that his sense of duty would let him do nothing less.

She tossed the covers aside and stood, wrapping the fur around her body. She lifted the parchment and read, feeling a stab of fear settle in her stomach. "They're coming," she whispered.

Kyran turned; their gazes locked. "I did not mean to wake you." He came and stood before her, cupping her cheek, caressing it with the pad of his thumb. " 'Tis still hours from dawn. You should sleep. I would have you well rested for our wedding."

"Our wedding?"

"Aye. If you'll have me, I will marry you at sunrise."

She reached up and kissed him. "I am eager to become your wife." She smiled then grew serious, more frightened than she thought she'd be. "But what if they attack?"

"Oddrum's no fool . . . impatient, perhaps. He knows the folly of laying siege on a castle of this size. Rock doesn't burn. There is no other entrance than through the gates in the outer bailey . . . is there, Sayrid?"

She swallowed. "Only one, my lord, and 'tis well hidden. I've used it on occasion to sneak into the castle. And since I'm confessing, there's another inside the castle that leads out to the sea."

"Indeed," Kyran replied, frowning. "You will show me—"

"You were explaining why Oddrum won't attack, and I'd really like to hear what you have to say." Another firm look from her beloved caused her insides to tighten even more.

"He won't attack because his men will be picked off like ducks on a pond by our archers."

Sayrid's eyes brightened. "Then let him. Let him lay siege. Whilst he starves, we will be together, safe from harm." She moved the furs aside. "Come, and let me warm you."

His smile told her he would if he could, but he merely kissed the tip of her nose, and pulled the furs up over her shoulders. He caught the ends together and pulled her close to receive his kiss, ignoring a barely audible, intolerant growl.

Frowning, she watched intently as the ghostly image of the dragon began to appear.

"What are you looking at?" Kyran asked.

"Do you not see him?"

"Nay, but I sense his presence."

She cast a quick glance at the corner of the chamber where the old dragon rested, his head resting on his front talons, impatiently tapping the tip of his arrowhead tail on the stone floor. "Aye, he is here, watching," she said, wondering why he wouldn't show himself in Kyran's company.

Kyran glanced around the room and smiled. "Shrewd he is, to let you see him, and I his Protector cannot." He felt the floor shake ever so slightly and suspected the dragon, if he looked anything like the tattoo on his chest, had stamped a hind foot, or perhaps his long, heavy tail. Kyran slipped his hand under

Sayrid's thick hair, curling his fingers around her neck to draw her to him. He kissed her again—a slow, passionate kiss. She leaned into him, ignoring the dragon's impatient sigh.

"Though I would prefer you stay, you are to follow the great one," she whispered once they parted.

"Aye, I sensed as much. I thought I felt his presence after the messenger left, and now I know I did." Kyran brushed a strand of her hair behind her ear. "You're beautiful with your hair all tangled. I asked that a hot bath be prepared that we could share, but plans have changed. Enjoy it, and I will return to you as soon as I can."

Out in the corridor, Kyran turned, hoping for a glimpse of the beast, but saw only the iridescent rock. Though he couldn't see the old dragon, he felt his spirit, heard a raspy whisper in the back of his mind. As directed, he followed the great one's directions. He went to the end of the corridor, pausing when there was nothing before him except solid rock. Slowly, magically, as if he'd willed it to open, a portion of the stone slid aside. Without flint or steel, a flame jumped to life on a stubby candle, revealing precipitous stone steps spiraling downward into a dark, seemingly endless abyss.

"You're certain I'm to do this?" Kyran muttered, none too pleased with the steep angle and lack of any type of balustrade. "A rope would've been appreciated."

A warm puff of air caused the small flame to cavort wildly followed by a low, forewarning growl.

"Very well," Kyran muttered, slightly annoyed that the beast refused to speak openly to him. He felt the stone vibrate with each step and knew the dragon had begun his descent. Through two more hidden passageways they went, until finally the last portal opened upon a massive chamber deep within the ancient castle.

It appeared to be a giant maw carved out of solid rock—filled with an orange-red glow yet too dark to see the ceiling or the walls. Before them glowed a large, smooth, oval almandine that had been embedded in the stone, surrounded by more symbols and runes. Runes and ancient symbols had been carved into every wall. Treasure of unspeakable value lay in piles around the chamber, twinkling with precious gems and stones. As he approached the almandine, the light emanating from it began to grow stronger, yet he felt compelled to get closer. As he got nearer, he was forced to shield his eyes.

Nearly blinded by the jewel's dazzling light, he leaned on the wide stone altar, drawing back when it felt as if he'd touched a hot coal. "You brought me here," Kyran began, slightly irritated. "Now what? What is it you want from me?"

The floor beneath his feet trembled, and the light grew even stronger, more painful. Slowly the transparent image of a large, iridescent bluish-green dragon appeared before him, growing in density until Kyran couldn't tell if it were real or still only a spirit. The dragon was huge, standing on all fours, his bat-shaped wings tucked closely to his scaly sides. Two ivory horns erupted from his skull at the top of a wide forehead and two smaller horns appeared above the dragon's flared nostrils.

Ivory spikes, shaped much like the iron spikes on the castle, protruded from the top of his broad head, trailed down the crest of his neck and along his spine, shrinking in size till they ended at the tip of his arrow-headed tail. The scales on his back were a brilliant iridescent blue, changing to a green on his sides to a greenish yellow on the inside of his muscular legs and underbelly.

The dragon narrowed his wise, yellow eyes and gave a beastly snort. Slowly, he squatted on his haunches. The dragon did not speak, but Kyran heard his thoughts: *Oddrum is on his way with ten thousand men, many of them heartless mercenaries.*

Kyran nodded, even though his heart sank with the news of so many. "Aye, so I've been told. Greed-filled man that he is, he refused Cyric's proposal, preferring war."

The dragon's image let loose an angry, knowledgeable growl. *There is naught to be done except to fight.*

"And, so I shall—to the last man if needs be."

As I knew you would. The dragon shook his head as if reluctant to continue. *Though I loathe war, I will see to the arming of your men.* He rose and then thudded toward the altar, lifted a scaled and calloused talon and, with a chipped, pointed nail, traced the runes around the almandine stone. *This cave—this chamber is a sacred place that holds the essence of my being. This castle was constructed to protect the people, yet more blood will spill. 'Tis not what I—what 'we' wished for, so many years ago. Should Dragon's Head fall, so will my spirit, never to rise again.* The beast turned and heaved a loud, long sigh, nearly blowing Kyran over with his warm breath. *You know what I ask of you?*

Kyran nodded. "Aye, great one. I recognize and accept my destiny willingly. On the morrow, I will defeat Oddrum in your honor."

The dragon gave a soft, appreciative growl. *We are well pleased with you, Kyran the Protector. The Ancient Ones and I will be watching.*

"I will not fail, I swear it." He sensed that their conversation was done and would have left, but the dragon's last words stopped him.

Remember that this is a sacred place where time stands still and the dead live again. Honor it as such and tell no one.

Sayrid stared at her reflection in the smooth oval disk Gwendolyn held while Rhonwyn looked on. The creamy-white gown they had dressed her in was gathered under her breasts with a golden sash, the long skirt fell in soft folds to the top of her matching slippers. Even though Kyran had told her earlier that the battle would begin tomorrow, she felt anxious and troubled.

"There is a rumor going around," Gwendolyn said as she pinned the matching mantle to Sayrid's shoulders with two bronze-and-topaz brooches, "that this gown was made by the Ancient Ones and worn at the very first marriage ceremony of the Protectors long ago, before the death of the dragons."

Sayrid smiled to hide her apprehension, sensing that they weren't alone in the room—that there were bright, yellow eyes watching her every move. Even the walls appeared to have changed from stone-gray to a luminous bluish-green; if she closed her eyes, she felt certain she could hear the dragon's steady breathing. But what soothed her anxiety the most was the love she felt—the dragon's love—a love so pure, she grew confident he wouldn't let anything bad happen to her beloved. The heaviness suddenly lifted from her heart.

"The embroidery is more beautiful than any I have seen." Rhonwyn's voice drew Sayrid's attention away from the walls. Her friend lifted her wrist and glanced at the intricately stitched golden squares around the cuff. "The same design adorns the neck and hem. In each square, a tiny topaz has been sewn, but so well done, I cannot see the stitches."

"And what shall we do with your hair?" Gwendolyn dragged a brush through the coppery curls. "There is a golden circlet for your brow. Perhaps we should braid it with ribbons."

"I would have it left down," Sayrid said, her voice barely over a whisper. She took a calming breath ready to argue—ready to reveal that Kyran wanted it that way.

"Aye, I think it would look wonderful that way, don't you, Rhonwyn?" Gwendolyn placed the golden circlet on Sayrid's head and smiled.

"Aye, Mother. It will surely be glorious in the sunrise." Rhonwyn's smile grew even brighter. "I probably shouldn't tell you this," she teased, "but the king—I mean, Kyran the Protector, is wearing a tunic that matches your gown, down to the embroidery and the jewels." Rhonwyn heaved a dreamy sigh. "Except for Cyric, he is the most handsome man in all of Dragon's Head . . . mayhap even all of Wales."

Gwendolyn reached into her pocket and took out a tiny carved dragon. "Dafydd made this for me for our marriage, and it would please me if you borrowed it today for yours."

"And," Rhonwyn added, pinning a small sprig of pine on Sayrid's left shoulder. "This will symbolize everlasting love, and the coin I placed in your slipper will ensure wealth and prosperity."

"And we must not forget the most important piece to finish your attire." Gwendolyn held out a small, golden purse that she attached to the bejeweled girdle around Sayrid's waist. " 'Tis filled with rosemary, marigolds and herbs for fertility and fidelity."

The older woman motioned for Sayrid to bend her head whilst she slipped the amulet over her head. "Forged as one, separated at the binding ceremony, and now, to finally be joined in love."

Sayrid's mouth fell open. "How did you know that?"

Gwendolyn's smile filled with warmth, but in her eyes lingered a flicker of sadness. "Because Dafydd and I were there."

A crisp autumn breeze blew in from the Irish Sea, spreading its pungent scent over the entire village. Sayrid took a deep, calming breath, watching the sun appear as a fiery orange ball far out on the horizon, spreading a sparkling orange light over the water. As a veil of golden light washed over her and her beloved, Cyric spoke the ancient words. "As it was at the beginning of time, and shall be till the end of time, we, the people—the sacred tribe of Dragon's Head, bear witness to this man and this woman and the joining of their lives."

Slowly, sunlight climbed the rocky face of the massive castle. It seemed to come alive, its cracks and crevasses disappearing to reveal a luminous emerald glow. To all who attended the ceremony, the walls appeared to change into the scales of the ancient dragon of centuries ago. In the bailey, under a canopy of marigold and wildflower garlands, Cyric tied the ceremonial knot in the soft hemp rope around Kyran and Sayrid's wrists. After he kissed her cheek, he grinned and pounded Kyran's back, his congratulatory words drowned out by the cheers of all their guests.

Sayrid smiled and accepted a small bouquet of wildflowers from Rhonwyn and other women from the village. By the time they'd made it over to where many tables had been laid with succulent delights, she had so many beautiful flowers, Kyran carried them for her.

"Shall I take them for you?" Rhonwyn asked Kyran, laughing as two more little girls raced up with more flowers. At first they looked at Sayrid, but, upon seeing Kyran with his arms full, they giggled. He bent so they could reach, and they placed the flowers on the top of his bundle. Rhonwyn laughed. "Here, give them to me."

Kyran gladly deposited the flowers in Rhonwyn's waiting arms. " 'Tis appreciated," he replied before he turned to his new wife. Her heart swelled with pride when he lifted her left hand, his thumb grazing the plain golden ring that matched the one on his finger.

"I have heard it said that, according to tradition, the third finger of the left hand is directly connected to the heart."

Sayrid smiled, remembering how not very long ago he infuriated her with his endless knowledge of so many topics. "You never cease to amaze me, my lord."

He kissed the back of her hand. "Nor you me, my lady. Come.

Our guests will devour everything on the table, and though you are a feast for mine eyes and wine for mine thirst, my belly still growls with hunger."

"And a poet, too." Again she laughed when she really didn't feel like laughing, accepting his offered arm and following him to their places at the head of the table. Though not like the feast she had attended days ago, platters of bread, roasted venison and boiled carrots were placed on the long trestle tables. Though it seemed as if everyone who had come to witness the marriage appeared to be having a good time, she felt certain that there was less laughter and more somber expressions, for everyone there knew that on the morrow their loved ones would face Oddrum's enormous army on the battlefield.

Sayrid had no appetite, and felt thankful when the meal finally ended. Perhaps now, she and her beloved could slip away and share a few more intimate moments alone.

"To Lady Sayrid," Bynor shouted over the clamor of the many guests. "Be she forest nymph or cunning sorceress, we may never know, but know this, my friends: she was, till now, the best kept secret of Dragon's Head."

Cups were raised and clanked together as toasts after toasts were recited. Lusty shouts of marriage and marriage beds drew soft gasps from many of the village women, and boisterous guffaws from many of Kyran's warriors.

After the tables were cleared, Sayrid frowned with curiosity when Kyran motioned to Bynor, who rose from the table and left. A few moments later he returned, leading a pure white mare, as beautiful as any she'd ever seen, with a long wavy mane. The mare's flowing tail nearly touched the grass with each prancing step.

"Do you like her?" Kyran asked, accepting a hug and a kiss.

"Aye, she's the most beautiful marriage gift I've ever seen."

"I'm pleased that you like her, and there's more."

Before Sayrid recovered from her surprise at receiving the mare, two young boys—the same two she remembered who had tended Kyran when he'd been wounded, carried over an intricately tooled leather saddle and matching bridle. Sayrid clasped her hands together in delight, then promptly turned and kissed her husband several more times, so many times in fact that the crowd began to applaud, and more lusty remarks were shouted over the happy laughter.

Sayrid felt a warm blush on her cheeks when she rose, stopping Kyran from standing with a firm hand on his shoulder. " 'Tis my turn to present you with a marriage gift."

As if on cue, two of Gwendolyn's youngest boys struggled with a silver breastplate upon which Dafydd had carved a dazzling likeness of a dragon. To her amazement, Dafydd had even managed to paint it to match the dragon residing within the castle walls. 'Twas so heavy, the boys nearly dropped it before Kyran caught an edge and helped them lift it to the table. Giggling, they raced back to their parents, to peek from behind their mother's skirt. Kyran stood, picked up the magnificent armor and held it high for all to see. Another cheer resounded around the bailey.

Much to Sayrid's amazement, Derwyn approached, and Sayrid wondered if the old woman would sense the magic in the armor and scold her for trying to save her beloved. When Derwyn didn't seem to notice, Sayrid relaxed. Her grandmother looked much younger wearing a sky-blue gown, lacy cap and matching shawl. She leaned heavily upon her favorite crooked walking stick, and carried a long, deerskin-wrapped bundle to the table and placed it before Kyran. "A special gift for my new grandson," she said, smiling. " 'Tis something to help you see what others cannot."

Kyran untied the leather straps on the pouch and removed what appeared to be a hollowed-out length of wood with some type of mirrored glass on both ends.

Derwyn pointed a knobby finger to the smaller end. " 'Tis a magical looking glass. Put that up tae your eye and tell me what you see?"

Kyran did as she asked, drawing back with a startled expression after his first try, only to do it again. He turned the cylinder toward the distant trees, blanching a moment before a smile spread across his face. "Here." He handed it to Sayrid. "Aim it at the trees."

She did and, like her husband, gasped when they appeared to jump out at her. As she scanned the forest, she could make out birds' nests in the trees that were too far away to see with the naked eye.

"Thank you, grandmother," Sayrid managed to say—the first words she'd spoken to the elderly sorceress since the day Derwyn revealed the prophecy.

Sayrid and Kyran had just tapped their goblets together after Bynor had given another toast, when a warning signal erupted from the forest. An answering blast came from the drum tower of Dragon's Head, the horn-trumpet cry resounding ominously over the valley. In the next instant, the bailey became a blur of men, ushering their women to safety inside the castle, as a flock of ravens flew overhead. Several men grabbed their bows and, taking aim, shot arrows at two of them—their bird-like bodies turned into men the moment they hit the ground, causing more panic.

Warriors scrambled to the battlement, grabbing their weapons as they took their places next to those who already stood guard. The huge gate was wrenched open, and more of Kyran's men, with help from the village men, rushed out to bring in the stock, the villagers' food supplies and anything else they could carry. As the people hurried to get inside, Kyran's soldiers hurried to arm themselves and get outside, lining up in tight formation to protect the stragglers.

"What is it?" Sayrid asked. Her heart pounded against her breast as she followed her brother, Kyran and Bynor to the battlements. She searched the forest for the threat, cursing herself that she'd been so involved with her own happiness, she'd failed to sense the approaching enemy.

"There," Cyric stated, pointing to a rise where the trees grew thin. "By the gods, 'tis Oddrum on that black horse, is it not?"

"Aye," Kyran answered, lifting the magical looking glass for a better look. He heaved an annoyed sigh and passed the glass to Bynor. "What say you?"

"According to our spies he has massed eight, maybe ten thousand men. I only see about a thousand." Bynor passed the glass to Cyric who raised it to his eye.

"How many days before the whole of them arrive?" Cyric asked. He handed the magical looking glass back to Kyran.

"Three, mayhap four at the most."

Sayrid's breath caught in her throat when Bynor agreed with her husband.

"I must go," Kyran told Sayrid, grasping her shoulders before he kissed her. "Cyric will see you safely inside."

She wanted to stop him, to plead with him to come inside the safety of the castle, but she knew he'd refuse. Silently, Sayrid followed Cyric down the steps to the bailey. Rhonwyn stood, white-faced, clutching her hands tightly together, apparently unsure of where to go and what to do. "Go to her," Sayrid encouraged. "I'll be all right."

She watched Cyric take Rhonwyn into his arms, offering her his strength and comfort. The urge to cry felt as if it would be more than she could bear. Mortified, Sayrid spun, nearly bumping into the giant Morven, clad in his usual Viking attire. She dared not look up, wishing to keep her dignity intact. She would have excused herself and stepped around him, but he took a step, blocking her path.

"Fear me not," he said tightly. "As I swore an oath to him"—he motioned with a swift nod to where Kyran stood talking with several of his captains—"so shall I swear an oath to you. As long as I live, I will protect you."

Sayrid looked up and met his steady gaze, seeing for the first time a flicker of compassion in their crystalline depths. Here stood a man she could confide in. Here was the man who could help her save Kyran. She went to speak, pausing to nervously clear her throat. " 'Tis not I who am in danger."

She took a breath to ease the tightness in her throat, finding it difficult to continue. She licked her suddenly dry lips. "Derwyn had a vision. Oddrum will attack, and, whilst fighting to protect us, Kyran will die."

Morven frowned so fiercely his bushy, reddish-gray brows met in the middle. "By the gods," he growled, placing a heavy hand on her shoulder. "By the gods, I will do everything within my power to prevent it."

"I—I know you will," Sayrid managed to say after she blinked back the sting of tears. "And so shall I."

"Kyran, a word if you please," Cyric said, finding his friend on the wall-walk by the gatehouse inspecting the barrels of water they would need should Oddrum try to burn the wooden gate down.

"The look on your face bodes ill. Out with it," Kyran demanded, checking a box filled with arrows.

"I noticed you didn't wear your amulet during the marriage ceremony." Cyric met his friend's firm gaze, unwilling to be put off. "Did you simply forget to wear it?"

Kyran turned back to his inspection. "Nay, I did not. Brynn pretended to be a villager—a serving maid, and none of us were any wiser. I suspect she may have taken it before she left."

Cyric heaved a disgruntled sigh. "I feared as much." He waited until Kyran finished. Then they both leaned their forearms on the railing and stared out over the cottages and recently harvested fields below. "You defeated Arcas without it. I suppose you'll not need it to defeat Oddrum."

"In due time, we shall know."

Cyric watched Kyran leave the wall-walk, wishing he could do something to help. Kyran was a strong and formidable warrior. Though he had great faith in his friend's ability, a little ember of fear flickered in the back of his mind—fear that, in the wrong hands, the amulet could reveal secrets best left unknown.

Oddrum inwardly scoffed. Whilst his army oiled their swords preparing to do battle, his sister had brought the means by which he could easily win the war. A flock of warrior ravens.

Gone was the innocent child filled with hopes and dreams. The woman who sat in his tent and stared at him now did so with a determined gleam in her defiant dark eyes. Several wild strands of black hair had come loose from his sister's braid to frame her creamy features.

Oddrum took a long drink before he spoke. "And what did they see whilst they soared above Dragon's Head?"

"Many things, but most importantly they saw a marriage," Brynn answered.

Oddrum threw back his head and gave a loud bark of laughter. "A marriage?" When he stopped laughing, he sighed as if bored. "So what?"

" 'Twas not an ordinary marriage," Brynn stated firmly. "A predestined marriage of two powerful people, bound together from childhood."

"Curse them," Oddrum snarled. "Think you I am afraid? Nay. I am not. Life-mates are mortal and die like mortals. I'll not stand idly by and let a young dog make a name for himself

232

at my expense. Never. He'll soon learn that he has taken hold of too big a bone."

Brynn wanted to volunteer her help—to share what she felt were important battle strategies, but his arrogant smirk crushed her good intentions.

"We've nothing to fear. I've squashed bigger bugs with my thumb." Oddrum stood, tossed the last of his wine down his throat and stormed from the tent, calling over his shoulder, "Let him come. I'll geld the self-righteous buck and send him back whence he came."

Brynn looked at Maldwyn, who sat quietly on a padded stool. He waited for a few moments before he stood, peered out the tent flap, and then sat in Oddrum's vacated comfortable chair.

Brynn met his gaze. "They know of the raven-warriors. Two did not return from patrol."

Maldwyn nodded. " 'Tis of no consequence. I have other means by which to aid your brother."

Brynn came to his side, kneeling as she put her hand on Maldwyn's knee. "Why aid him at all? If he's killed, his kingdom will be mine . . . ours."

Maldwyn cupped her cheek and smiled. How easy this would be, to bend her to his will. "Are you serious?" he asked, pretending to be surprised.

"Aye, I am. I'm sick of Oddrum's pompous ranting. He's arrogant and a fool to think Dragon's Head will fall so easily." She stood, and Maldwyn saw the truth of her words glittering in her eyes. "After the battle starts, if he were to take an arrow in the heart, no one would know from whose bow it came."

"And if he's dead when he hits the ground, there would be no need to remove it—no one would discover it to be a broadhead." Maldwyn nodded again, pleased with her plan, but unwilling to show it. "We must beware, little one. These thin walls have ears and 'tis most dangerous to plot the death of a king."

Maldwyn slipped his hand in his pouch and pulled out Kyran's amulet. The moment he opened his fingers, the stone began to glow. He smiled, closing his eyes and reliving the vision.

"What do you see?" Brynn asked anxiously. "Tell me, what do you see?"

"Patience, my dear, patience." He heaved a contented sigh. After a few more moments, his fingers slowly curled over the medallion.

"I see a battle, but 'tis not of the past, but the future. I see your brother fall—"

"Aye, I knew it," Brynn cried excitedly.

Maldwyn held up his hand to quiet her, leaning slightly forward to get her full attention. "I see you as queen of Dragon's Head, married to Cyric."

Brynn frowned. "Marriage . . . to Cyric." A slow smile curved the corners of her mouth. "A mouse married to a cat."

Maldwyn chuckled at her jest. "Aye, but there's more. I see a death. I see a death that is unexpected and ultimately will be the ruin of Dragon's Head."

"Ruined?" Brynn asked. "I do not want it ruined."

"Hush, my little witch. 'Twill do no good to vex yourself. I care little if the spirit of the dragon dies. Good riddance. The castle is filled with treasure embedded in a mountain." Maldwyn slipped the amulet back into the deep pouch hidden in his robe. "Nay, the legend may perish, but the castle will remain forever, and you, my dear, will rule her and the people as Cyric's queen."

Sayrid shivered. She wasn't prepared for the drop in temperature as the sun disappeared on the horizon. She wrapped a fur more tightly around her body, stepping out upon the balcony, aware that Kyran had finished tending the fire and followed her out.

"Look over yonder. What is that?" Sayrid asked, pointing to the east where an eerie glow rose up from the clearing and the surrounding forest. "I've had no visions of such, yet Derwyn warned me that Maldwyn is a very powerful wizard and could block my powers."

Kyran came up behind her, wrapping her in his arms. She turned slightly and blinked up at him. "Do you think he conjured up this display in order to frighten us?"

" 'Tis definitely designed to frighten us, but 'tis no wizard's magic, just simply a battle strategy." He placed a kiss on her temple when she turned back to the disturbing sight. "Those are campfires. 'Tis known, the more you see, the more men there are to tend them. I have used the same strategy to intimidate my enemies."

She shivered again. "It seems to work," she murmured, frowning. "It appears as if the entire forest is ablaze."

Had she not been so intent on the fires, she would have noticed the idea she'd just delivered had caused his dark brows to snap together. When she turned, her eyes widened at the look on his face.

"What is it?" Sayrid asked, annoyed that he'd too quickly learned how to block her from reading his thoughts. She accepted his kiss, momentarily closing her eyes and forgetting their worries.

"I needs speak with Bynor."

"Wait," she cried, taking a calming breath. "Your amulet . . . you're not wearing it."

Kyran touched his chest where the amulet would have been. "Aye," he grinned, but she sensed it was only for her benefit. "After all the trouble you went through to return it, I seem to have lost it." He kissed her again, then left her standing alone on the balcony wearing a very worried frown.

Morning dawned, damp and cold with thick fog hugging the ground, stretching into the forest and out to the sea behind the old castle. Bynor had assembled their army of five thousand men in the valley on the recently harvested fields, and, with his shouted commands, told them of their strategy.

As the old dragon had promised, each man, except Morven, wore an oyster-colored surcoat, adorned with the image of a bluish-green dragon—another mysterious gift that suddenly appeared in the great hall of Dragon's Head. The men were armed with spears, swords and shields of a silver-like metal unknown to Kyran. He watched Sayrid ride her white palfrey out of the small postern gate, following the rocky path to the rise south of the Dragon's Head, where the wall fell over the edge of the cliff, but the rocks and grass formed a platform several hundred feet above the valley from which to observe.

" 'Tis cold for autumn," she murmured, pulling her blue mantle more closely around her body.

" 'Twill warm once the sun is high." Kyran forced a smile, letting his appreciative gaze slowly wash over his new wife. Even though her forehead was marred with a worried frown, she was a true beauty, he thought, both inside and out. Though he preferred it down, her hair had been tied back in a loose braid, held with a bronze clip. The golden circlet she'd worn to their wedding held the curly wisps that had escaped away from her smooth features.

He had tried to soothe her worries when they first awoke just before dawn. Even when she pretended to understand his strategies, he sensed she still wanted to find another way to convince Oddrum that Cyric's plan, as distasteful as it was, would prevent the death of thousands.

"The women have gathered many stacks of cloths for

bandages, extra furs, and made extra pallets for the wounded." She took a breath, turning slightly in the saddle to face him. "Derwyn and I have prepared potions for fever and pain. After Morven filled the larder, I asked him to go to the river where the healing mud is found and gather as much as he could carry." She turned back to look out over the army below. "We will be ready . . . as ready as your army."

"You asked Morven, and he obeyed?" Kyran asked, trying to tease her out of her gloomy mood.

"Aye. Though I didn't expect it, he swore his allegiance to me."

Kyran tried hard not to laugh, covering his mirth with a cough. "I see. How gallant of him."

"Has there been any word from the messenger you sent to Oddrum last night?" She turned, her troubled gaze fusing with his, her chin lifting in preparation for bad news. "Do not lie to me. I believe I already know the truth."

Kyran took a long deep breath. "The messenger's body was found this morning on the path leading into the forest. He'd been drawn and quartered and left as a feast for wild boars."

"By the gods," Sayrid whispered, covering her mouth in dismay. "I pray his death will be avenged this day."

"I will see to it personally and take his family King Oddrum's head." Though he thought it an honorable gesture, her repulsed shiver caused him to rethink his decision. "Perhaps I should only take them Oddrum's crown."

"Th-that would suffice, I'm certain." She took a long deep breath of crisp air and let it out slowly. "How many now?"

"I can't be sure—perhaps five or six thousand."

She wanted to comment, to ask him again to reconsider, but Bynor approached on horseback. "The men are ready and eager, my lord." Clad much like Kyran, Bynor pressed his closed fist to his heart in salute to Kyran before he bowed his head to Sayrid. "My lady."

"Captain," she acknowledged with another strained smile.

"I await your orders," Bynor said stiffly.

Kyran returned the greeting. "We wait until they come to us, agreed?"

"Aye, it will be as we discussed last night, down to each detail."

"May I know your battle plans?" Sayrid asked.

Bynor coughed uneasily.

Kyran nudged his stallion a little closer and pointed to the grassy rise. "In addition to our men in formation below us in the valley, behind that rise, just barely out of sight, are a thousand mounted warriors waiting, as we are, for the right time to attack. Over there, hidden in the trees on our side of the forest are more, armed with spears. Now, look high in the trees."

"Are those archers?" she asked.

"Aye. You can barely see them."

"What are they wearing?" She turned with a puzzled frown.

Kyran grinned at his wife. "I got the idea from a garment I remembered you wore—one that looked like vines and leaves. If it worked for you, fooling Aswyn all those years, it's certain to work for me and fool Oddrum as well."

"If you look closely, my lady," Bynor began, his excitement to begin the battle dancing in his blue eyes. "The men's shields are highly polished. If we were to choose a battlefield, we would have chosen one that put the sun to our backs. As you can see, that option is not available to us by the lay of the land. Oddrum has noticed this as well, but he's in for a surprise. As soon as the sun rises, our men will use their shields to catch the light and blind his army."

Bynor puffed out his chest. "Brilliant, is it not?"

Sayrid forced a smile. "Aye."

Before she could ask more questions and learn things Kyran

didn't want her to learn, he leaned slightly over and took her hand, squeezing her fingers. " 'Twill be morning soon. You must go back to the castle and keep the women calm if Oddrum chooses to attack."

"Why wait until all his men have arrived? Are not our chances for victory better if we attack a smaller army?"

"Aye, in many ways that's true, but then our warriors would be worn down from fighting, and Oddrum would have fresh warriors arriving before ours could regroup." He leaned over and kissed her. "Now go."

Kyran watched her leave before he turned back to Bynor. "You told the men that should they see a raven or black bird of any size to strike it dead without question, even if it means they compromise their position?"

Bynor nodded. "Aye. Though they fear the old wizard's wrath, they will obey."

"And Morven?" Kyran shifted his weight and adjusted his reins.

"Morven has hidden himself in Derwyn's old cave where he has a hot fire, many torches and a barrel of pitch. If their archers take to the trees, they'll soon regret it."

"Then we're ready," Kyran stated flatly. He stopped Bynor from leaving. "There is one more thing I would have you do for me."

Bynor's features grew more serious. "Anything, my friend."

"Be certain, for once it is done, there is no turning back."

CHAPTER FOURTEEN

Sayrid paced before the hearth in the great hall—Derwyn's prediction a constant in her thoughts. Was this morning the last time she would gaze at her beloved? Was his brief, gentle squeeze on her fingers the last time she'd experience his touch?

She pressed her fingertips to her temples, willing away her tears as a thousand questions flittered like dragonflies in her head. Derwyn's prediction couldn't be right. She herself had admitted she was old and her powers growing weak. And what of Kyran's amulet? Did not Derwyn tell her many times to wear it for protection? Surely if hers protected her from Aswyn, Kyran's would have protected him from Oddrum.

Her fingers brushed against her own amulet, and instantly she saw an old man with a long white beard. Although she'd never seen him before, she knew with certainty 'twas Maldwyn, the wizard Derwyn had told her about. In his palm rested Kyran's amulet.

Alarmed, Sayrid ran up the stairs to the chamber she shared with Kyran. Once inside, she leaned back against the door, drawing in a ragged breath, trying to gather her thoughts—to think of a way to leave Dragon's Head.

He asked you to stay . . . to tend the wounded when they come, yet here you are, planning your escape.

Sayrid jumped then turned toward the dragon's deep, gravelly voice. "He asks the impossible," she snapped, her emotions too raw to be civil.

His destiny was decided for him a long time ago when he was born with my mark on his shoulder. He is the Protector, not only of you and our people, but of Dragon's Head. He has passed the mark on to another in preparation for his death.

"Then tell me, great one, why he must die?"

Warriors die in war.

She pushed away from the door, moving to stand before the ghostly image of the dragon. "Tell me why, with all your power and all your magic, why this war has to happen?"

The dragon heaved a long, tired sigh, rustling Sayrid's skirts and causing wisps of hair to swirl around her face. *I cannot control evil men and the deeds they hide in their evil hearts.*

Sayrid met the dragon's gaze. "I have loved you, protected you, but what have you done for me?"

She blanched when he tossed his massive horned head back and gave an angry roar. *You dare question me? I am Dragon's Head. Without me this*—he motioned with a wide sweep of his sharply clawed talons, curling his long scaly fingers into a beastly fist—*none of this would exist.* He took a lumbering step closer, and lightly poked one long talon on her chest. *You and all who call themselves "the people" would not exist. 'Tis what I sacrificed—to protect "my" people. And you, little one, who for many years had no memory of family, who lay in a cold chamber with nothing but her fear to cling to. 'Twas I who kept you warm—rocked you to sleep, guided you to the secret passageways in mine castle and showed you the means to escape.*

He growled, low in his throat, giving her a disapproving look. *'Twas I who gave you Kyran—'twas I—part of me in your amulet—who kept you safe till he came for you.* He turned and lumbered back toward the corner of the room, part of him disappearing into the wall before he glanced over his scaly shoulder. *Never again ask what I've done for you.*

"Maldwyn has Kyran's amulet," she blurted out, her fear for

her beloved fueling her courage. "I must get it back before it's too late."

The dragon's yellow eyes narrowed as his chest rumbled with another low growl. *It may already be too late.*

He vanished before she could question him further. Feeling even more wretched, she sank to her knees, buried her face in her hands and wept.

Sayrid wasn't sure how long she lay on the cold stone floor, only aware that she must have cried herself to sleep. Slowly she opened her eyes, blinking to clear them when she saw her vine-like overgown under the bed. She reached under and pulled it out before she got to her feet. Faint traces of smoke hung in the air. As the fog cleared from her head, she went to the balcony and looked out, startled to see the sun high, but relieved that the smoke appeared to be coming from cook fires started by Kyran's men.

She hurried to dress and quickly braided her hair, securing it back with her leather circlet. Tucking a dagger in her leather girdle, she went to the trunk by the side of the bed and dug down to where she'd hidden the small pouch containing the poisonous plants she'd collected the day Brynn poisoned Cyric. She slipped the pouch into the deep pocket of her russet gown and then left using the hidden passageway.

Moments later, just outside the stone portal, she closed her eyes, concentrating on the giant Viking's whereabouts, surprised to see a vision of him sitting in Derwyn's small cave. A rabbit carcass sat on a chipped plate, and Morven sat on Derwyn's rickety stool eating a loaf of bread and drinking from a jug of ale.

Careful to keep hidden, she slipped from tree to tree, once again thankful for her ability to blend in with the foliage. When she stood before Derwyn's door, she hesitated a moment before she knocked. What if Morven wasn't in the mood for visitors? She frowned, remembering his pledge of loyalty, and knocked before she lost her nerve.

Morven threw open the door, stooping to look out, grumbling like a hibernating bear that had been rousted from his den.

"How did you find me?" Morven asked. He stepped out, towering over her with the half-eaten bread clutched in his fist.

Sayrid took a calming breath. "Did not you, yourself, say I'm a witch?" She inwardly laughed at the spark of fear she thought she saw in the depths of the big man's eyes. "Then surely you'd know how I knew. I need your help or I'll. . . ." What? She wondered. What could she possibly do that would convince him to disobey his orders and leave this cottage to follow her? "I'll be forced to use some of my magic on you."

She had doubted Morven could appear more frightening, but the look he gave her and the stance he assumed banished that thought.

A slight movement caught her attention. One of Oddrum's ravens landed silently on the ground and immediately became a fully armed warrior. He drew his sword and rushed Morven with a frightening battle cry.

Reflex caused Sayrid to hold out her hand to ward him off— feeling the power build within it. "Nay," she said, horrified at the same time a bolt of pure-white light shot from her palm, startling her as well as Morven.

They both stood, stunned as the light hit the man in the chest as if it were a great arrow loosened from a magical bow. It knocked him back, lifting him slightly before it slammed him into the trunk of a tree. The man gave a painful grunt before he fell, face first, to the ground.

Morven gave her a sideways glance, crossed the short distance to the base of the tree, and used his staff to roll the man over. "By the gods," he muttered, stepping back. "He is dead."

The man's chest smoked as if he'd been on fire, but his clothing had not been burned. Sayrid slowly lifted her hand and examined her palm as if she didn't believe what had just transpired. Morven glared at her, but she knew it wasn't out of anger. Nay, she sensed his fear a moment before her knees gave out and she sank to the ground, too weak to stand. Morven took a step toward her then stopped, eyeing her as if she had grown two heads.

"I won't hurt you," she said, trying to put him at ease. "I doubt I could if I wanted to. I have no strength left." She pressed the heel of her hand to her forehead, feeling dizzy. "I—I don't know how it happened . . . or why it happened."

"It happened because you are a witch," Morven supplied, nodding his shaggy head. He braced his thick legs apart, jammed the end of his staff in the moist soil and bowed his head. "I am your servant."

"My servant?" she repeated in disbelief, trying to stand, but still too weak to accomplish it. Morven was instantly at her side, his bear-like grip easily lifting her to her feet. She swayed ever so slightly, but was able to remain standing with his help. She turned and looked at him. "You've pledged your loyalty to me. Isn't that enough?"

Morven's frown grew deeper—even more frightening. "You saved my life. Good or evil, I am your servant—my life is yours."

Sayrid shook her head, trying to clear the last of the fog from it. Here was Morven the Red, a giant of a man, pledging his servitude. "Very well, if you insist, then help me. Time is of an essence. An evil wizard has Kyran's amulet, and we must get it back."

Morven raised one shaggy brow. "Where is this wizard?"

Sayrid pointed toward the distant mound where Oddrum had set up his tents. "There."

"There?" Morven gave a disgusted snort. "Then let him keep

it. 'Twould be suicide to try to retrieve it."

"Perhaps, but I have a plan." Sayrid started walking, stopping when Morven didn't budge. "Just moments ago, did you not say that your life is mine?"

"Aye, I did, but—"

"Then I order you to follow, or I'll turn you into the bear you already resemble."

Kyran's fingers tightened on his stallion's reins. Far to the west on a huge hump of grass dotted with trees, Oddrum's mounted warriors were preceded by archers, and behind the horsemen gathered the foot soldiers for as far as the eye could see. Kyran accepted his helm from a young warrior, put it on and adjusted the nose-guard. Two . . . maybe three to one, he surmised, remembering he'd faced worse odds with inferior equipment and fewer supplies.

But something nagged at him. When he killed Arcas, he and his men fought for their freedom—freedom from years of slavery. They had nothing to lose, no one to protect except each other. Their minds were set on getting the battle won.

Things were different now. Like himself, many of his men had taken wives; some even acquired young children through the unions and eagerly accepted roles as fathers. This time lives of the villagers, young and old, women and children, hung in the balance, and the knowledge weighed heavily upon his mind.

The thought that he might never see Sayrid again nearly consumed him, but he shook it aside. Had he not always known his life would end this way? Had he not said many times 'twas better to die in battle than in chains and under the lash? Aye, he silently affirmed. To die defending Dragon's Head was an honorable death.

He glanced at the sky, at the pink streaks announcing the sun's rise. Though it promised to be a typical fall day, dark thunderheads squatted on the horizon, far out over the sea. If needed, he'd call upon his powers and bring them ashore. Foul weather never hindered his ability to wield a sword, but hopefully Oddrum's army had an aversion to fighting in a cold, pelting rain.

Under the cover of night much had been done, undetectable to the inexperienced eyes of his wife when she came to bid him a speedy victory. He'd expended a fair amount of energy blocking her from reading his thoughts. He frowned, wondering what she would've said to him if she knew he planned to burn most of the forest of Dragon's Head to flush out Oddrum's men. He heaved an annoyed sigh. 'Twas not what he wanted, but what had to be done, and it distressed him the most.

While he watched Oddrum's army assemble and make ready to ride, another storm with dark, ominous clouds, illuminated with occasional arcs of lightning, hovered behind Oddrum's army. No doubt, a creation of Maldwyn's intended to frighten the men of Dragon's Head. Kyran could have laughed if their situation hadn't been so grim.

"Let them come," he muttered, lifting his hand to signal the archers to get ready for battle.

Sayrid huddled down behind a copse of wild currant bushes, watching as four men played a game of dice while roasting a hare over a fire. The smell of roasted meat wafted over her, causing her mouth to water, reminding her she'd had nothing substantial to eat since her wedding feast. Her stomach rumbled. Keeping the men in sight, she plucked a few currants and popped them into her mouth.

Breathing in the savory smell of the meat, she watched one of the men leave the game to tend to the food whilst another picked up a skin and took a long drink, passing it to his friends. She was so engrossed in watching, she didn't hear Morven approach. She jumped when he squatted down next to her. "You nearly frightened me to death," she whispered harshly.

Morven gave her a dark look. "Think you are the only one who knows this forest?" He parted the branches of the bush to get a better look. "Shall I kill them?" he asked.

Sayrid's mouth dropped open. "Not if there's another way."

He drew his brows together, grabbed her arm and quietly dragged her away from the men. "There is only one way to get to the wizard and that is to kill the men who guard him."

"Morven," she began, uncertain what to say. "You're a smart man to have survived this many years and battles. Surely you can think of something other than their deaths to defeat them."

"Are you certain this will work?" Sayrid asked with a doubtful look.

"Just do as I say," Morven muttered. He gave her a little shove. "Do it—now."

"I—I shall . . . just don't push . . . I'm going." She stepped out of the trees into the small clearing, startling the men.

"By the gods," the short one mumbled, drawing his sword.

His taller companion put a hand on the short one's arm. " 'Tis a snip of a woman, you fool."

"M-my horse . . . my horse is tied to a tree a few paces back. I—I think he's gone lame," she stammered. "Can one of you help me? I have coin to pay for your trouble."

A sick feeling came over her as a heavyset man stood and grinned, showing yellow and broken teeth. "Lame, you say?" He nudged his friend in the ribs with his elbow. "You stay and help with the hare. Euan, come with me and we'll see if we can help this poor woman."

"You're both so kind," Sayrid said as she hurried ahead, doubting the wisdom of not allowing Morven to kill them. "I'll show you where I have her tied. It's just up ahead."

"Slow down a bit," the man called. "We don't want to lose sight of you. How—"

Sayrid had only gone a short distance when she heard a loud crack, and then another. She didn't have to look to know that Morven had knocked both men unconscious with his staff. Terribly relieved, she sank down on a flat rock before her trembling knees gave out.

"Now what?" she asked when he returned.

"Do it again," Morven ordered.

Sayrid stood with her feet rooted to the ground, feeling a little desperate. "Nay, they will never believe me a second time."

"Say something different."

By his stance, Sayrid knew he wouldn't listen to any argument she might present. She heaved a defeated sigh. "What . . . what should I say? Follow me into the forest so a giant can bash in your brains?"

Morven didn't answer. He just grabbed her arm and dragged her closer to the clearing. Before she could protest, he shoved her out from the protection of the bushes.

"Ah . . . your friend . . . the fat one. . . ." Sayrid composed herself, tucking a wayward strand of hair back into her braid at the same time she frantically tried to think of something to say. Her gaze drifted to the fire and the cooking hare. It dawned on her that the sooner she got the man into the forest, the sooner she'd eat. She licked her lips and swallowed. "Your friend frightened my horse, and she kicked him in the head. He's bleeding, and the one called Euan told me to come back and ask you to help."

Both men stood. The short one who attended the fire took a step toward her. "Where are they?"

She took a step back, but he caught her arm and twisted it behind her back, drawing her up against his chest. His breath was foul, his hair matted and dirty. She shoved against him, surprised when he lost his grip. "You bitch, what have you—"

Sayrid felt it happening, the spark of sensation that felt hot and tingling on her palms. The man made as if to strike her, but she held out her hand to deflect the blow—knocking him back with a bolt of light. Had she not been so frightened, she would have smiled at the startled look on his face as his feet left the ground and he flew backwards till he hit a tree, sliding down the trunk in a dazed stupor.

Behind her, she heard the ringing sound of a sword sliding from its scabbard and the other man's muffled curse as Morven stepped into the clearing, wielding his staff. It wasn't but a moment later when she heard the familiar crack of wood against skull, and then the scuffling stopped. While she sat on the grass regaining her strength, Morven went to the fire and tested the meat for doneness before he lifted the skewer and began to blow on the food.

"Kyran's life could be in danger, and you'd rather fill your belly?" she asked in angry disbelief—disbelief that he'd gotten to the food before her. Her stomach rumbled again while she watched him take a large bite, letting the juice dribble down into his beard.

" 'Tis foolish to waste it," he said over a mouthful of meat. He tore off a leg and held it out to her. "Eat. You are pale and weak. This will help you regain your strength." He took another large bite, his words barely audible whilst he chewed. "I do not want to carry you up that mound to the wizard's tent."

More hungry than she cared to admit, she accepted the food and began to eat. The meat was done to perfection and tasted wonderful. She had just finished when the man she'd slammed against the tree began to stir. She turned, frowning at the same time she tossed the bone into some bushes. "I thought I had killed him," she murmured in disbelief, wiping off her hands on her skirt.

"I'll do it," Morven grumbled. Holding the carcass in one hand, he picked up his staff and began walking toward the dazed man.

"Wait," Sayrid asked. "Let me try something."

Morven's brows shot up in surprise, and she sensed he was pleased with her heartlessness. But she'd soon disappoint him. She stared at the man, thinking about Kyran and the war and the prophecy and soon her palms began to burn. The next moment, she held out her hand and loosed another bolt of light. It slammed into the man's chest. Although he appeared dead, she knew he wasn't. She didn't feel as weak this time, either, and she attributed the weakness to the degree of power she expended. The more powerful the bolt, the more it drained her strength.

Morven finished his meal, threw the carcass aside and grabbed a skin of wine. When his thirst was quenched, he dragged his hand across his mouth, belched, and held it out to her. She waved it away and stood, pleased that she felt perfectly fine.

"Come," she said softly. "We still have a ways to travel."

Sayrid stopped so quickly, Morven nearly bumped into her. "On second thought, I will have that skin and the other as well." Morven grumbled something under his breath, but picked them both up and slung them over his shoulder.

Sayrid followed Morven through the forest. For the size of the man, he moved with fluid grace. Silently, dodging scouting patrols, they made their way to the mound where many tents had been erected. "Which one?" Morven asked in a harsh whisper.

Sayrid lifted her amulet and pressed it into her palm. The stone began to glow before an image appeared. Taking care not to show herself to the guards, she pointed at a red-and-black-striped structure set apart from the others—an elaborate tent with black fringe. A flap, held aloft by two carved poles, acted as a canopy over the entrance. "That one."

Morven began to walk toward it, but she caught his arm. "Wait. I have a plan."

She reached into her pocket and pulled out a small leather pouch, taking two dried, brownish leaves the size of her little finger. "Uncork the wine."

When Morven did as she asked, she put one leaf in each skin, capped them and then shook them for several moments. She expected Morven to ask her about the wine, but he seemed uninterested. Certain the drug she'd added to the wine would render unconscious anyone who drank it, she gave the two skins back to the Viking with orders to pretend he was one of Oddrum's men who came to deliver wine.

She couldn't tell by his dark expression if he approved or disapproved. But he grabbed the skins and walked with no hesitation, directly toward the guards. Though she strained to hear, she was too far away. She noticed that the guards appeared cautious at first, but, after seeing Morven was a Viking and not a warrior of Dragon's Head, they allowed him to approach. He handed them the skins, and they put down their spears and drank, seeming to enjoy it. As she knew it would, the potion worked quickly; after only a few sips each, they slumped to the ground. Without a moment's hesitation, Morven relieved them of their daggers, their purses, and their spears. He turned and motioned for her to follow.

"What are you going to do with those?" she asked.

"We may need them," was all he said, marching straight toward Maldwyn's tent.

Once again, Sayrid caught his arm, lifted her amulet and stared at it for several moments before she smiled. "He's not in there. Come," she said, running the last few yards. "We must hurry."

Maldwyn's tent was every bit as elaborate on the inside as it was on the outside. A soft pallet of fine cloth and rich furs had been placed on the east wall of the square tent, a small table and two padded stools stood in the middle and a large trunk squatted on the south wall. "Keep your eyes open, whilst I search the trunk," whispered Sayrid.

The hinges squeaked when she lifted the heavy lid, but she paid no attention. She had to find Kyran's amulet.

Maldwyn heaved a bored sigh. He moved his bishop twice, placing the king in peril, and still Oddrum hadn't placed him in check. He supposed it was a good thing. Oddrum's mind should be on the morrow's battle, not on a silly game of chess. Maldwyn yawned before he could stop himself.

"Are we boring you?" Oddrum asked, raising one disapproving black brow.

"Forgive me, my lord. I did not sleep well."

Oddrum gave an impatient snort. "Then take your leave. This game has lost its appeal."

Pleased that he'd gotten off so easily, Maldwyn rose from the stool and headed toward the tent's opening, stopping when Oddrum called after him. "And make yourself a sleeping potion. I will need you alert on the morrow."

Maldwyn nodded politely, but, once outside, his white bushy brows drew closer together as he glanced in the direction of his tent. The warriors he'd left to guard his belongings seemed to be lying on the ground . . . asleep. He knelt by the nearest man. Upon seeing a tiny fleck of dried foam on the man's lips, he stood, his face mottled with rage.

"Curse you," Maldwyn muttered angrily as he stormed up the rise and across the grassy clearing. He grabbed a fistful of the flap and threw it open.

★ ★ ★ ★ ★

For his size, Morven traveled with the speed of a young buck. Sayrid struggled to keep up, pressing the heel of her palm against her side to ease the annoying pain. Though she longed to rest, she sensed that Maldwyn had returned to find Kyran's medallion missing. The next moment, she felt certain of it, when a fierce gust of wind circled around them, pelting them with bits of leaves and debris.

Using his body as a shield, Morven grabbed her wrist and hauled her with him through the forest, heedless of the fury of the wind. Much to her relief, they broke through the worst of the storm and made it to the path that led through the fields and toward the village.

Soldiers on the wall-walk shouted several warnings to stop. However, once Morven raised his staff, the men hurried to offer their help, covering Sayrid with their cloaks to protect her from the wind and flying dirt. The moment she stepped inside the bailey, the wind ended in a puff of smoke, kicking up a few leaves before it vanished altogether.

Bynor came running. "What's happening here?" he asked, and by the tone of his voice Sayrid knew he wasn't very happy. "You had your orders."

She stuck her head out of the cloaks. "If you must know, he was helping me."

Bynor muttered something under his breath, then gently grasped her arm and led her toward the keep. "You can explain it all to Kyran. Since he discovered you missing several hours ago, he's been beyond worried." Bynor stopped and nodded, his frown contradicting the amusement she noticed in his eyes. "Aye, he's way beyond worried. I would say he's furious. Come. This should be interesting."

Kyran met her at the door, yanking it open before Bynor's

fingers touched the huge bronze rings. "Where have you been?" he demanded, his features so fierce, she flinched.

"I—I. . . ." She tried to think of something to say that would, in his eyes, justify her actions, but couldn't think. His feeling of anger and frustration hit her much like a wave crashing on the rocks below Dragon's Head, and suddenly she knew how much she'd frightened him.

"Forgive me," she said, reaching up to cup his cheek. She was just about to tell him everything that had happened when he grabbed her and nearly crushed her in his embrace.

"Ah . . . I'll go and see to the men," Bynor muttered uncomfortably. She heard the heavy door close before Kyran finally released his hold.

He held her at arm's length. "I thought Oddrum. . . ." He closed his eyes in an effort to regain control. " 'Tis of no importance. You are here now, and that's all that matters. Come, you look tired."

Taking her hand, he started toward the stairs, but she pulled back. When he turned, his expression revealed his confusion, but that wasn't all she saw in his eyes. The love she saw and felt nearly brought her to tears. With trembling fingers, she slipped her hand into the small pouch tied to her belt and slowly lifted out his amulet. It began to vibrate in her hand. "I thought you might need this . . . before you face Oddrum on the battlefield."

"By the gods. . . ." He didn't finish; he just pulled her into his embrace, holding her as if he never wanted to let her go, and she melted against him, closing her eyes and willing her mind and body to memorize the moment.

CHAPTER FIFTEEN

Kyran removed his helm and dragged his arm across his forehead, wiping away the sweat that stung his eyes. He'd fought hard the last two days; they all had. 'Twas his turn to take a few hours' reprieve from the carnage. Many of Oddrum's men had deserted, and Kyran suspected 'twas because mercenaries have no loyalty except to their purse. He'd seen the bulge of coins in the pouches of several warriors he'd dispatched to their deaths, and thought Oddrum a fool for paying them before the battle started. Mayhap they refused to fight—insisting on getting paid first lest it ended badly.

Kyran dismounted, tossing his reins to a boy just as Cyric hurried down the steps of the keep to greet him. "Thank the gods, you are here. I had heard you were wounded." His gaze fell on Kyran's leg, above the knee where a makeshift bandage had been tied. Cyric offered a shoulder to lean on. "Can you walk, or should I call for a litter?"

"Nay, 'tis only a minor wound. I can walk."

"Sayrid will have that better before the sun rises on the morrow, I am sure. You should be proud of her and the way she tends the wounded. Without her, many would have died."

"She is what keeps me going," Kyran said wearily. He accepted a tankard of mead, drinking it down before he said, "Thank you. My thirst was great."

Kyran glanced around the great hall of Dragon's Head. Everywhere he looked, wounded men rested on fur pallets that practically covered the floor. Others slept in beds that had been placed on the benches. Tables were piled with pitchers, basins and bandages. When a man called for a drink, his request was quickly answered by one of the many women who tended to the wounded warriors.

Kyran walked slowly among them, stopping to offer words of praise and comfort and to assure them that victory was just a few days away. By the time he reached the stairs, he felt their pain as if it were his own. Chilled to the bone, he closed his eyes for a moment's reprieve and saw Sayrid, dragging a brush though her thick hair before a warm fire. In his vision, she turned and smiled brightly, motioning to a large tub of steaming-hot water. Suddenly he felt revived and began to climb the stairs to his chamber.

"You look tired," she said when he stepped inside and leaned back against the door for a moment. She came and took his helm, placing it on the table before she filled a goblet with warm, spiced wine. "Drink. I have added herbs that will make you feel better and help your pain."

He accepted the wine, took several sips, and then gave it back to her, too weary to move away from the door for several moments. After she put his goblet down, she returned and turned him so she could reach the leather laces of his breastplate. By her guarded expression, he knew the blood smeared across the intricate dragon and the marks and dents from numerous blows distressed her, but she never wavered from her task. Nor did she question him about the war, and he assumed she knew having read his thoughts.

The breastplate was heavy for her to manage alone, so he helped her lift it over his head, and together they carried it to the corner where he leaned it against the wall. He unbuckled his sword belt, adding that to the pile with his dagger and shirt of mail. When he fumbled with the ties of his padded gambeson, she caught his hands in hers, inspecting the broken blisters before she undid the laces, easing the garment off his bruised and battered body.

"How they have hurt you," she said, her voice filled with compassion, her eyes filling with tears. She smoothed her fingers lightly over his shoulders, down the bulging muscles of his upper arms, then back over his chest, smiling slightly when his nipples hardened against her palm. She stopped her caress on a purple bruise discoloring his side.

"Your rib is broken," she whispered. She closed her eyes, pressing her hand against the bruise, whimpering slightly before she took a calming breath and let it out slowly.

Was it the wine, or simply her touch that eased his pain? He cared little which one, only that he could finally draw a breath without hurting. Next she knelt and loosened the makeshift bandage around his thigh, frowning when she examined the wound. " 'Twill have to be sewn." Tears glistened in her eyes. "All I have are the herbs in the wine. The magical mud must be saved for the badly wounded."

"As it should be."

She gazed up at him and would have embraced him, but he caught her gently by the upper arms and held her away. " 'Twould be foolish to let the water grow cold. Come, help me bathe, then you can sew my leg and then. . . ." He smiled.

Sayrid raised a reddish brow. "You can barely stand. I doubt you could do much more than fall into bed, my lord."

"Aye, and, once we are abed, I will show you how to pleasure a weary warrior."

And he did. With a few softly spoken words of instruction, Sayrid straddled his hips, leaning forward till her nipples brushed against his chest before she kissed him. Softly at first, then more forcefully, nipping at his lips until he opened his mouth and their tongues entwined, teasing and tasting. Liquid fire filled her belly, but she waited to fulfill her own needs, easing down on his hardened shaft, then up again, till he groaned deep in his throat, caught her hips in his bandaged hands and held her down, filling her completely.

Tiny jolts of pleasure became powerful surges of primal delight with each potent thrust of his shaft into her sheath. No sooner had she decided to hold back her own enjoyment for his, when he moved a little faster—a little deeper, and her body tightened around his. The throbbing ecstasy of his shaft rubbing against her womanhood shattered her good intentions. She arched her back, driving him deeper and crying out his name. In the next instant, she felt him shudder, his fingers biting into her hips, holding her down until he gave a satisfied groan. Slowly, his eyes opened, and he smiled at her before he relaxed back against the feathered mattress and fell asleep.

Though Kyran's steady breathing told her he slept without pain, Sayrid couldn't sleep. She sat up in bed with a fur over her shoulders, resting her chin on her knees, watching his chest rise slowly up and down. How young he looked in slumber. Gone were the lines of fatigue she'd seen around his eyes. Gone was the tight set of his jaw that caused a tiny muscle low on his cheek to jump spasmodically. She yawned, but refused to close her eyes—memorizing every inch of him, every mark, every line, and every scar. Gently, she traced the dragon on Kyran's chest, and the dragon appeared, as if she had summoned him.

He is a true warrior, fearless, swift and relentless.

Sayrid looked over her bare shoulder. "He is loving and kind. He has kept me from reading his thoughts to spare me the details of war. He does not deserve to die."

He is the Protector.

"He is my husband, my life-mate. If he dies, so shall I perish." She felt the bed vibrate with the great one's roar. She tossed him a dark look. "Shush, you will wake him, and he needs to sleep."

Then do not speak foolishness, little one. You will not die. Your powers are too strong, and I forbid it.

She lifted her chin in open defiance. "You forbid it?" she scoffed. "Then spare him to save me."

The dragon stamped his foot down hard on the stone. *You try my patience. I cannot—will not change what must come to pass. The prophecy must be fulfilled. The people must be united, or we will all perish.*

Sayrid rounded on the dragon. "Are you prepared to face the consequences if you and Derwyn are wrong? If his death doesn't end this foolish war?"

Heed my words, little one. Do not interfere. What will be, will be, and no one, not even you, can stop the wheels of fate now that they've begun to turn. His image started to fade, causing her to jump off the bed to face him.

"Nothing is certain in life, great one," she cried. "Nothing."

Sayrid pretended to be asleep when Kyran rose and walked stiffly to the hearth and added another log. While the room warmed, he dressed in the clean clothing a boy had brought the previous night. Through half-closed eyes, she watched him effortlessly don his armor before he came back to the side of the bed and gently drew his knuckles down her cheek. Still, she forced away the desire to rise and beg him not to go, for it was a futile thought and would only serve to distract him when he needed his mind alert for another day of fighting. When he went to the door and opened it, pausing to buckle his sword around his waist before he pulled it closed, the urge to weep became more than she could bear.

After she regained control, she rose and splashed some water on her face. She calmly brushed her tangled hair and braided it. When she finished, she went to the trunk and opened it, finding her old gown and vine-like overgown. She slipped her amulet over her head, tucking it safely under her gown. 'Twas better if no one caught sight of it. Her bow had been brought from her cottage and hung in a place of honor over the hearth, her arrows and quiver beneath it. She reached up and took two plain arrows from the quiver, then gathering her paint and her dagger, she sat before the fire and began to carve and paint a special design.

Sayrid couldn't get the shot she wanted from where she stood; there was too much in her line of sight, too many bushes and trees—the only ones left standing after Kyran had burned much of the Mystical Forest. Though she knew the reason, and many of their men had lived because of it, it pained her to see the charred remains.

Determined to save her beloved, she took a steadying breath and crept closer, staying hidden as best she could. She lifted the two special arrows from the quiver on her back. After she nocked them both and put them on the arrow rest, her fingers tingled on the string, the pounding of her anxious heart thudding in her ears. She offered a quick prayer to the goddess of the forest to give her the strength to have a steady hand, and forgiveness for what she was about to do.

Composed, she raised her magical bow, took aim and loosed her arrows.

Protected by a copse of scorched, sapling birch trees, Brynn took a black-feathered arrow from her quiver and nocked her bow, patiently taking aim as a slow and menacing smile spread across her ivory features. Her self-confident target stood exposed, clearly and completely in her sights.

Oddrum gasped and nearly tumbled from the back of his horse

as two arrows slammed into his chest. With wild, disbelieving eyes, he glanced at the manner by which he'd lost his life, noticing first the arrow painted and carved with runes, then the one with telltale raven feathers. "Brynn," he rasped, clutching his horse's mane to steady his spinning world—his last coherent thought was that Maldwyn had taken an arrow in the chest too. Darkness clouded Oddrum's vision as he slipped from the back of his horse—dead before he hit the ground.

Maldwyn wrenched Sayrid's arrow from his chest, relieved to discover she'd used a bodkin. Silly girl, he thought, as a vision of her whereabouts drew his eyes to where she stood on the rise, barely visible, dressed in a most unusual gown that appeared to be twisted vines and leaves.

"Cursed bitch," he murmured. Blood oozed from the small hole. While he pressed his palm against the wound, he had yet another vision—one of Brynn nocking her bow with another black-feathered arrow that had been dipped in a deadly poison, taking aim—not on any of their enemies—but on him.

Rising to his full height in a fit of rage, a fierce wind swirled around his body, slightly lifting his beard and causing his long white hair to swirl eerily around his head. Brynn knew the moment he found her—his eyes fusing with hers as the arrow took flight. In horrified wonder, she watched as Maldwyn held up his hand. The arrow magically turned, and her mouth grew suddenly dry. Too frightened to move, she closed her eyes and braced herself, expecting at any moment to feel the broadhead sink into her chest, ending her life.

Kyran's heart hammered against his chest the moment his gaze landed on Sayrid through the magical looking glass. "No," he rasped, trying to get to her, hacking his way through the throng of fighting men. Why had she put her life in danger? But, with sickening assurance, he knew.

A swordsman rendered another wound, slicing into Kyran's arm, but he felt no pain. He felt Sayrid's determination, and nothing but his death would stop him from reaching her. He spun his destrier, sending those trying to get close to him scrambling away from powerful hooves, cursing him as they dodged Kyran's sword. It felt as if he'd made no progress at all, but finally he arrived at the bottom of the rise. Putting spur to flank, his stallion reared then bolted up the rocky slope.

"Sayrid," Kyran shouted, jumping from his horse the moment they reached the summit. She turned, lowered her bow and smiled. "Sayrid," he cried again, running to her.

Time felt suspended, hanging in the air like the thick smoke of the burning thatch on the cottages. Men shouted to Brynn's left—from the rise. Slowly she opened her eyes and turned, amazed and relieved to see Sayrid suddenly stop, arching slightly when a black-feathered arrow sank deeply into her back.

Using the last of his strength, Maldwyn changed into his raven form. He had just taken flight when he had another vision—one of Brynn, nocking her bow again with another arrow. He soared high, caught an updraft and swiftly disappeared over the top of Dragon's Head Castle out of arrow range, and soon out of sight.

Kyran's mouth grew dry when Sayrid took a step toward him and then stopped. She jerked slightly before her smile quickly faded. Ignoring the burning pain between his shoulder blades, he caught her when she reached out to him, his heart tearing into pieces as he felt her confusion at first—confusion that quickly turned into understanding. Drawing in a shaky breath, she forced a wobbly smile and gazed lovingly up at him at the same time she clutched her amulet, whispering for him to take it.

The moment Oddrum fell, mercenaries spilled down from the mound, waving swords and spears as they began to flood the valley, spreading death and destruction—striking down anything in their path.

"By the gods, have mercy," Bynor muttered to Morven as the big man dodged a spear. Bynor raised his hand and signaled for his men to retreat.

Fighting his way to the base of the rise, he turned to help Cyric when suddenly the ground began to shake—small tremors that quickly turned violent. Horror-struck, he watched as a crack appeared in the soil, twenty feet from where he and his men stood, splitting the valley in half—he and what was left of his army on one side, the mercenaries on the other.

The fracture widened, devouring burned trees, fields and empty cottages like a hungry beast as it spread to a fifty-foot-wide chasm that spat flames high into the air—the fire roared with ear-shattering intensity. Instantly, roiling black clouds appeared overhead, slamming blinding bolts of lightning into the earth, incinerating anything in their path. Oddrum's men scrambled to avoid being killed, but they couldn't escape death.

Just when Bynor thought the worst was over, a giant whirlwind erupted from the flaming gorge, lifting those who didn't run for their lives high into the air, and then dropping them into the gaping jaws of the inferno. When only a few of Oddrum's warriors remained, the chasm closed, silencing the screams of the dying.

Kyran opened his eyes and slowly uncurled his fingers where he'd grasped Sayrid's amulet. He carefully eased Sayrid down, rolling her slightly toward him. With a quick snap, he broke the arrow's shaft, glanced at it and tossed it aside, ignoring the blood that covered his hand. His breath came in painful pants as his chest tightened, making it difficult to breathe. Hot tears burned the back of his eyes, and he knew with horrifying certainty the wound was fatal.

"Sayrid," he said softly, brushing a strand of curly red hair from her cheek. "Sayrid, my love, my life."

His wife managed a weak smile and reached up to touch a tear that trickled down his cheek. "Do not," she began, catching her breath—relaxing when he took her hand and placed a kiss in the palm. "Do not weep for me, beloved."

A gust of wind tousled his hair, followed by the sound of distant thunder. Somewhere in the distance a horn sounded, and then another and another, joined by the shouts and cheers of men.

"Do you hear that?" he asked in a broken whisper, holding her tightly, afraid if he didn't she'd simply disappear. "Oddrum is dead—his army has surrendered—the war is over."

"Our people . . . ," she murmured. "Our people are finally united. The prophecy has been fulfilled."

"No," he said angrily. A gust of wind tousled his hair. " 'Twas not supposed to be like this. 'Twas my death your grandmother foretold."

When Sayrid closed her eyes, he felt her pain lessen and knew there wasn't much time. "You are a great sorceress . . . ," he said frantically. Lightning arced wildly across the darkening sky. "There has to be something we can do, some spell—a chant to reverse what has been done. Tell me what to say to prevent this," he cried.

She stopped his hopeless tirade with the touch of her fingers against his mouth. A sob caught in his throat, but, instead of venting against the injustice of it all, he forced a stiff smile to show her he would survive. He sensed that his friends, Cyric and Bynor, had arrived and stood quietly by to help if needed.

"I. . . ." The light in her wise, enchanting eyes grew dim. "I die happily for you . . . for you . . . and Dragon's Head."

Stunned with the finality of losing her, Kyran cradled Sayrid in his arms, staring at her flawless face, pale yet peaceful in death.

A steady rain began to fall, softly at first, but turning quickly into a downpour, soaking him, his friends, and a few of his warriors who had lingered behind to assist him. He heard Bynor ask Cyric and the others to leave; although he sensed their reluctance to do so, they began to disburse. Bynor caught Kyran's horse, and held him while the rain continued to soak their clothing. Kyran sat, gently rocking Sayrid's body, oblivious to the low, mournful growl that rumbled from the keep—a growl that was soft at first, but soon spread to encompass the entire valley.

Bynor couldn't be certain how long he stood in the rain, holding Kyran's horse. He was numb, both emotionally and from the cold. He touched his left shoulder—the area on his chest where it burned and tingled, but not from a wound. His chest hurt from the mark Kyran had passed on to him—the mark of the dragon.

Slowly, Kyran lifted his head, his voice barely over a whisper. "The dragon . . . he . . . there is a chamber deep inside the castle. . . ." He slumped over his wife, unmoving.

A jolt of fear cut into Bynor's heart when he put his hand on Kyran's shoulder to rouse him and nothing happened. He tightened his fingers and gave Kyran a firm shake, and still nothing happened.

"No, by the gods, no," Bynor rasped before he stood and yelled for Morven and Cyric.

★ ★ ★ ★ ★

Inside the keep, the mournful howl started softly, barely audible at first, almost as if the walls wept. Derwyn suddenly felt cold. With trembling fingers, she put down a cup of marigold tea that Rhonwyn had brought, and she tugged her shawl a little closer.

Something was amiss. She closed her eyes and found Cyric speaking with some men in the warriors' quarters. She sighed with relief. But when she tried to find Sayrid, her heart tightened with dread. "Nay," she cried, wrapping her arms tightly about herself. "This cannot be."

"Rhonwyn, dear, put another log on the fire," Gwendolyn asked with a worried frown. "Derwyn's not looking well."

Rhonwyn stood to do as she was asked when the floor began to move—vibrating the table near Derwyn's bench till her cup fell to the floor and smashed into pieces.

"Mother?" Rhonwyn asked, her voice revealing her fear. "What's happening?"

"I do not know, but try not to be afraid." Gwendolyn sat down next to Derwyn to offer some comfort and find out why the keep seemed to shudder. "Tell us, Derwyn, what's happening, and what it is you see?"

Derwyn raised watery blue eyes to Gwendolyn. "The great one is suffering. He's lost someone he loves. . . ." Derwyn gasped and clutched her shawl tighter. "Sayrid . . . he's hurting and grieves for Sayrid." Derwyn pressed her knobby fingers to her forehead. " 'Twas not supposed to be like this. I saw his death, not hers."

"Whose death?" Gwendolyn asked softly.

"Kyran, the Protector. He was supposed to sacrifice his life to end the war . . . to fulfill the prophecy."

"The prophecy?" Mother and daughter exchanged anxious glances.

"His death would have united the tribes and finally brought

peace to Dragon's Head . . . to all of Wales." Derwyn shook her head as tears streamed down her wrinkled cheeks. "She's gone, Gwen. My precious grandchild is dead. By the gods, what am I to do without her? What will we all do without her?"

Stunned by Derwyn's announcement, Gwendolyn's hand trembled as she held it out to Rhonwyn. The young woman grasped it and knelt before her mother. "Rhonwyn, go and find your father."

"But you look so pale," Rhonwyn cried.

"Go now, and hurry."

Rhonwyn had no sooner left the castle when the doors burst open again. Cyric, Bynor and Morven were soaked to the bone, but 'twas not their appearance that frightened Gwendolyn and caused Derwyn to wail. It was Sayrid's limp body in Bynor's arms, and Kyran's motionless body over Morven's shoulder. Cyric hollered for the servants to hurry and make ready Kyran's bed, but stopped Bynor from following. Swallowing hard, Cyric approached, nodded a swift greeting to Gwendolyn, and then knelt before Derwyn.

"Grandmother," he began, his voice sounding hoarse. He paused and cleared his throat, and Gwendolyn wondered if tears lingered on his cheeks or if the moisture was just from the rain. "Grandmother, tell me what to do. Sayrid is. . . ." He squeezed his eyes tightly closed as if what he was about to say caused him great pain. "Sayrid is dead. Kyran has fallen ill, and I can't tell if it's from his wounds . . . or something unexplainable." He swallowed and then continued. "I need you to tell me what to do . . . where do I take her, and how do I help him?"

Gwendolyn felt his pain, and put her arm around the old woman to offer some comfort, and encourage her to compose herself so she could help her grandson. "Derwyn, you know the old ways, the ways of the Ancient Ones. Concentrate. You heard the spirit of the dragon only moments ago. Try and give us some direction."

Cyric took a calming breath. "Bynor said Kyran spoke of a dragon and a sacred chamber."

Derwyn slowly stood and with Gwendolyn's help made it over to where Bynor stood. He appeared as if made of stone, stiff and unmoving—his tormented gaze fixed ahead, cradling Sayrid in his arms. Derwyn lifted a shaky hand and cupped her granddaughter's pale cheek, moving a strand of wet hair, before she looked up at Bynor. " 'Twas not supposed to be like this," she cried.

Bynor's eyes fused with Derwyn's. "Help her," was all he said in a voice barely audible before he clamped his jaw tight and looked down at Sayrid.

"Aye, Grandmother," Cyric interjected. "Help her . . . help us to know what to do."

Derwyn looked at Cyric, and then held her arms out to him, wrapping him in her embrace the moment he came forward. "We must prepare her body." She turned to Gwendolyn. "I will need your help and Rhonwyn's too."

"Aye, anything," Gwendolyn replied.

Derwyn turned back to Cyric. "I needs to see Kyran. 'Tis imperative to keep him alive until the ceremony."

"Ceremony?" Cyric asked. His brow furrowed in grief and confusion. "I don't understand. Speak you of her funeral?"

"Nay, my child, not her funeral, her rebirth. 'Tis only legend and, as far as I know, has never been done except by the power of the Ancient Ones, but we must try to save her, for if we fail, I fear we will lose Kyran as well."

The entire castle felt as if it trembled, and Derwyn knew she must try to summon the dragon. "Now, hurry. There is a place I must go before we go to Kyran."

Gwendolyn waited until they left, then motioned to Bynor as the castle shuddered again and a low rumble echoed throughout the great hall. "Come, follow me."

They were halfway up the steps when Dafydd burst through the door, Rhonwyn right behind him. "Gwendolyn, what has happened?"

She hurried down the steps and into her husband's arms, taking a moment to gather her courage for the task that lay ahead. Slowly she looked up at Dafydd, and he tightened his hold when the floor shook. Gwendolyn and Dafydd exchanged worried glances before she spoke, "I do not know the details, but Sayrid is dead, and Kyran is dying. And"—she took a steadying breath—"I sense the spirit of the dragon is dying, too. There is little time. I need the trunk we hid in the forest a long time ago."

Morven's frown increased when the whole castle felt as if it trembled, causing him to momentarily lose his balance. After he waited a moment to make sure it didn't happen again, he gently laid Kyran down on the bed, staring at him for several moments. The big man sniffed and dragged his arm across his watery eyes, then turned and added several logs to the hot, glowing coals. He filled a small cauldron with water and placed it close to the flames.

Moving slowly, methodically, he removed Kyran's armor, pausing when his fingers touched the amulet. His wet, bushy brows came tightly together. He'd seen it before, but not like this. The stone was dark, cracked and lacked any luster. Morven lifted it off and placed it on the bedside table, and then he removed Kyran's soiled clothing. He filled a basin with warm water and bathed away the grime of battle and the smeared blood from his wounds.

"You are soft," Morven grumbled, rinsing out the cloth and carefully dabbing at the fresh wound on his friend's arm before he bound it with a clean cloth. "You have no serious wounds to speak of. I have sustained far worse. 'Tis that witch you married, and the evil spell she's cast upon you."

After he finished bandaging Kyran's hands, he lifted him, pulled the furs aside and placed him in the bed, tucking the fur carefully around his chest. "I warned you. Now look at you. Powerless to resist."

He sniffed again and once more dragged his arm across his eyes before he pulled the fur a little higher to make sure his friend stayed warm. "You should have listened when I told you she was a witch."

CHAPTER SIXTEEN

Derwyn hobbled down the long corridor, past Kyran's chamber. Near the end was another door. By the looks of the dust on the latch, it hadn't been opened in ages. She tried to open it, but it wouldn't budge.

"Let me, Grandmother," Cyric said, placing his shoulder against the wooden door. After two tries, he finally forced the rusty hinges open and they both stepped inside, brushing at a cobweb. "I fear when we cleaned, we must have missed this room," he muttered.

"Aye, but only because the door's invisible to all except our family." Derwyn hurried to the mantel. She found a small chunk of flint and steel, and set a spark to a candle. Cyric found another candle, adding enough light to look around. A fair-size chamber, it contained an elegantly carved wardrobe and matching trunk.

Though everything was covered in a thick layer of dust, there were two elegant chairs that appeared to have the seats covered with light-colored furs, the wooden backs carved with the likeness of two harts, a doe and a stag with two smaller fawns.

"Was this your room when our family lived here?" Cyric asked, glancing around. He had never seen so many runes—the stone walls were nearly covered in them. He touched his finger to them, tracing the ancient symbols. "It appears not to be a bedchamber."

"Aye," Derwyn answered, pressing her hand against the wall.

271

The stones felt alive, vibrating at the same time the chamber filled with a low, heart-wrenching groan. " 'Tis a place to come and pray."

Cyric watched Derwyn go to the other side of the chamber, where a small wooden altar stood. She took a taper and touched it to four narrow candles, then closed her eyes and began to speak in a language foreign to him. After she had spoken several words, she chanted very softly—her voice wafting up to the ceiling in a mellow, pleasing tone.

The floor beneath his feet convulsed, forcing him to brace himself against the wall to keep from falling. His grandmother appeared oblivious to the shakes and shudders and groans of the old castle, so he remained quiet though a thousand questions sprang to mind. He glanced at a darkened corner, blinking several times to make sure he wasn't imagining what he saw. As the filmy image grew larger, he wrapped his fingers around the hilt of his dagger, and tapped his grandmother lightly on the shoulder. "I believe the dragon Kyran spoke of has come."

His grandmother spun, reaching back and grasping his hand before she composed herself. "Aye, it appears so." She gave his fingers a little squeeze. " 'Tis been many years since I've seen him. Watch, listen and learn."

Cyric took a calming breath and watched as the image of the dragon grew larger, as more of his body came though the wall. As frightening as the dragon appeared, Cyric sensed there was no danger—only overwhelming pain and sorrow.

Derwyn, my old friend. Welcome home.

Cyric frowned. Had he heard the beast's thoughts? He must have, for when his grandmother answered he knew what she would say before her lips moved.

"I misread the signs great one . . . I failed to understand the true meaning. I thought the Protector would sacrifice his life, but I was wrong. Instead Sayrid died . . . for him and for all of us."

Cyric couldn't believe his eyes. The old dragon hung his head and gave a mournful sigh. Two tears ran down his scaly cheeks, and splashed on the floor—the droplets instantly turned into tiny almandines. *I cannot bear to go on without her.*

Derwyn went to him and placed a comforting hand on his horned snout. "Nay, you cannot die. I cannot do this alone. I need your help, wise one. We must take Sayrid to the hidden chamber and try to perform the sacred ceremony—to ask the Ancient Ones to return her soul."

The beast gave an uncertain shake of his head, at the same time a low rumble emanated from his chest. *As far back as I can remember, it has never been done. There have been others who have tried, but none were successful.*

"Aye, but none have been as powerful as Sayrid. Not her mother. Not I. She is special, and, by the gods, I can still sense her presence. I know that she will be special again. We must try. If you love her as you say, you must help me. The Protector is dying as well. If you perish, so will Dragon's Head and the people."

The dragon gave an angry growl. *I gave my life for the people, and still they fight and deny the prophecy. Now Sayrid has sacrificed her life for them as well, yet still there is much unrest. Oddrum is dead, his people without a leader. In time they will have forgotten what happened here today and hunger once again for Dragon's Head.*

Cyric stepped forward. "Nay, wise one. I will not allow that to happen. Although many were killed with the mercenaries, I have already sent some men with food and supplies to the survivors where they've made camp on the mound. I've offered them sanctuary. I've offered them and their families a home here at Dragon's Head, where they can live with us in peace. We will clear the burned forest to make room for more fields and more cottages."

The beast gave a loud, sad sigh, his warm breath drying Cyric's damp clothing and rustling his hair. *Very well, if you are determined to fulfill the prophecy, then I shall do all I can to help. I will guide you to the hidden chamber, but we must move quickly. My powers are weakening.*

Morven stood after checking Kyran, stretching stiff muscles before he went to the table and filled a pewter goblet with spiced wine. The Viking drank it down before he crumpled the cup in his fist and threw it angrily against the wall, just as Cyric and the old sorceress walked into the room.

Cyric met Morven's irritated gaze a moment before he glanced at the bed. "Tell me he still lives."

"For now," Morven grumbled. "But for how much longer depends on the depth of the evil spell her granddaughter put him under."

Derwyn met Morven's angry gaze. "Foolish man, 'tis not a spell. He is dying of a broken heart—because his life-mate has died." Derwyn looked at Kyran and then back at the giant Norseman. "There is still time to save him, but we must hurry."

She went to the bedside. Upon seeing the amulet, she snatched it up and clutched it in her hand while she held her other hand over Kyran's chest. A tiny light sparked for a moment in the almandine, and then slowly faded. "If you want him to live, bring him and be quick about it."

Bynor had stood quietly by the chamber door while Gwendolyn and Rhonwyn had washed and prepared Sayrid for the ceremony. When they were through, Sayrid's long red hair had been brushed free of tangles and left down around her shoulders, held in place by the gold circlet she'd worn at her wedding.

Gone were the smudges of dirt and mud. Her blood-soaked russet gown had been discarded, the arrow in her back carefully removed and the wound packed with the healing mud before it was covered with a clean, white bandage.

Her skin had been rubbed with sweetly scented oil, and they'd dressed her in a soft, long-sleeved gown of oyster-white—simple in design and, in Bynor's opinion, resembling more an elegant robe than a woman's dress. When they finished with the last few touches, Sayrid looked as beautiful as she had looked on her wedding day, though still unmoving and pale.

He forced himself to look away, the sight of her too agonizing. He swallowed down his sadness, wondering how Kyran fared. So deeply was he lost in thought, he started slightly when there came a soft knock on the door.

"Who goes there," he said, opening the portal a crack to see. Relief washed over him and he pulled it open. By Cyric's expression, there was still some hope.

Bynor cautiously entered the massive cave-like chamber hidden deep within the bowels of Dragon's Head. He had heard rumors about such a chamber but had doubted it existed, because the description usually came from songs sung by minstrels—and he too far in his cups to remember the words. He took a step and felt the stone floor vibrate—a strange orange-red glow gave enough light for him to see his way to the altar but not enough for him to see the ceiling or where the walls ended.

Behind the altar, a large, oval almandine appeared to be embedded into the stone and was surrounded by more symbols and runes like those on the walls. But 'twas not the ancient symbols that drew his attention: 'twas the treasure laying in various-sized piles around the chamber, twinkling in the eerie light.

"Put her here," Derwyn commanded. She was clad in a robe

similar to Sayrid's, but the back was adorned with the image of a fierce, iridescent-blue dragon. The floor beneath his feet trembled as he gently laid Sayrid on the altar in the sacred chamber, pausing only to look upon her beautiful face one last time, aware that if the ceremony failed, her body would be purified by fire and her soul carried to the Otherworld by the Ancient Ones.

Morven entered next, carrying Kyran in his arms. Like Sayrid, Kyran had been dressed in a long, oyster-white robe, tied at the waist with a golden cord. He, too, had been bathed and all signs of battle removed except two clean bandages around his hands, covering what Bynor knew were broken blisters from wielding a broadsword. His own palms bore bandages. He frowned when he noticed that neither Sayrid nor Kyran wore their amulets.

A pain not completely from sadness sliced through Bynor's chest, residing deep in his shoulder where the mark Kyran had passed on to him still burned as it very slowly took the shape of a dragon. Placing his palm against the ache, he watched as Derwyn told Morven to put Kyran next to Sayrid. She smoothed the couple's clothing, then took Kyran's left hand and Sayrid's right hand, tying them together with another ceremonial cord.

Morven joined Bynor close to the door, but the Viking's eyes narrowed and slowly scanned the room. Staying in the shadows and out of the way, they watched Cyric enter with Rhonwyn on his arm, both dressed in robes with golden rope belts. Cyric wore a jewel-encrusted crown, Rhonwyn a simple golden circlet to hold her long, wavy brown hair in place. Gwendolyn and Dafydd were the last to enter. Like the others, they were dressed in ceremonial garments, though only Gwendolyn carried a small golden pillow, and upon it sat Sayrid's and Kyran's amulets.

Derwyn hurried to greet them, taking the amulets. The two couples formed a semicircle around the altar and bowed their heads. The next instant, heavy footfalls shook the floor. The sound grew louder with each step until the entire chamber began to vibrate. "Join hands," Derwyn commanded. She closed her eyes and began to chant.

Bynor couldn't look away even though the light radiating from the almandine grew stronger and stronger with a brilliant, dazzling light. Shielding his eyes, he tried to watch. Derwyn held out the two amulets, but the longer he stared at the light the more it felt as if it were slicing into his head. He heard Morven's heavy breathing and knew the same was happening to him. Pressing his hands to his head, Bynor sank to his knees. Morven soon followed, the big man grunting as he collapsed face down on the vibrating stone floor. Bynor tried to fight off the effects of the light, but it seemed to grow even brighter. Groaning, he rolled to his side and collapsed, certain he heard the roar of the spirit of the dragon before darkness filled his head and took his pain.

Kyran slowly opened his eyes, but felt too weak to move. He appeared to be surrounded by a brilliant white light as memories swam in his head. *I recognize and accept my destiny willingly,* he heard himself say, but he knew he hadn't moved his mouth.

We are well pleased with you, Kyran the Protector. The Ancient Ones and I will be watching . . . watching . . . watching. . . . The dragon's voice faded into light that filled every inch of the chamber.

"I will not fail you, I swear it," Kyran cried aloud, trying again to rise, but his body wouldn't obey his mind. Lifting heavy lids, he turned and saw his beloved lying beside him, her face peaceful in rest. Derwyn stood beside them, her eyes closed, her lips moving rapidly, but he couldn't make out the words or hear any sound. She held their amulets—one in each hand, facing each other. He felt Cyric's presence and others as well, but they too were just diminished images consumed by the light.

He flinched when a stream of orange-gold light shot from his amulet into Sayrid's and held fast, burning into the stone until he felt certain the bronze would melt. His head hurt even more as he watched the light. He closed his eyes for a moment, seeing the dragon. The beast narrowed his wise, yellow eyes before he gave a beastly roar—a terrifying sound that reverberated painfully in Kyran's skull. *Remember that this is a sacred place where time stands still and the dead live again . . . the dead live again. . . .*

The orange-gold light intensified. It felt as if it burned inside his body, swelling and ebbing—tiny pinpricks of light that grew stronger—more excruciating.

"Sayrid," he called in a broken whisper, fighting the urge to vent his agony. He clamped his jaw down tight and stared at his wife, willing her to turn her head and open her eyes. "Sayrid," he said through clenched teeth. "On all that's holy, come back to me—help me."

As if the gods answered his prayer, little by little he felt her respond. Her cold fingers twitched, then brushed against his, easing a little of his pain. He grasped them and gave them a firm but gentle squeeze. The lights continued their agonizing torture, but he focused on her beautiful face, his mind calling to hers.

Gradually, she turned her head and slowly opened her eyes. "My beloved," she whispered, smiling at him. She gave a sleepy, contented sigh. At that moment, his agony ended.

Sayrid rolled over in bed, tucking her pillow under her head so she could watch her husband sleep. Though she had no memory of the ceremony, afterwards she'd been taken to another chamber away from Kyran, where she asked about her unusual garments and learned from Derwyn what had transpired. While there, the dragon had come to her and shared the stories of his beginning and the creation of Dragon's Head and its importance to the people.

She jumped when Kyran spoke, drawing her back from her thoughts.

"You're wakeful," he murmured, his eyes still closed. The moment his hand came around her neck, she leaned forward to accept his kiss.

"You knave, you frightened me," she said, smiling when he opened his eyes. "I thought you were asleep."

"I was, but then I sensed you were watching me." He reached up and kissed her again, pulling her down so that her head rested upon his shoulder.

" 'Tis well past morning. We cannot stay abed all day."

"Why not?" he asked, before she felt him place a kiss in her hair. "What have you to do that's so important? The war is over. Oddrum is dead, and his people are united with our people."

"I worry that Maldwyn and Brynn escaped." Her eyes were serenely compelling.

"There's nothing to fear from them." He pulled her closer and gave a contented sigh when she snuggled closer. "I could stay like this forever."

Sayrid lifted her head. "Have you forgotten so soon?"

"Forgotten what?"

She gave an exasperated sigh. "Cyric and Rhonwyn are getting married today. You and I are to bear witness. And, afterwards, there will be a feast and dancing."

Kyran yawned. "I thought you didn't like to dance."

"I didn't, but then you showed me it wasn't anything more than walking around in a circle, remember? You stopped me from leaving. You said, 'A dance before you depart.' "

"I did?"

"Aye, you did, don't you remember?" She frowned. "Walking in a circle," she repeated skeptically. She paused for several moments. "You didn't care about dancing, did you?" She didn't give him time to answer. " 'Twas a ploy to get me to stay, wasn't it? You wanted me to stay—to share your bed."

Her husband raised his brows in feigned innocence, then rolled on top of her and smiled. "I confess," he said, his eyes twinkling with mischief. "I lusted after you. Of course I wanted you in my bed—from the very first time I saw you." His smile widened. "And I usually get what I want."

"And I lusted after you," she added. "I couldn't sleep—I had no appetite. I couldn't stop thinking about you. But if we don't get up, we'll be late," she murmured against his lips, tipping her head as he spread kisses over her face, down her neck and on her shoulder.

He spread her legs with his knee, and she arched to meet his thrust. "Only if you keep talking, my beloved."

ABOUT THE AUTHOR

Donna MacQuigg is a second-generation native of New Mexico. She has previously published six historical romances and one contemporary Western romance. *The Dragon's Secret* is her first fantasy romance and the first in a series of fantasy books by this author. See more by visiting her Web site at www .donnamacquigg.com. Donna enjoys receiving your comments at knightwriter@comcast.net or at donnamacquigg@yahoo.com.